The
STRETCHMAN

Debra Zaech

BLACK BED
SHEET

The Stretchman
A Black Bed Sheet/Diverse Media Book
November 2022

Copyright © 2022 by Debra Zaech
All rights reserved.

Cover art by Stephan Zaech and
Copyright © 2022 Debra Zaech

ISBN-10: 1-946874-88-4
ISBN-13: 978-1-946874-88-7

The Stretchman

A Black Bed Sheet/Diverse Media Book
Antelope, CA

a little sticky entering my nose, while simultaneously, I felt two medium-sized boulders pounding on my chest. It was enough to wake the dead. I was thrust upon my hands and knees. I landed with a tremendous thump. The air was forced out of my body, along with the demonic possession.

The next thing I remember was rolling onto my back, looking up and spotting a big black nose and a lolling tongue staring into my eyes.

I hugged Dakota. I wanted to sit there with her, never releasing my hold. She wagged her tail, but still whined softly. I made sure to pet her, telling her she was a good girl. It's important to appreciate her efforts, even though her cardiopulmonary resuscitation skills are somewhat faulty.

I got up and headed for the bathroom to wash my face and breathe in some fresh air. I doubted myself. Did I have a bad dream? I could still smell the stench of the mucky water. I took a shower and realize it was more than a stench. My body was covered with sand and grimy residue, stuck to me like maggots on dead skin. I let the hot water cleanse the filth. I felt the dirt and grime slough down the drain diminishing my fear and anxiety. I glimpsed down to the left and saw a black nose with a white strip sticking through the shower curtain.

"OK, Dakota, come on in." It seemed two of us needed a satisfying shower. Dakota had a great time trying to bite the water as it peppered through the showerhead. I soaped her up and gave her a proper scrubbing. She loved when I massaged the soap into her backside. Her whole body wiggled in delight like a dancer performing her solo. I allowed her to stay in the shower a little longer while I dried off, changed into some clothes and dried my hair.

The Stretchman

A Black Bed Sheet/Diverse Media Book
Antelope, CA

☼
Dedication

To my family,
Sven, Alex, Stephan, Andrew and Monica,
You encouraged me to, "get a hobby, do something with your free time or write a book."
So, I did, and I thank you.

A special thanks to Nicholas Grabowsky and Black Bed Sheet Books for giving me this great opportunity.

Chapter
ONE
Lucy and Dakota

My dog would always growl to alert me of danger. Little did I know how useful she would be in the near future. I first met Dakota at The Plainledge Animal Shelter. She is a Bernese Mountain dog. Her owner developed Alzheimer's disease and could no longer care for her. I found her at the shelter, where she rescued me.

Dakota is a beautiful Berner with a black coat; a fluffy black tail with a white tip. It looked like someone dipped the top of her tail in a can of white paint. She has a white strip between her eyes that continue up to the middle of her forehead and down and around her nose. She has brown "dashes" above each eye that look like tattooed eyebrows. Her legs are ombre style, starting with black, turning to brown then white. Her back reaches my waist and she weighs a solid 120 pounds

Dakota saved me for the first of many times when I was coming home from work. I am in my early forties and I work as an Administrative Assistant at The Paul-Anthony Waldron's construction company. I took the scenic route home, passing The Plainledge Animal Shelter. I looked at the sign and contemplated, *"Hmmm, a dog..."* I decided to go in and look around.

I parked on the side of the huge square building that had enough room for, at least, fifty cars. The

1

building was made of concrete with a large blue sign indicating, *"Plainledge Animal Shelter."* It was a beautiful, cool October afternoon. The perfect weather for walking a dog!

I walked into the shelter and immediately heard excited barking and yelling. Oh, so many wagging tails and drooling tongues. An animal lover's delight. I could live here! Each bark exhibited its best voice and begged me to select them. This was both an exciting and miserable experience. The special dog selected becomes a life-long best friend, but I had to leave the others behind. I did not expect to see any pure-breeds. However, when I spotted the area to the right of the cashier, used for the older dogs, and laid my eyes on the beautiful Berner, I was astounded. She looked so similar to the Berner I previously owned. Chase was a male Berner and my best friend for 9 years. Could she replace him? Would there be too many expectations?

I hesitantly walked over to her. I poked my head around the corner and spotted her. She was lying on her stomach with her big head on her front paws. Her head was facing forward, but her eyes looked directly at me. Her dashes were so expressive; one raised upward, the other relaxed.

I saw the woman sneaking up on me to take a peek. She was older, in her late 30s, maybe early 40s. She had shoulder length brown-red hair and soft brown eyes. She wasn't too heavy. This may be a good thing, as she had better be able to run around after me, fetch a ball and go on long walks. She appeared tall for a woman, but it was hard to tell because she was doing this weird half-bent down position as if she was trying to be invisible. Doesn't she know I could smell her as soon as she walked in the door? Humans…. Anyway, I wanted to make sure she was the right one for me so I did the staring

2

contest to monitor her reaction. I looked especially cute with my one eyebrow raised and my head on my paws.

"Oh, my goodness, you are so beautiful. You look just like Chase."

Who the heck is Chase? I don't want to be Chase or anyone else. I'm Dakota. OK, one strike against. I kept staring, giving her another chance, but was also mindful of keeping my own options open.

"Can I pet you baby? What a good girl."

Then she scratched me behind my ears. I felt my whole body tingle. A scratch behind the ears for us is like a total body massage for humans. I couldn't help myself. I got up and started zooming around the cage. I ran in circles, probably broke the doggie book of world records for circling inside a pen at massive speed. I included jumping on and off my bed to show off my superb agility. She must have like the show because she took out her phone to take a picture. Remember I told you how old she was. Well, she didn't know how to take a video. I give her credit for trying, but by the time she figured it out, I was all zoomed out. She may be behind the eight ball in technology, but I loved that she laughed when she saw my display of perfection.

It was the zoomies that got to me. She was so excited to show off. Of course, if my kids acted like this, I'd insist they take some anti-anxiety medication, or perhaps some Xanax, but what can you expect from a dog? They can't speak Human, so they have to use their body language.

I approached the woman at the counter. She was standing, slumped over the counter, reading a magazine. She didn't notice me at first. She was busy reading and chewing gum. The way she chomped on that gum sounded like hungry pigs waiting for their overdue dinner. She was probably only in her 20s, but presented as if she was ten years older. She was exceedingly tall for a woman and scrawny, reaching almost 6 feet tall, weighing about 140 pounds. She wore a pair of green cat-style reading glasses, green and white flowered, bell-bottom pants. Her white long-sleeve shirt with peasant sleeves made it look like she was wearing bell-bottom pants on her upper body as well. She wore a green flowered headband that matched her pants perfectly. Her died curly yellow hair fell around her headband curly at shoulder-length. Her bangs were stiff and unmoving like wheat growing out of her hairline. She said her name was "Shaggy," which I found humorous, since she worked in a dog shelter. She didn't find anything humorous and didn't even ask for my name.

I inquired for additional information. Dakota was the Berner's name. I liked and she responded well to this name, so I decided to keep the name. Her file claims she is about three years old and she gets along well with other people and other animals. She had all of her shots and received a perfect bill of health from The Plainledge Shelter veterinarian. Unfortunately, the Berner has a life expectancy of 8 years, so we will have to make good use of each day.

I chose a red collar and a blue leash. I bought a dog tag from a machine. I punched in her name and my phone number in case she ever runs off without me. I bought all of the necessities plus some toys, biscuits and a dog bed.

Shaggy waited at the counter while I selected my purchases. She was so underwhelmed I had to laugh. Dakota gave a quick yap. Shaggy responded with a look like my mother used to give me when I snuck a piece of my boiled chicken dinner to my dog who waited patiently under the table.

I was so happy to leave that place. Shaggy was not a nice lady. She never spoke to us or pet us. She never even cuddled the new puppies. She ignored us unless she had to feed us. She would slop a minimum amount of dog food into our bowls, never offering any cookies or snacks. She'd only fill our water bowls when they were empty. Most of the time we drank warm water.

I listened intently to find out my human's name. She was called Lucy. She lives alone in a small house in an old neighborhood, which had a few families, some children and a few dogs. Is she kidding me? Does she know I am a Bernese Mountain dog? I like people, other dogs and I need a LOT of room. A small house will not do for me. I need bigger, better, more. Where will I zoom, who will I jump on? Who will play with me? How will I be entertained all day? I need constant attention. She should have chosen a Chihuahua.

I'm not sure we could define each day we had thereafter as "good," perhaps, "interesting," "unbelievable," or "haunting" may be better choices.

I took Dakota home on Oct. 25. I lived in Plainledge, in my new home for a few short weeks. My house was the second one on the block. It was a three-bedroom, one-bathroom ranch. You enter the small hallway as you enter the house. The Great Room, which was a combination living room and dining room, was on the right. There was a bay window with a view to the front yard. The kitchen was a few steps in back of the hallway and to the right. There was an atrium door that opened up into a small screened in patio. It was somewhat run-down with old blinds and a timeworn tile floor. Further down the hallway was a bathroom. To the right was the master bedroom. As you walked into the master bedroom, a closet with mirrored doors stood to the left. A television stood on an old-fashioned TV stand and a large dresser stood to its right. There were two other small bedrooms to the left of the hallway. Neither was used except to store some currently unused items.

One faced the front of the house, the other to the side of the house. To the left of the Great Room was a closet and a small den. The den had a big window facing the side of the front yard. Continuing through the den was a smaller room I used as another storage space. It was a rectangular space without a closet. I planned to eventually use this as a walk-in closet. There was a window facing the front yard.

It had an unfinished basement, which was musty and dank. I only went down there during the walk-through with my realtor. The one-car garage and sat on a ¼-acre property. The yard was fenced in, one of those old-fashioned red and white slotted chain-linked fences, so Dakota was able to run around without running away. I enclosed off a section where she could do her business. There were a few bushes in the rear of the yard. She learned quickly to run to the bushes and dance around to scratch her own back. I referred to them as "the Ass Scratching Bushes."

My new home came into sight. I had to wait in the car until Lucy put the leash on my collar. I think she needs occupational therapy. She struggled for 15 minutes to click the leash on the collar. Geez, I could check out the entire neighborhood in that time. She took me to the backyard first. The yard was bigger than I thought. There was substantial room for running and playing. I was elated. The unfriendly girl at The Plainledge Animal shelter rarely permitted much outdoor time for exercise and play.

I did my business all over the yard. It felt great to run around and pee all over the trees and bushes. I think I like this place. Many people don't know that female dogs mark their territory, but we do and I did! I finally decided to follow Lucy inside. As soon as I walked into the house, I smelled something wrong. My hair stood up on its end, my ears perked and my eyes dilated. I felt scared, but couldn't see anything to justify the emotion. The feeling that someone was there, an unearthly presence, seized my ability to think clearly. I know Lucy sensed it too because she looked around and said, "It's OK girl." But I don't think she believed that, nor did I. As she showed me around the rest of the house, I noticed she purposely opened all of the closets, took a good look inside each of them, looked under all the beds and out the windows. I detected a stale pungent odor when she lifted her comforter and looked under the bed. I whimpered and jumped back. My first instinct was to run, get out of the room, so I ran to the front door. Then I realized I was there to protect her, so I pulled myself up from my white paws, puffed up my chest, stuck my nose in the air and swaggered back into her bedroom. Oh, woof, I found her passed out on the floor! I ran over and licked her face. I made sure I got my tongue in her nose. Then I took my two front paws and jumped on her chest. I know she appreciated my revival skills because she woke up laughing and yelling, "What the heck…?"

I saw Dakota sprint out of the room and I heard her whimper. It only took another second before I caught the overwhelming odor. It smelled like a rotting corpse. The combination of the stench and the fear was enough to cause me to pass out. I lived in this house for a year and never experienced this sudden olfactory attack. I would have thought Dakota needed a good bath, but the horrific odor was not present in the shelter, nor the car.

I saw a dark blue light around my peripheral, slowly engulfing me. As the light closed in, I felt nauseous and dizzy. An uncomfortable anxiety swept over me. I felt like I was on a rowboat that unknowingly circled right into a storm. The waves washed over me, suffocating me, leaving me helpless as if I lost the oars and the control of the boat. The rocking waves of nausea and inability to regulate the

7

swaying motion increased my nausea. I was unable to take another breath and must have passed out.

I felt myself falling through a black tunnel like an underwater tornado. I was pushed down, circling upside down and right side up. I was terrified. The water pressure made me move downward agonizingly slow. My hands and legs reached upward while my backside pulled me down. I felt like I was being plunged into a depth below the Earth, beyond any place imaginable. Rocks pulled me down from my midsection. My destination could not be any worse than where I was now. After what seemed like time stopped and I was doomed to a continuous fall into the abyss, I hit the bottom. I landed on a grimy wet floor. It wasn't ice cold, but cold enough where a sweater and a cup of hot tea would have been a benefit. I started scrambling around on my knees, looking for an escape route. The rocky, sandy floor scraped my knees and hands. I felt my flesh cutting like incessant paper-cuts, burning through my extremities. The wounds healed as quickly as they opened, only to repeat this process again and again. The new cuts inflicted additional pain, making my journey intolerable. My fear increased, but I could not move. I tried to scream, but only bubbles escaped my mouth. Somehow, I was able to breathe, with some difficulty. It was like being buried in a coffin with a straw tube inserted in my mouth, allowing the air to enter painstakingly slowly.

Suddenly, the motion subsided. I could vaguely see some dark shapes in the sunlight reaching down through the water. There were five of them. They were mostly dark, but transparent. I imagined them to be a family, as the taller and heavier one may have been the father. He was about six feet tall and gaunt.

8

He took the lead and the rest followed him like a mother duck and her dead, soaking wet ducklings trailing behind. The mother was shorter than the father. She kept looking around, slowly, side to side. Was she looking for an escape route, an enemy or trying to protect her children? She looked like the figure in the painting *"The Scream"* by Edvard Munch. The three trailing ducks were even more dreadful. They were half-floaters and half-human. They had the same ghost-like spirit of their parents, but their arms and legs had more definition. I'm not sure if they hadn't fully advanced into their final macabre apparition or if they were stuck between both worlds indefinitely.

The mother tried to bump the older child toward me. His arm reached out to me. I was confused. My desire to help and conflicted feelings of loathing for the decrepit shape clouded my judgement. I leaned backward to avoid the child's arm, not moving my feet. The touch was airy like a plume but hit me like a cinder block. I shuddered at the pressure. I entered an altered state of consciousness. I was someone in between reality and a dream. I should have fled. I had no power over my own body. I was aware of my external environment, but something took control of my ability to act. I felt pressured to follow the family. My head ached. I wasn't able to blink and tears streamed down my face. The same two words repeated in my mind, *"you must, you must."* I struggled against the force directing me to remain here with that family. I realized Dakota was not with me. I did not, would not leave her alone in our house.

I heard growling in the background. It was low and growing quickly into deafening barks. I was attacked from behind. I felt something warm, wet and a little sticky entering my nose, while simultaneously, I felt two medium-sized boulders pounding on my chest. It was enough to wake the dead. I was thrust upon my hands and knees. I landed with a tremendous thump. The air was forced out of my body, along with the demonic possession.

The next thing I remember was rolling onto my back, looking up and spotting a big black nose and a lolling tongue staring into my eyes.

I hugged Dakota. I wanted to sit there with her, never releasing my hold. She wagged her tail, but still whined softly. I made sure to pet her, telling her she was a good girl. It's important to appreciate her efforts, even though her cardiopulmonary resuscitation skills are somewhat faulty.

I got up and headed for the bathroom to wash my face and breathe in some fresh air. I doubted myself. Did I have a bad dream? I could still smell the stench of the mucky water. I took a shower and realize it was more than a stench. My body was covered with sand and grimy residue, stuck to me like maggots on dead skin. I let the hot water cleanse the filth. I felt the dirt and grime slough down the drain diminishing my fear and anxiety. I glimpsed down to the left and saw a black nose with a white strip sticking through the shower curtain.

"OK, Dakota, come on in." It seemed two of us needed a satisfying shower. Dakota had a great time trying to bite the water as it peppered through the showerhead. I soaped her up and gave her a proper scrubbing. She loved when I massaged the soap into her backside. Her whole body wiggled in delight like a dancer performing her solo. I allowed her to stay in the shower a little longer while I dried off, changed into some clothes and dried my hair.

Did she not know what dogs do when they are wet?

Dakota was finished and jumped out by herself. She proceeded to wring herself out and shake the water off her body onto the sink, the floor, the walls and my dry hair and clothes. I didn't mind. She was so cute and lovable; I couldn't get angry with her. I changed into another dry outfit and made a cup of peppermint herbal tea for me and a cool bowl of water and a large dog biscuit for Dakota. My friend Karen loved making homemade, limited ingredient dog biscuits. She made a batch for Dakota as a "Gotcha Day" surprise. I carried them on our walks and trips to the dog parks. They were great reinforcers for training. We shared them with Dakota's dog friends. They sparked many conversations. Dakota and I developed many friendships due to the biscuits. They were especially helpful when a child was hesitant to pet a huge dog. I would hand the child a cookie to offer Dakota. Dakota would sit still until the child extended her hand. She gently took the cookie from the child's hand, wagged her tail and nudged the child's hand with her nose. The child would instantly fall in love with Dakota. She taught them to trust dogs and how easy it was for a dog to love them in return. I give Karen credit for these accomplishments.

Karen loved baking as much as she loved dogs. She loved dogs more than she loved people. Whenever she visited a friend or attended a party, she'd bake dog biscuits rather than buy a gift for the hostess. Her dog biscuits would prove extremely helpful in the months ahead.

Chapter
TWO
Cathy, Janet and Yukon

Janet and Cathy lived next door to Lucy in a three-bedroom ranch. They lived there for six years. You enter the house and immediately step into a large living area. It was a comfortable room with a television, a sprawling black microfiber sectional sofa, two white sherpa chairs and two black and white checkered end tables. To the left is the country kitchen decorated with a chicken décor. The border of eggshell white yellow-wheat-colored chickens covered the middle of the walls.   The wooden kitchen table sat in the left corner. It was adorned with a lovely two-pace service for two. The plates and glasses had matching little chickadees painted on them. Yellow cloth napkins were shaped into triangles, neatly placed next to each plate. Silver plated antique flatware lay on top of the napkins. Behind the living area were three bedrooms facing the backyard. A full bathroom was situation in the rear of the kitchen.

They welcomed Lucy and Dakota into the neighborhood the first day she moved in. They went over with a beautifully-wrapped tray of homemade cookies, an antique teapot and an assorted box of herbal teas. They sat on the ledge of the Bay Window in the Great Room and chatted over tea and cookies while the moving men carried in her furniture and belongings.

Janet and Cathy met in college and married two years ago. They had an opportunity to rescue a dog and make their family complete.

Cathy is a dog groomer. She is five feet four inches tall, 140 pounds, with shoulder length brown hair and matching brown eyes. She has a wonderful, bright smile that always make others return the smile. She has many friends, but some people judged her when they found out she is a lesbian.

She works at Plainledge Animal Shelter full time for 5 years. She loves shampooing the dogs, cutting their nails, brushing their teeth and brushing their fur. She would arrive early everyday so she could clean her work area and plan her day for her furry friends. The Plainledge Animal Shelter was a small shop where Lucy rescued Dakota. They sold pet food and supplies. As you walked into the shop, the cashier station was on the left, up in front of the shop. The food and supplies were straight ahead and the grooming station was to the left of the cashier. The station had glass enclosures so the humans could check on the quality of care their fur babies received. Cathy was in her element when grooming the dogs. The unconditional love she received was more than she could ask for in a job. People were not always as kind. Janet and Cathy are lesbians. Cathy was bullied throughout high school. It was difficult to understand why anyone would have a problem with two people loving each other.

Cathy was in ninth grade when the first incidence happened. The ninth-grade dance was in two months. The students were wondering whom to ask or who will ask them to the dance. Cathy wanted to ask Mary to the dance at that time, but felt uncomfortable and knew there would be repercussions. Jack asked her to the dance on a dare from one of his friends. Jack was the quarterback of the football team. He was "The Big Man on Campus," the one all the girls wanted to date. He was six feet tall with dark brown hair and blue eyes. He was currently dating Jill the head cheerleader. She was five feet eight, 120 pounds with red hair and green eyes. Neither had an academic average above a 70, but were the most popular couple in the school. Jack followed her to her locker after the last period bell rang. The halls were crowded with students packing their backpacks, laughing and rushing to catch the buses.

Jack yelled, "Quiet everyone; I have a question to ask Cathy." The hallway immediately fell silent. Everyone stared at her, while Jack got down on one knee,

"Will you go to the dance this me?" Cathy turned a deep shade of rose. She felt all eyes upon her like a fish in a glass bowl. She had no time to respond when Jack said, "Or would you rather go with Jill?"

The entire hallway erupted in laughter. Jack tumbled over the knee on the ground, landed on his back and laughed so hard tears were streaming down his face. After a minute or two, he collected himself and simply got up and walked away. The other students stared for a minute longer then continued on to the school buses. No one tried to console or sympathize with Cathy. She remembers those situations with a deep hurt in the pit of her stomach and is eternally thankful for her job and the dogs at The Plainledge Animal Shelter.

Dogs are not similar to people in that respect. They are loyal until their last breath. They don't judge, blame or bully. They harbor an innate ability to love unconditionally.

On this sunny warm October morning last year, her favorite customer, Marion, came in with Yukon, her 130-pound Greater Swiss Mountain Dog. Yukon was black with a white strip down his nose and up to the top of his head. His legs were black with white at the bottom, appearing as though he was wearing boots. His tail was thin and black with a whit tip at the end. Although a gigantic breed, Yukon was a friendly giant who loved everyone he met. Cathy never minded a big wet sloppy kiss on her face from Yukon. After grooming Yukon, she walked him out of the room to find Marion. It was strange that Marion wasn't outside the door waiting to take Yukon home. Yukon and Cathy walked through the aisles. Yukon stole a couple of unwrapped dog biscuits that were on the shelf at nose height. They were his favorite limited ingredient dog biscuits. He didn't see any signage stating, "If you eat it, you pay." A woman named Karen created her own recipe and donated them to the shelter.

However, Yukon did see two human feet and two human legs lying out from one of the aisles. He romped over, but stopped in mid-romp. He recognized Marion's smell immediately. She was lying still on the floor. Yukon tried licking Marion's face. He tried moving her with his nose; he tried whimpering in her ear, all to no avail. Cathy heard Yukon's distressed sounds and found him hovering over Marion's body. She dialed 9-1-1 and waited for the paramedics to arrive.

The paramedics listened for a heartbeat and felt for a pulse. Unfortunately, Marion had died of a heart attack. She was only 70 years old. The wretched howling noises exploding from Yukon was more than Cathy could endure. Tears began forming in her eyes and slowing falling down her checks. She sat on the floor and scooped Yukon into her arms. He put his head on her shoulder. His thunderous howling simmered down to gentle wailing. They sat there for twenty minutes. Yukon exhausted himself and fell asleep. Cathy hung a "closed" sign on the front door, took a blanket from the supplies shelf and laid down next to Yukon. They slept for hours. When Yukon woke up, she gave him some fresh cool water, which he drank and a special dog treat, which he did not eat.

Yukon wouldn't leave her side. At 7 pm, she called Janet and explained the incident. Before she could finish her question, Janet replied, "Of course we'll take him." Cathy purchased the necessities for Yukon, dog food, treat, a dog bed, a blanket and a stuffed squeaky gopher toy. She helped Yukon into her Mini-Cooper, which was a task in itself and they went onward to their new lives together.

I couldn't believe Marion wasn't listening to me. I tried licking her and pushing on her chest, to no avail. I was getting angry with her; I didn't like this game she was playing. Nevertheless, I started to get nervous when Cathy started yelling and called 9-1-1. When the men in the ambulance arrived, Cathy said they were paramedics and I started to howl. They breathed into her mouth and pumped her chest. They said she had no pulse and it looked like she had a heart attack. Who would have attacked her heart? Marion was such a nice lady. They put her on a weird bed that started low to the ground, then popped up to my height when they placed Marion on it. Out the door they went with Marion lying stiffly upon the bizarre bed. Where were they taking her? I should go too. What was I supposed to do when she was gone? How could I protect her? Those stupid dog-hating paramedics weren't listening to me.

They took her away as my howling became more desperate. "Come back Marion, don't leave me alone. I need you. I love you"

Janet was a happy positive person. She was five feet, three inches, about 130 pounds, with a gorgeous mane of black hair and dark brown eyes. She attended St. Katharine's University and obtained her undergraduate degree in psychology. She decided to continue and earned her Master's degree in social work at the same university. She accepted a position in the Foster Care system. She tirelessly worked to place children in loving homes. The job fit her perfectly, as she was a true empath.

She felt the same love for dogs. She audited a course at St. Katharine's. Professor Babs taught a course about dogs and their importance. Dogs and children were helpless without people. Janet was motivated to offer assistance to all species, but held a special fondness to the young children and abandoned dogs. She often volunteered at The Plainledge Animal shelter where Cathy worked. She enjoyed playing in the yard with the dogs.

There were many instances when Janet collected a few of the children from The Foster Care agency, load them into the company bus and spend the day with them at the shelter. She noticed such a positive change in the children's behavior and mood after they shared the day with the dogs. The shy children had no difficulty talking to the pups. They chatted and laughed, their suffering disappearing for a few hours. The children on the spectrum felt at ease; petting the dogs, sitting on the floor with them and allowing them to cuddle with them. This was a tremendous accomplishment. Janet's heart exploded with joy. The dogs also benefitted with these visits. They adored children; they often had more energy than the adults did, which was a perfect match for the spirited puppies.

Janet was confident enough to come out of the closet at an early age and did not care what people thought of her. She always knew she liked the girls instead of the boys. When she was in fifth grade, she had a crush on Becky. Becky was quiet and shy, but beautiful to look at. Janet was fairly certain the shyness was due to Becky's fear of being ridiculed if she admitted she was gay. However, hiding her true self was oppressive and energy draining. Janet sat next to Becky one day during the lunch period. The cafeteria was packed, but Becky sat by herself.

Janet approached Becky and said,

"Hey, is this spot taken?" Becky simply shook her head.

Janet removed her sandwich, thermos of milk, cookies and chocolate pudding from her lunch box. She unpacked the wrapping for the sandwich, lifted the cover off the chocolate pudding snack cup, poured milk into the thermos top that substituted for a cup and said, "Boy am I hungry."

Becky raised her head and smiled at Janet. She said,

"You better be."

They both laughed, shared their lunch and the friendship blossomed. They did not display any overt affection in school. However, they often walked home together, holding hands and chatting. Janet helped Becky feel less concerned about what other people thought and more concerned about her own happiness and satisfaction.

The following years, the girls entered Junior High School. Becky's confidence grew. She wound up breaking up with Janet for another girl in her class. Janet was sad to lose Becky. However, she was thrilled Becky began to assert herself and found her own path.

Janet had a few close friends who validated and supported her and she needed no more. Her parents accepted her unconditionally. She learned kindness, love and understanding through her wonderful parents.

It took Yukon a while to grieve, but he slowly began to eat, play and run around. By the end of the first year living with Cathy and Janet, he felt right at home. In fact, the house, the furniture and all items within his reach belonged to him. He took up the entire space on the couch and their bed. He snatched whatever food was in his reach, including the snacks he could jump up and snag. Anything that fell on the floor…his. If the garbage can was open, the discarded items…his. He would grab an object, make eye contact with Cathy or Janet and run to the couch. They would try to take it away from him and he would grip it tighter and growl at them. He loved playing that game with them. Even though they trusted him, they were hesitant to take anything from his mouth.

I discovered a game I could play with Cathy and Janet. The three of us loved to play. I would steal something from the table or the garbage can and I would sprint away and carry it to my couch. I made sure one of my humans watched me so they would join in the fun. Cathy or Janet would chase me and pretend they wanted me to surrender the item. I would playfully growl and wag my tail simultaneously. Sometime they would reward me and offer me a cookie if I traded with the stolen object. Other times they would quit the game, walk away and declare me the winner.

One day when Yukon stole Cathy's shoe and took it to her bed, he noticed a strange smell emanating from the room. Their house seemed lovely, lively and comfortable, except for that smell in the bedroom.

Yukon followed the smell and Cathy followed Yukon. As he got closer to the bedroom, his whining became more agitated. He started to gag. Cathy had to pet him and tried to convince him that nothing was out of the ordinary. However, she started to smell the foul order herself. She never noticed it until she rescued Yukon. She bent down and gave Yukon a big sniff...nope it wasn't him. Yukon bent down to get a good look under the bed. His big head couldn't fit, but his stuffed his nose underneath as far as he could. Cathy waved her hand under the bed, feeling for any abnormalities, toys or anything that may emit such an odor. She detected a large, circular damp area. She threw the mattress to the side to broaden her view. Sure enough, a damp brown spot was smoldering below. She touched it and quickly pulled back her hand. It felt, she couldn't explain, *uncomfortable*. A mysterious feeling coursed through her body in an instant, surging outward as soon as her hand departed. Yukon growled, sensing a disturbance.

The rancid smell permeated throughout the bedroom. The circle expanded, bubbling with smoke and grime. The windows and door slammed shut with a bang that shook the room. It was pitch black. Cathy was petrified. She bent down beside Yukon, gently holding his collar...and they started to fall. They were sucked into the massive smoldering portal. They fell through a dark tunnel. They pounded into the ragged, sharp edges without feeling any pain, just fear. They fell quickly, but it felt like slow motion. Their bodies fell upside down, around and around, spinning furiously. Dizziness and fear mounted. The darkness was overwhelming, like jumping out of a plane in a terror-nado, whipping around, making it difficult to breathe, trying to call out and reach for each other, but unable to do so. It ended abruptly as they landed safely on the ground. They bumped down violently, but were unharmed. Their feet touched upon a hard, moist surface like packed wet sand on the beach during low tide. The smell was consistent with the texture. It smelled rotten like molded mushrooms, like soggy seaweed washed up on the shore, like damp garbage in a landfill.

They took a few deep breaths and tried to quell the nausea that threatened to erupt. There was just enough light to make out their surroundings. Night vision glasses would have helped. However, it may have been an advantage not to see the intricate details of their underground dwelling. They appeared to land within the lobby of a cave with six tunnels. Their immediate location was oblong, like a gloomy dome. Three tunnels on their right side, one curving to the front, one to the side and one to the back. The left side was composed of the same structure. There was a second area straight-ahead, shaped like a small circular enclosure. Cathy envisioned the layout as a giant subterranean beetle.

The tunnels narrowed into a space not even big enough for Yukon to squeeze through. Fortunately, the space ahead had the most luminous light source, so they decided to choose that direction first. The sides of the space were fragile. As Cathy touched the wall, the wet, rocky material crumbled allowing enough space for Yukon to fit. It sounded like the wall was crying. Each time she scraped more of the wall; more voices cried. Desperate whimpering, cries of pain and torture, cries for help. She continued to whittle away at the wall, shredding some of the sides, only making enough room for her and Yukon to fit...she couldn't afford to crop off any more of the wall, as the sobbing became unbearable. She would have to figure out where they were, why there were here and how to help them escape.

Yukon followed behind Cathy. They walked about one hundred yards when they stopped short. They entered a room exactly like her and Janet's bedroom. Well, almost exactly. This room was like "The Dark Side." Instead of the bed in the back of the room as they walked in, it was immediately in the front. Where the dresser was to the left of the door in her and Janet's reality, here the dresser was on the right. That wasn't the worst part. The bed, dresser and window were covered with the same wet rocky material as the cave walls. Everything was murky, soggy and decaying. Cathy heard the same echoing when she touched "her" furniture. Sounds like people crying. Horrible pleas of pain and hopelessness, where time stood still. This time Cathy heard an additional strange sound, a dog's soft howl. It also seemed to originate from the walls. It was probably more than one dog. It was difficult to determine how many people and dogs were trapped due to the echoing, the dim light and our own fear. Yukon heard the howling and returned a sad whine.

A disturbing vision added to the unnerving wailing. A ghostly apparition sailed through the gloomy abode. Half-human, half-spirit, this vision was angry and terrifying. Its legs were short, but they stretched as it walked. It reminded Cathy of "Stretch Armstrong," a toy she played with when she was young. The arms and legs were short, but could be extended to lengths five times their original size. Its face was elongated, like a melted hourglass figure. Its eyes were massive and hollowed out. His mouth was open wide. It looked similar to his eyes, empty but threatening. His nose jutted straight out from his gaunt face. It was lengthy and pointed, crooked like a witch's nose. His lips were barely visible.

As this Stretchman moved, its leg grew longer, giving it the ability to move in great strides as it took each step. Its head grew longer than its body, which was at first level with Cathy, now reached up to the celling and down to its knees. It was over seven feet tall. Its arms struggled to keep up the pace. They cracked, popped and bent at unusual angles as they reached downward and touched the ground. It had no feet; short shredded stumps took their place. It had five long fingers on each hand. It floated about three inches from the ground. It continued to grow until its head had to bend at an irrational angel to accommodate the ceiling. It had to be nine or ten feet tall. Its lips developed and grew thick as if it just had a Botox injection. They spread out in a menacing toothless grin. It began to laugh. It was a small sound, considering its size. It was as if it had the hiccups and needed a quick breath between snorts of laughter. It had difficulty producing any sound, but found it important to try. Yukon issued a menacing growl, but Cathy held him back. She had no idea what this beast was capable of doing, although it was obviously evil.

The beast lifted its right arm and pointed its extended finger to Cathy and Yukon. Then it twirled around in a counter-clockwise direction. Its twirling grew faster and faster, spinning and spinning, hiccupping and laughing. It changed hands, pointing at them with the right hand, then with the left as its body rotated. Its head bent at irregular angles as the celling interfered with its spinning. Lolling to one side then the other, its tongue hanging out of its mouth, it began moving in the direction of its head.

Cathy froze, staring at the apparition. She was so horrified and perturbed, she couldn't think, move or breathe. She stood for a few minutes focused on the horror growing in front of her. She reached for Yukon without taking her eyes off the monster. He was shaking, but tried to be brave and protect her. She whispered, "It's okay boy. We have to get out of here." She was trying to convince herself as much as Yukon.

I had an eager obligation to protect Cathy and Janet since the day they rescued me. I had no idea what I was getting myself into. Dogs have more olfactory receptors in our noses, so we have the natural ability to detect odors more easily than humans do. As soon as I walked into the house, I perceived a peculiar odor, something sinister, not your average household smell. I wasn't happy about entering the bedroom, but I had to guard Cathy. I barked a warning, hoping she'd retreat from the hole and run out of the house, but she did not heed my warning. At least she held onto my collar so I was able to follow her through the portal. I will admit, I did not like the tumbling feeling. I couldn't get my paws on the ground. I couldn't grasp Cathy and I didn't know which way was up.

Once again, I smelled the demon before Cathy sensed it. I wanted to attack it, sink my teeth into it, grab its neck and shake until it broke. However, it kept stretching, so I changed my mind. I wasn't afraid, dogs are too brave to get scared. I'm not afraid of anything or anyone. I stood next to Cathy and growled the most valiant, courageous growl any dog ever mustered. Luckily, Cathy grabbed my collar and demanded I heel.

The Stretchman stopped when it heard Cathy's voice. It faced her and Yukon and mimed a circular motion with his hands. Yukon and Cathy began to spin. The nauseous feeling began again. The momentum of the spinning forced them upward as if they were vacuumed into an ascending force. They landed back into the bedroom from where they came. The windows and door were ajar, the lighting laminated the room in a typical fashion and the revolting smell had vanished. Nonetheless, Cathy snatched her car keys, clipped on Yukon's leash and headed for her car. She drove to The Plainledge Animal Shelter where she would feed Yukon, give him some fresh water and give him some of Karen's homemade dog biscuits. She would decompress while she chatted with her co-workers the customers and the other dogs. She would discuss the situation with Janet later. Janet was a great listener and would help her process the event and possibly explore the portal beneath the bed.

Chapter
THREE
Seth and Trista

The Ravana family lived in Plainledge for twelve years. Their house was to the left of my block, on the end of a dead-end street. I first heard about them from Cathy and Janet. I had not met them until I took Dakota for a walk around the neighborhood a few weeks after I rescued her from the shelter.

No one was particularly fond of the Ravanas. Their lawn was unkempt with yellow dandelions infused like polka dots. The grass grew in some areas ranging a foot tall, while other areas were patches of dirt, holes and mold, barren of any grass. The house was a standard size ranch in further disrepair. There was a crack in the stoop big enough to see from the side of the road when I walked Dakota. The curtains on the front windows were filthy, devoid of once probably lively colors. They looked like hanging shrouds of crêpe paper. It was always dark; no decorations, lawn ornaments or holiday lights.

Trista Ravana was married to Seth Ravana Trista was a petite woman at 5 feet tall and 100 pounds. She had mousy brown hair and tired brown eyes. She walked with her head down, never making contact with others. She rarely left the house and had no social life. Seth was the only person with whom she had contact.

26

Seth was an alcoholic and a bully. He was six feet four inches tall and weighed two hundred and fifty pounds. He had black hair and blue eyes. He was voted "Best Looking" in Plainledge High School and he agreed with the title. He played football at St. Katharine's University, which afforded him popularity with both his male and female classmates. He abused Trista and made her life miserable. He called to her as, "Wife," never using her first name or other name of adoration. He forbade her to leave the house. She was not allowed to have friends, talk to anyone other than him and their son. She was not permitted to own a cell phone. She was a prisoner in her own home. Seth would even allow her to rescue a dog.

Seth hated dogs. After staring on his university's football team, he was drafted to play in the Major Leagues. He would play linebacker for the New York Sharks. They offered him a salary he never thought possible. He had his eye on a mansion in the city. He pictured his future, living in the city house, driving a Mustang and dating gorgeous women without making any commitments. Of course, he would have to watch his diet and drinking, maintaining his muscular physique and optimal physical fitness, but he could always indulge after the season.

Life didn't turn out as planned. He and his football cronies planned a "Beer Olympics" at the local park. They decided to walk to the location knowing they would not be able to drive themselves homes after drinking all evening. They played beer-pong, beer-poker and created other great beer-drinking games. Seth jumped on the kiddie spinner after his first ten beers. His cries to stop went unanswered as his friends spun him around and around. He saw the trees whirl, the ground seemed to rise and the moon moved from left to right over and over again. He lost his clutch on the metal bar and flew off the apparatus. He wobbled a few steps, bent over and spewed vomit all over his pants, his sneakers and a few crushed beer cans spread out beneath him. The Beer Olympics ended on that note and the boys scattered, walking home in different directions.

Seth took a short cut through a deserted ally where he happened upon a small pack of three feral dogs. The Doberman was the biggest of the three, about 24 inches tall weighing 90 pounds. The two smaller dogs would not have been worrisome, but together they created a wild pack. They growled at him and bared their teeth, but stood in their places. They were passively protecting their territory. Seth accepted a challenge when he faced one. Drunk and stupid, he picked up some rocks and shards of glass and hurled them at the dogs. He grabbed an old rusty garbage can cover and smashed it on the Doberman's head. The dogs charged, defending themselves. The provoked Doberman latched onto Seth's ankle biting into his flesh, sinking his teeth deeper, thrashing his head side to side. Seth tried to punch and kick, but the angry dog was too much of a match for him. He slipped. He twisted his injured ankle and fell to the ground landing on fragments of sharp objects, trash, and various rubble. The pain in his ankle was enormous. He never felt such excruciating pain. He was always the one dolling out the pain, never on the receiving end.

I am a Doberman. My name is Loki. The three of us lived together in a puppy mill with many other unfortunate dogs and humans who abused them. The female dogs were bred continuously. The poor girls were neglected, fed only enough to survive and produce milk for the litter, never loved or shown

28

affection. My two friends, Cody, Jenna and I escaped one night. Cody and Jenna were small white dogs. They may have been littermates, as they arrived together and tried to stay in close contact whenever possible. We heard the police officer ring the doorbell. While he chatted with the ringleader, we chewed each other ropes, released our bonds and squeezed ourselves out the small opening in the window. We vowed to return to liberate the others, but fate stepped in for us.

Many neighbors complained about the barking and whimpering, the filth and the constant flow of traffic on the property. The police obtained a search warrant and forced their way into the house of misery. They discovered the basement full of captive dogs, living in squalor. They immediately called the local animal control center, called The Plainledge Animal Shelter. The great man called Helmuth took all of the dogs to his shop. The lovely Babs bathed them, fed them and gave them comfortable lodging until they were adopted. It was too late for us. We could not be found; we ran too far.

We hung out together from that day onward. We searched for food near the dumpster on a nightly basis. One night a drunken man sauntered through. His demeanor reminded us of the ringleader, so we showed him our intimidating teeth, but backed away from him. We had enough trouble in our recent past, we didn't wish for more. We were stunned when this loser launched harmful items in our direction. We were ready to vacate the premise until he hit me over the head with a heavy object. I couldn't tolerate the unwarranted assault. I attacked. I lunged, I bit, I chewed. I allowed all of my pent-up rage, anger and pain unleash on this abominable man. Scenes of abuse, powerlessness, neglect and hunger flashed before my eyes and left me incapable of controlling myself. I continued my rampage until I was exhausted. I released my grip and ran off with my two companions.

Seth was forced to walk home on his damaged ankle and aching body. He took a warm bath, cleaned his wounds and went to bed. He slept fitfully as the pain was intolerable. He drove himself to the Emergency Room early the next morning. His winced in pain if he accelerated, so the drive to the hospital took double time. He was able to step on the gas and brake pedals with his right foot, but he was unable to use his left foot to change the manual gears. He was forced to continue in first gear. He felt humiliated hopping through the hospital doors. The voluptuous nurse with the big boobs was uncharacteristically uninterested in Seth's sex appeal. She simply rolled over a wheelchair and plopped him down. He glanced downward, unable to face the world in his mutilated condition.

The doctor ordered x-rays and blood tests. The nurse helped Seth onto the bed and hooked him up with an IV drip. The blood tests showed an unspecified bacterial infection. A few nights in the hospital were necessary.

The doctor reviewed the x-rays and discussed the results with Seth. The injuries were life-changing. The ankle was not only broken, but shattered. They could operate, but Seth would most likely walk with a limp. He would need months of physical therapy, bedrest and pain medication. His professional football career was over before it began. He vowed to take revenge on any animal that crossed his path, but mainly dogs. Those repulsive, hideous, ill-tempered beasts deserved every bad fortune Seth could muster.

It wasn't always so maddening for Trista. When she reminisced, she regrets the day she met Seth. They were attending St. Katharine's University. It was a beautiful campus on Long Island. Trista was majoring in Child Study. She was the President of the Child Study club and worked in the University Tutoring

Center. Seth was majoring in Business and played football on the Division I football team. He was the offensive linebacker, as he was the most massive player on the team. Neither were dating anyone when they met at an After-Game party. Tristan was shy and hadn't dated much in her life. She felt honored that Seth actually approached her and spoke to her. She couldn't believe he stayed with her for the most of the evening. He was so sweet, laughing with her, lightly touching her arm, bringing her drinks and snacks. She had never felt quite so special.

Seth was the big-man-on-campus. He had the talent and good-looks that made the young ladies swoon over him. He took advantage of these qualities, as he dated a different girl every Friday and Saturday night. He knew how to compliment and manipulate them into bed at his desire. He had his eyes on Trista. She was innocent and unpopular so he knew he could have his way with her with a few compliments, jokes and his infamous appeal. He even surprised himself how easy it was to hook her with his charms. He made certain she drank enough to become inebriated, loosen her inhibitions and fall for his prowess. She followed him to his 1965 Mustang.

The car was his dream. The man who previously owned the car drove it to Aaron's Auto-Body Shop. Aaron, Seth's father, owned the shop. The shop was situated at the beginning of the town's line. As Mustang Man looked in, he was impressed. The mechanic had an ideal layout. The expansive garage held ten cars. The doors remained open for a full view of the repairs and restorations. The customers were permitted to watch their old wrecks morph into beauties. Three mechanics worked full time, seven days per week. Aaron paid his son and two other students to work as part-time employees during the busier seasons. The restroom resided in the back right corner of the garage. The separate room accommodated a register, a few aisles of cookies, household items, coffee and donuts. A small table and four chairs offered a sitting space for those waiting for their vehicles.

Aaron purchased and sold used cars and restored the classics. He wanted the Mustang pimped-out. However, when Seth laid his eyes on the car, he fell in love. It was a red two-door convertible with a white top. It had red interior leather bucket seats and manual roll down windows.

Seth begged his father to purchase it. He promised to work in the shop until he covered the payments. His father offered the man more money than it was worth, but his son was the school football star and he deserved it. Seth kept it as close to the original as possible, containing only an AM/FM radio, no air-conditioning and a three-speed manual transmission. Seth never coughed up the money for even one payment.

Trista thought it was just about the coolest car she ever laid eyes on. Seth took her for a ride with the convertible top down. All of the friends at the party watched them drive by and cheered them on. Trista was in her glory. She loved how people stared at her and Seth. Wow, is her popularity going to increase ten-fold...

Trista felt a bit nervous when Seth parked the car behind Aaron's auto-body shop. Aaron required Seth's help a few hours a week. However, Seth was the authority figure in the house. If he didn't show up for work, there were no consequences. Of course, he never clocked in.

It was dark and deserted. Seth told her how beautiful she was and how he wanted to kiss her when he first saw her at the party. He leaned in for the kiss.

Trista hesitated at first, then obliged. She was so excited to be with Seth, she did not dare dissuade him. She kept thinking about how popular she would be. Spending time with Seth would automatically secure her place with the sought-after cliques. Trista closed her eyes. It felt wonderful, a warm delightful feeling overcame her. She felt desirable and safe; comfortable and calm.

But Seth suddenly changed. His warm smile became a smirk. His hand moved up her shirt. She asked him to stop, but he didn't pay her any attention. He pushed her down on the seat and straddled on top of her. She couldn't believe what was happening. She yelled and begged him to stop. He ripped her underwear from her body and pulled her stockings down to her ankles. She started to cry and squirm, but he was too heavy for her to move or get away. She punched and clawed to no avail. Her face streaked with tears and sweat as he continued to plunge from her most private place. She fantasized about her first time and never imagined it would be so awful, so degrading. When he was finished, he told her to pull up her stockings, wipe her face and fix her hair. He simple started the car and drove her home.

When they arrived at her house, he threatened her. If she told anyone, he would find her and repeat the incident again and again. She was terrified. Her whole body was sore. She walked slowly into her house, one painful step at a time, trying to calm herself so as not to raise any suspicions. She took a scalding hot shower and tried to wipe off the dirt, sweat and impurities as well as the humiliation and degradation.

It hurt to wash, to bend, to move. She let the water run at full throttle while she cried and cried and cried some more. After twenty minutes or so, she dried herself off and fell into bed. The sheets that were normally so soft, comfortable and clean now felt rough, stiff and soiled. She slept fitfully reliving the nightmare both in her dreams and upon waking. She didn't want to miss school the next day as to avoid any potential gossip.

Her plan didn't proceed as she expected. She arrived on campus to a quad of people whispering behind her back. As she passed each group, the murmuring stopped and they stared at her, covering their mouths with their hands, giggling in silence. It hurt to sit. She held the arm of the chair and cautiously declined, trying not to bump her bruised and swollen body. She trembled during the day, barely able to sit in the classrooms without having a full-blown panic attack. When she opened her backpack to look for a pen, she saw a package of condoms. The class erupted in giggles. Trista wasn't amused. She hadn't considered that vital fact. Seth didn't use a condom. She ruminated with this thought for three weeks. Not a moment passed that she relaxed. After four weeks, the worry increased. Six weeks passed without a period. Trista was too fearful to confide in anyone, even her parents. She entered the nearest drug store and spotted the Early Pregnancy Tests. She looked around, did not see anyone in the aisle, and slipped a kit in her backpack.

Chapter
FOUR
Helmuth

Helmuth received the call from the police He sped through the town ignoring all stop signs, yellow traffic lights and yield signs and arrived at the house of misery in record time. He was devastated to see the animal cruelty. Cages piled on top of each other, excrement falling in the cages below. Bloodied ropes tied to poles, dead tiny puppies thrown in cardboard boxes, dog carcasses lying against the back wall. He would not tolerate this abuse, but first he must take care of those who managed to stay alive.

He picked up each dog, stroked him or her and calmly explained where he was going to take him or her. He gently loaded the dogs into individual crates, placed them tenderly into his van and drove them to The Plainledge Animal Shelter.

Babs was waiting for them when they arrived. She prepared cages with blankets and toys, warm baths and bowls of fresh food and water. She also had the vaccinations ready to inoculate the new arrivals for rabies, distemper, Parvovirus and Hepatitis. The lights were dimmed to facilitate relaxation. Babs was pleasantly surprised to see Shaggy run through the door before Helmuth arrived.

Babs and Shaggy worked passionately until they finished bathing every dog. They fed, inoculated and cuddled them. They chose to remain in the building with the terrified pups. They used blankets and dog beds from the shelves and set up three makeshift beds for themselves and for Helmuth, in the cage area. They left the cages open. Some dogs felt safer in the cages, others yearned for human contact and slept on the floor next to Babs and Shaggy. It was probably the first painless night these poor creatures had ever experienced.

Helmuth pretended he had to return to the site to verify no dog was left behind. He promised he would return as soon as possible and would sleep with them and the pups for the night. Helmuth did indeed return to the house of misery. However, he had an ulterior motive. He planned on doing more than just checking on the remaining dogs. He arrived at the house in minutes and was instantly horrified.

He walked into the small ranch. The kitchen was in view from the front door. He saw filthy dishes, pots and pans, glasses and utensils dumped into a sink full of murky water. To the right was a long hall. Three bedrooms extended outward, one on the left and two on the right. They were in complete disarray. The comforters, pillows and sheet were strewn around the floor. The dresser drawers were broken and remained ajar. The two empty closet doors hung on one hinge and drooped to the side. A wooden staircase behind a basement door led to a lower level. Gelatinous goop covered each step.

The stench turned his stomach. His imagination ran wild. Who could treat innocent animals so gravely? The police officer explained regretfully how the ringleader managed to get away undetected. However, they caught the two assistants, retrained them in the basement while the cops wrote up their reports, and sectioned off the area.

Helmuth casually sneaked to the lower level. Dried blood discolored the knives and old urine soaked the rags dispersed around the room. Broken tennis balls and large rocks harboring rusty stains scattered nearby. He saw the two men sitting in the grime, zip tied to the radiator. He took two tennis balls while he told the men how the dogs must have been grateful for playtime. They would have loved to play fetch with the balls. He bounced them up and down and against the walls, playing a game of catch with himself. He stopped, took a good look at the tennis balls and swiftly jammed them in the men's mouths.

He sarcastically mentioned how the dogs must have appreciated the blankets and soft cotton materials that kept them warm and comfortable. He picked up two bloody rags from the dirty floor. He studied them, contemplating their benefits, "Hmm, let's see, aha!"

He tied the rags securely around the men's mouths, stuffing the tennis balls further down their throats, causing the men to gag. Helmuth gained some satisfaction seeing the men struggle to breathe. The men screamed beneath the tattered cloths, but Helmuth only heard muffled moans.

He told the men how the dogs must have appreciated feeding time. They must have wagged their tails when they saw their dog bowls approaching. He continued his sneering tone; acknowledge the men's concern for the pups, how nice it was for them to take such good care of the animals.

Helmuth picked up two cracked dog bowls, filled them with additional strips of cloth, and placed them under the radiator. He hummed happily as he pulled out his lighter from his pants pocket. He tossed it into the broken dog bowls, stayed for a while and watched the fire spread throughout the room. He watched the men struggle to free their bonds, twisting and squirming, their eyes wide with fright, their pupils dilated like black full moons.

One tried to use a sharp piece of the dog bowl to cut himself free, but it liquefied in his grasp, the plastic sticking to his hand, burning a hole in his palm. Their hair and eyebrows sizzled and disappeared. Their clothes caught on fire and sizzled from their bodies. Their ears and noses melted, elongated and dripped from their faces. The tennis balls and rags tied securely to their scorched faces muffled their cries.

Helmuth, the only one who heard them, inconspicuously strolled up the stairs and out the doors. He delighted in the irony. The two men, like the dogs they tortured, cried in agony for help, to no avail.

Chapter
FIVE
Samael's Beginnings

The pregnancy was emotionally difficult. I was torn between keeping the child who deserves a life and terminating the pregnancy. I was afraid the baby would be an ever-present reminder of the vicious attack. I was young and confused. I wasn't certain I could love the child. I wound up without a choice. My mother, Jean, forbade me to have an abortion. She said I made a decision to have unprotected sexual relations with a man I hardly knew; therefore, I was responsible to take care of and raise the child. Jean monitored my every move. She home-schooled me, cooked my meals and watched me eat. She slept with me in my bedroom and locked me in so she was aware of my movements throughout the night. She was determined to punish me for my mistake. I felt guilty and I was afraid to disobey her commands. I progressed through the months like a robot.

Samael was born six months later. He was premature, weighing only 2 pounds and eleven inches long. My mother rushed me to the hospital when my water broke. She abandoned me in the labor and delivery room. I was terrified. The pain was intolerable and I felt so alone. The labor lasted twelve hours. I pushed for three hours. I was exhausted. Samael emerged without a sound. The nurses whisked him away. I didn't see him for hours and I was grateful for the nap. They told me not to worry and I didn't. A part of me wished he would die. I didn't want to raise the spawn of a rapist. My mother, Jean. would not entertain the thought of adoption. She wanted me to suffer this consequence for the rest of my life. I wasn't sure I would be able to consistently care for his basic needs. The problem was, I only had my mother and she was no help to me.

The first time I held Samael, he was so small, and I thought he would break. I often had the urge to crush his bones with my bare hands or suffocate his face in my bosom. I felt no bond with him, no love.

The nurse and lactation specialist, Ginny, showed me how to breastfeed. I placed my nipple in his mouth and he began to suck. The pain sent a rippling sensation from my breast to my head. My eyes teared.

I did not feel a mothering connection to the baby. He always reminded me of the rape. I pushed Sam away and he tumbled to the floor. The nurse gasped. I mustered some crocodile tears and pretended to be troubled with my own reaction. Ginny picked up Sam, checked him for injuries and comforted him. He stopped crying quickly, confirming Ginny's assessment that he was unharmed. I didn't care. Ginny claims she understood the volatile emotions of a new mother and the hormone imbalance that caused my regrettable response. She encouraged me to try again. She explained how my body would grow accustomed to a wide range of sensations and feelings. I wondered if homicide was one of them. I continued breastfeeding because I could not afford formula and my mother insisted. She monitored the feedings, ensuring Sam received enough milk to provide him the proper quantity for his optimal development. I wished for any opportunity to flee from Jean. As the saying goes, "Be careful what you wish for."

We arrived home and my mother continued to shadow me, so I rebelled. I often left Sam in his crib crying. I didn't change his diaper until I smelled a foul order emanating from him. Even then, I would wait for my mother to scold me or change him herself. Sometimes when he cried out in hunger. I would curl up in a fetal position and sob until I fell asleep.

Seth showed up a few days later demanding to meet his son. Jean gladly invited him in for a cup of tea and called me to join them. I introduced Seth to Samael and he leaped back from the table. He was surprised the baby was so small and crinkly. He asked if I was positive, if he was the father. I turned and observed my mother grin and Seth laughed. I burst into tears. Seth yelled at me saying he didn't need two babies. He asked me to settle down, he had some good news he wanted to share.

Seth asked me to marry him so we could live together at his parents' house, as a family. My mother screeched, "Yes!" before I could respond. She scooted upstairs, threw my belongings into a few suitcases and trudged them down one at a time.

We moved into Seth's parents' house. Aaron and Joanie were gracious enough to split the space with us. They offered to live upstairs while the younger generation may live on the main floor. Seth wouldn't allow his parents to visit us. He banned them from the kitchen. They had to purchase a microwave and deep fryer to prepare their own meals.

Aaron and Joanie loved Samael. They helped me with the feedings; they bathed him and changed his diapers. They bought formula and accessories for the baby. They even bought some clothing for me.

Seth enjoyed abusing Samael and I. He loved the living arrangements. It was convenient for him to live without rent. He would wait for his parents to leave for work before inflicting any abuse. It angered Seth when Samael cried. Seth would lift the baby up by the ankles and bop him up and down like a yo-yo. As the baby's wailings increased so did the frequency of the bouncing. Fortunately, Seth tired of this hilarious game.

He turned Sam right-side up, carried him over to the kitchen and prepared his bottle. Seth was never at a loss for new exciting creative games. He found a delightful approach to feed a baby. Occasionally he would heat the milk until it was scalding. The baby would suck quickly and burn his mouth. Other times, Seth would add ice cubes to the bottle. He laughed when the baby flailed his arms and legs and choked on the frozen milk. This was one of Seth's favorite games. He liked it almost as much as football.

On a rare occasion, Seth would heat up the milk appropriately. Samael contently suckled on the milk bottle. Seth would wait a minute then take the bottle away from Sam. The baby would cry and Seth would laugh. He laughed so hard; tears fell from his eyes. He continued with his macabre game and start hitting the baby on the head with the bottle. This caused a bout of uncontrollable giggles. His abuse became too much for me.

One day at feeding time, Seth took the bottle from the baby's mouth. When he started to laugh, I yelled at him. That was a colossal mistake. Seth whipped off the baby's filthy diaper and smeared it all over my face. He wouldn't allow me to clean myself until he finished feeding Samael. I was allowed to clean my face with a hand towel after he forced me to licked as much off as I could with my tongue. It felt as abhorrent as the first time I met Seth; that brutal gruesome day he raped me. I only obeyed for fear of further repercussions. I sat silently in excrement, unable to protect myself. My faced flushed as I boiled with anger and hostility. I festered for an hour, my brain poisoned with resentment and hostility. I was completely drained of emotion and energy. I conked out and fell over.

Samael never attended preschool. When he started kindergarten, he was at a disadvantage socially, emotionally and intellectually. The other children mocked him. He went to school in grimy clothes; without lunch or snacks and he gave off a foul-smelling odor. The stench not only kept the children away, but caused further ridicule. He was much smaller than the other students were because he never ate enough. He was always hungry. He tried to ignore the emptiness in his stomach, which resembled the emptiness in his life. This was difficult. His stomach growled as he watched the other children eat their lunch and drink their milk. No one ever offered him a morsel. Sam was too shy to ask for a bite of their sandwich or a sip of their drink, but he would have gladly accepted if they offered. The teacher ate lunch with her co-workers. She was not concerned enough to notice Sam did not have food or drink.

He desperately wanted to have a friend. Sam was always the one with the "cooties." He was lonely, isolated and miserable. He didn't even have a dog to play with.

Sam's teacher wasn't even fond of Sam. She would never ask him to come up and write on the board. When she passed out crayons, she offered him the box after all the other children selected their three favorite colored crayons from the box. Sam was always left with brown, tan and beige. He didn't have a favorite color anyway, so it probably didn't matter. He often colored pictures of tan and beige dogs. He would have even settled for a stuffed animal, something soft and cuddly and friendly to hold until he grew up and rescued his own dog.

Many of the children brought their favorite toys on the day of show-and-tell. A few children asked their parents to take their dogs to show the class. Sam fell in love with Gail's French Bulldog. He was a rich chocolate color with a white stripe down his chest. He was about a foot tall, not counting his head. Sam loved the little perky ears and the sweet black eyes.

He asked Gail if he could pet her dog. She said, "No, I don't want him to smell like you." She said it loud enough so the entire class heard her. The boys and girls started laughing at him. The teacher and Gail's mother tried not to laugh. They held their hands over their mouths to hide their reaction to Gail's hysterical comment.

However, Seth could see the evil smile lurking behind their hands. It's difficult for a five-year-old to understand another child's cruelty, but to witness an adult act in the same heinous manner is absolutely unbearable. He understood at an early age that children learn their behaviors from their parents.

Sam slumped in his chair. Tears rolled down his face. He cried silently, hoping none of the children would notice. He thought, "One day I will have my own dog. He's all I will need. I will feed him and give him fresh water. I will take him for walks and play ball with him. I will buy him toys and a nice soft dog bed. *I hate these children; I hate this teacher. I even hate my parents…*"

Chapter
SIX
Aaron and Joanie Ravana

Aaron and Joanie Ravana lived in Plainledge their entire lives. Aaron was six feet tall with black hair and brown eyes. The constant work at the garage promoted his slim but muscular build. Aaron inherited the auto-body shop when his father passed away. His father taught him how to repair the cars, how to conduct a thorough inventory, order supplies and manage a successful business. Aaron enjoyed changing a wrecked car into an object of beauty. He would arrive early, put on his mechanic uniform and jump right in. It was not unusual for Aaron to work a ten- or twelve-hour shift. Once he entered the zone, time passed quickly.

Joanie was a schoolteacher at Plainledge Elementary school. She enjoyed spending her days with the children. She was five feet nine inches. She suffered from severe anxiety since she became a mother. She was constantly nervous and had difficulty eating without upsetting her stomach. She maintained meager 120 pounds.

Joanie and Aaron attending Plainledge school together and were friendly since kindergarten. They were married for two years when the found out the exciting news. They were pregnant with twins, a boy and a girl.

Joanie's pregnancy was stressful. The male baby developed mush more quickly than the female. Joanie had a sonogram after six months of stomach pain and vomiting. The doctor detected a heart murmur in the female baby. Further tests indicated no heart defect, but the parents would have to closely monitor the child after birth. They would report any breathing difficulties or discoloration of the skin. The male child was healthy and active. The sonogram displayed pictures of what was interpreted as the male kicking the female. They laughed at the time, thinking it was the beginning of a normal sibling rivalry.

Seth and Sarah were born at 35 weeks. Seth entered the world first at nineteen inches long, weighing six pounds. He screamed with a loud healthy voice, his fists clenched, and his face beat-red. Sarah arrived thirty minutes later. Joan had difficulty delivering her. Unlike her brother, Sarah didn't wasn't eager to introduce herself. She was sixteen inches long and weighed four pounds.

Although Sarah fed nicely and was always satisfied afterwards, Joan had problems breastfeeding Seth. He suckled for thirty minutes and still was not satiated. She had to supplement his feedings with baby formula. Aaron was delighted with the bottle-feeding. It offered him the opportunity to help Joanie and bond early with Seth. The twins differed in personality. Sarah was quiet but smiled often whereas Seth was irritable and fussy.

Seth was jealous of Sarah and the attention lavished upon her. Joanie and Aaron provided her with more affection because she was more interactive and enjoyed the engagement. They hovered over her due to her heart murmur which resulted in breathing issues. Seth would kick, pinch her and knock her down whenever the mood struck him. The mood struck him a few times each day. His parents worried about his behavior but only believed in reinforcements. They would never punish Seth, only encourage him. "Be nice to your sister." He never obeyed them.

A week after the twins' fifth birthday, Joanie and Aaron were jolted from their sleep from a terrifying scream coming from Sarah's bedroom. They dashed to her room to comfort her. She was sitting at the edge of her bed wringing her hands and sobbing. She was inconsolable and found it difficult to breath. She shook more violently when they asked her what happened, and she refused to speak. They assumed she had a bad dream. They remained in her room for hours until she finally sobbed herself to sleep. Joanie decided to spend the night in Sarah's room. She tucked herself in the bed next to Sarah, but laid still with her eyes open, staring at the ceiling. She couldn't figure out what frightened her daughter so badly.

Aaron let out a screech on his way out. He stepped on a sharp object which stuck in his foot and lodged deeper as he stepped down. Joanie sat up and put her hand to her mouth, silently instructing him to be quiet. Aaron sat down and pulled out the pin embedded in his big toe. He held it up for Joanie to see, turned around to make sure he did not disturb Sarah and stood to leave the room. Fortunately, Sarah was asleep, unalarmed. Joanie shrugged her shoulders and laid her head back on the pillow. She wasn't stupid. She had her suspicions. They terrified her. *Could it be possible her own…could Seth…?* She couldn't face the possibility. A mother's love for their children is powerful. Denial is an effective coping skill, but at what costs?

Seth despised his sister. She was small and weak and demanded too much attention. Seth didn't want any recognition. He just felt sickened in the manner his parents treated Sarah. Their relationship with her was overbearing. He deemed it intolerable how they encouraged her dependent personality.

Seth was especially angry on their fifth birthday. His parents sang happy birthday and sang Sarah's name first. He was born first; he was the boy; they should sing his name first because he was number one.

He waited patiently for a night when his parents went to bed early. He selected a few large pins from his mother's sewing kit. He held two pins in each hand between his thumbs and forefingers and tiptoed into Sarah's room. He would have liked to use more, but they fell from his grasp. He had to settle with his still too-small hands. He slinked over to Sarah's bed and attacked her with the pins. He pulsed upon her back as if it was a drum. He thought he may even grow up and study music. The percussion was invigorating. He felt powerful, inflicting pain on a weak, helpless creature.

As soon as Sarah opened her eyes she started to scream. She felt the sharp pointy jolts of pain pulsating upon her back. She immediately knew the perpetrator was her awful brother, but was too afraid to tell her parents Seth rushed out of her room. He leaped onto his bed, covered himself with his blanket and pretended to sleep through the chaos. He took advantage of the fact that Sarah was afraid of him. She wouldn't dare have the gumption to tattle on him.

Seth continued to find means to cause Sarah misery. The teenage years were his favorite. He was very interested in Sarah's body as she developed. He

48

was entitled to observe, touch and use his twin in any manner he desired. He proceeded slowly, hiding in her closet while she undressed. He would wait for her to take her clothes off before he giggled. He loved the sight of her face when she realized he was hiding in the closet. She quickly covered her breasts with her right arm and covered her pubic area with left hand. He walked over to her slowly while she tried to reach for the clothes she recently threw on the floor. She yelled for Mom and Dad. Mom glared at Set, but said nothing. She was also frightened of him, so did not broach the subject. She escorted Sarah downstairs for a cup of tea. Aaron told Seth it wasn't nice to tease his sister.

Seth allowed a few months to pass. Mom and Dad never raised the issue again. It was all a silly incident in the past. Sarah had a tendency for overdramatizing every trivial situation.

Joanie and Aaron attended a wedding celebration on July 4th and the twins were alone. Seth waited eagerly for this opportunity. Sarah planned to attend her friend's Independence Day party. It was evening, fireworks displays were just beginning. She went upstairs to don her new bikini. Seth didn't wait in the closet. He forced her door open and charged in just as she put on the bathing suit. He knocked her down and slid on top of her. She yelled for help, but the neighbors were out shooting off fireworks. He ripped off her bikini top and stuffed it in her mouth. He pulled down the bathing suit bottom. The neighbors may not have heard her screams, but they were annoying to Seth. He touched her, he tasted her, and he raped her until he was exhausted. Sarah fought at first, kicking and scratching at him, begging and pleading for him to stop. After what seemed like hours, she simply laid there and received the assault uncontested. Her faced was streaked with the cosmetics that were meant to make her beautiful. Her new bathing suit ripped and discarded on the floor and her life as it was before this evening, was irrevocably destroyed.

She waited for Seth to leave the house. She gingerly lifted herself from the floor. There was blood and dirt caked upon her body. Bodily fluids dripped down her legs. She walked slowly to the bathroom and filled the bathtub with warm soapy water. She took a razor blade from the medicine cabinet, lowered herself into the tub and slit her left arm from the wrist to the elbow. She didn't feel any pain, just a relief, a letting go, an escape. She transferred the blade to her right hand and repeated the mutilation to her left arm. She rested in that spot, staring at the ceiling, tears staining her face as the blood drained her body and her life.

Aaron and Joanie returned from their 4th of July party after midnight. They sat in the kitchen. Joanie put on the teakettle to relax with a cup of herbal tea before going to bed. Aaron took two cups and a bottle of honey from the cupboard. Joanie poured the two cups with Mint herbal tea and joined Aaron at the table. She heard water running, but assumed one of the kids woke up to use the bathroom. However, she felt uneasy when they finished their tea and she realized the sound of the water continued to stream through the pipes.

She immediately sensed something was amiss and dashed up the stairs. Aaron yelled for her. When she didn't answer, he charged after her. The bathroom door was locked. Joanie screamed for Sarah. She knew it was her daughter, not her son. The hall was silent except for the running water. Joanie pounded and cried out. Aaron pushed her aside and kicked the door repeatedly until the lock broke and the door cracked open.

Aaron reached the tub first, straining to pull Sarah out. Joanie screamed, grabbed hold of the counter to steady herself, and then sprang into action. They lifted Sarah from the water and placed her onto the floor. Joanie fought with her sanity, called 9-1-1 and shut off the faucet while Aaron administered CPR.

Joanie heard the sound of the siren in the distance. She mistakenly believed the paramedics would arrive and revive her daughter. She probably realized there was no hope, but the alternate was too difficult to accept. The paramedics and police arrived. Aaron frantically continued to compress Sarah's chest persistently. Sweat poured down his face. His breath was shallow, his pulse racing. The police officer had no choice but to pry Aaron away from the body.

They pronounced Sarah dead. They estimated she died at least seven or eight hours ago.

Joanie produced sounds only a parent could generate after losing a child. The gut-wrenching wailing echoed across the house. The police officer was unable to conceal her own sobbing and forced to excuse herself before she contributed to the turmoil.

The EMT hoisted Sarah's body onto the gurney, strapped her to the mattress and carried her down the flight of stairs. The technician allowed Aaron and Joanie to drive with their daughter in the ambulance.

Chapter
SEVEN
Lucy and Dakota

Halloween was tomorrow. I wasn't sure how Dakota would react to all of the trick-or-treaters. I had a little time to take her around the neighborhood and introduce her to the neighbors, their children and their dogs. After yesterday's plunge into darkness, I was somewhat edgy myself.

We visited The Plainledge Animal Shelter for a costume for Dakota. She was a good sport and sat patiently while I dressed her in a few costumes. They were fashioned to accommodate the most restless dog. I didn't have to cover her entire body. I just lifted the clothing over her head and tied the two strings in a knot. The rest of the outfit hung down her chest and front legs. It created the illusion that she was actually wearing an entire costume.

I decided on the angel costume. She was the cutest angel I ever saw. Shaggy was at the register. She wasn't very happy. The shelter was full of Halloween-themed customers and their dogs. Costumes laid opened in every aisle. Not only did Shaggy have to ring up the sales, but she had to continuously bag and re-shelve the costumes for further sales.

I approached her and asked her if she would like some help with the littered items. She smiled for the first time since I entered the store. She said she would really appreciate my help and bent down to tap Dakota's head. I folded and packaged all of the discarded items and displayed them on the appropriate racks. Dakota did not follow me. She remained with Shaggy. I returned to the counter; mission accomplished. Shaggy was talking quietly to Dakota. She spoke in a high-pitched, childlike fashion, in the same manner many of us speak to our dogs. When she noticed me, her voice changed. She was more serious, less friendly. She asked me if I wanted to work with her at the shelter. She told me her parents owned it and they were looking for help. I accepted the job, part-time on weekends. I remained full-time at Paul-Anthony Waldron's Construction Company and worked weekends at the Plainledge Animal Shelter. Dakota was allowed to join me. She loved playing with the dogs and greeting the customers.

The first costumed family arrived at 3 pm the next day. There were three children, a Princess, a Superhero and a Pumpkin. They were accompanied by their mother, who wore a witch's hat. Dakota jumped up and stood at my side. She was whimpering and slightly shaking. I decided it may be best to take her outside and let her meet the children. I opened the door and held up my index finger, silently mouthing the words, "One minute."

I clipped on Dakota's leash, opened the door, picked up the bowl of candy and took her outside. The children were delighted. They overlooked the candy and asked if they were allowed to pet my dog and wanted to know her name. I told the kids her name is Dakota and I bent down to ask Dakota if she would like the children to pet her. At first, she seemed hesitant. However, she sensed they were friendly and meant her no harm. The girl in the Princess costume watched me bend down and mimicked my behavior.

She said, "What a beautiful doggy," and scratched behind Dakota's ears. Dakota loved her immediately.

The Superhero stroked Dakota's head. The little pumpkin held back, hiding behind her mother. Dakota laid down by the little one and put her head on her mother's foot. The pumpkin giggled, slowly inching downward to pet Dakota.

She touched her ear, then her head, and then sat down on the ground, put her head on Dakota's body and simply said, "Nice doggie." It was a successful beginning to Dakota's first Halloween in her new home.

What the heck was happening? Lucy answered the door to three disguised little tykes and goofy woman donning a witch's hat. Were they in the Witness Protection Program? Did they somehow turn into these creatures? Did Lucy have a cure; did she have the ability to change them back to their original form? Lucy grabbed a bowl of treats. I hoped they included dog biscuits. To my dismay, the bowl was full of candy. I heard the little creatures ask if they could pet me. I was confused. They smelled harmless and had adorable smiles, but why did they knock on my door in such ridiculous garb? Was the candy a weapon in case they attacked us? I had to proceed on instinct. I bowed down next to the one that resembled a pumpkin and allowed her to touch me. Wow, my instincts were correct. Her touch was magical. My doubt melted from my body seeping into the cement below me. I never thought I would have a chance to say, I was overjoyed sitting outside with a pumpkin.

The rest of the day went well until late evening. I thought the trick-or-treating was finished for the day. However, I remembered, there was always one late knocker. Dakota was excited to see another guest, as the doorbell was quiet for some time. Dakota ran to the door as I took the bowl to deliver the last pieces of candy. When we opened the door, we were confused. No one was standing there. It was probably a late-night Halloween prank. I stepped on the doormat to see if anyone was around. It was foggy and I couldn't see far, but I heard Dakota's all-familiar whining sound, signaling danger.

I closed the door so she couldn't get out. I took another step as I thought I saw something in the fog. The more I squinted, the more visible the shape developed. Dakota's whining became louder, more terrifying. I backed into the house to retreat from the maleficent shape and to comfort Dakota. I locked the door, shut the lights and took Dakota into the small rectangular room near the den. I dared not enter the bedroom.

As we sat in the front room, the fog spread through the window, obstructing any available light. However, there was a strange luminescent light breaking through the fog. We could see the fog, at first a mist of nothingness. It began to move. On the right, a stick shape formed, quickly changing into a more detailed, "No, no, it can't be. That's impossible." It was developing into an arm. To the left, another arm began to develop. They were vague without much detail. We had no choice but to focus on the iridescent light source.

A figure of a body appeared between the arms, and then two legs appeared. Dakota and I witnessed this same apparition in The Dark Place beneath my bed. I remember the legs ending in shredded stumps barren of feet. We met this Stretchman yesterday. The eyeless head pressed up against the window.

Vapors clouded the window with wet mist. The head continued to grow until the empty eye socket covered the entire window. We were sucked into the eyeless void dragging us magically through the window without any pain. The terrifying fear returned as we began to fall again.

We landed in the same dark place as yesterday. I took hold of Dakota's leash and knelt down to stay close to her. I noticed numerous holes embedded in the clammy ground. It looked like an abandoned golf course attacked by gophers. The holes were riddled with scratch marks, long indentations hastily made by an animal, probably a dog.

Dogs are both clever and protective. I saw the scratch marks; the holes were deep enough for a dog and his human to hide. It probably signified a dog had been digging for his and his human's protection. I was forced to suppress my fear. I search deep in my soul and mustered all of my bravery and strength. I started digging my own hole for me and Lucy. We needed to hide until we could figure out how to help the other captors escape. I scratched and clawed until my paws bled. Lucy stopped me and finished digging the massive hole herself. She took the clip out of her hair to scoop out more dirt in a shorter amount of time. However, the hairclip broke and she had to use her own nails. When we were both exhausted and bleeding, we jumped in the hole.

Dakota's idea was perfect albeit uncomfortable. We huddled together listening to Stretchman above us. It was groaning and sniffing to no avail. The moist dirt must have covered our scent, making it impossible for it to detect us. The sound of it shuffling back and forth was chilling. It bent down to scratch the ground. It had a temper tantrum, clumping and clomping from one area to the next, never far from our hiding place. It finally moved past us, sniffing out further locations. We waited a few minutes for it to float away from us before we ventured out of our self-made coffin. We slowly swished the dirt from our heads and crawled gradually out of the hole. I allowed Dakota to join me when the coast was clear.

I found it helpful to keep contact with the wall as we followed the path toward the Stretchman. I kept my right hand on the wall while my left hand held onto Dakota's leash. The last thing I needed was to lose contact with her.

Dakota stopped and stuck her nose in one of the holes. She would not move from her position. She could be very stubborn, but I knew something was wrong. She uttered the familiar whining noise indicating something was amiss. I looked down to a new horror. I saw three dark little fingers sticking out of the loosely covered dirt hole. A thumb, an index finger and a middle finger, wiggling nervously. I quickly brushed the few inches of dirt of the fingers and kept digging. The little fingers were attached to a small hand. I pulled the hand up gently and a head, body and the rest of the child emerged. She was covered in dirt and grim. Her brown skin and chocolate brown eyes were wide-open, fear causing her pupils to dilate. Her brunette hair looked tangled and snarled. She must have been 4 years old. She was, shy of 3 feet tall, weighing about 30 pounds. I cleaned her off as best I could. She was able to speak, but only in whispers. Her body had not yet decomposed into the zombie-like ghost. I hugged her close to me and noticed a leash in her hand. I asked her where was her dog and she pointed toward the hole.

I gently pulled at the leash while I swiped away more of the dirt. A furry head with tan curly hair emerged, so I kept moving the dirt away from the poor creature. The little girl started to cry with delight as the two triangular ears appeared, followed by a round hairy head with two little black eyes and a black nose. He looked like a small wooly brown bear. I brushed some of the dirt off his fur and I handed him to the little girl. He was about 11 inches tall and weighed about 3 pounds. She had no problem holding him. This must have been a normal routine for her. She tried to say her name, but she was only able to make the "B" sound. It was difficult for her to speak. However, when I asked her what was the dog's name; she smiled and whispered, "Cody." I asked her if there were more dogs or people buried in the dirt. She nodded. Dakota helped me dig out until we reached the others. It wasn't too difficult to dig, as the people were not buried too deeply.

We reached the boy first. He was older than the girl was, probably 7 years old. He was about 3 ½ feet tall, weighing about 40 pounds. He shared the same deep brown skin, chocolate brown eyes and brunette hair as the girl. He stared at me, looking confused. I introduced Dakota and myself. Dakota stuck her head under his hand, giving him the opportunity to pet her. He responded immediately. He knelt down and wrapped himself around Dakota and stuffed his head into her body. His love for dogs evaporated his fear immediately, if not temporarily. Like the girl, his body had not yet deteriorated. He was not afraid to speak, but did so quietly. He said his name was Connor. The girl was his sister, Bella. His brother, Kevin was also hiding in the hole with his mother and father. He said their names were "Mommy" and "Daddy."

We found Kevin next. He was approximately 10 years old, 4 ½ feet tall, weighing only 60 pounds. He had similar skin, eyes and hair color as his siblings, but his color was fading. His body had minor deterioration. I was able to see a boyish figure, but his arms and legs were less visible. He was in the early process of turning into a half-human-half-spirit. He spoke very slowly as if time was distorted.

"Mmmyy nnamme iiss Keevviinn." It was painful to watch him struggle with his words. Connor volunteered to speak for the three of them. The boys stepped near their sister and all gently touched the dog. I noticed a slight change as Kevin stood next to his siblings and touched the dog. Unless my imagination was over-reacting, I could swear his arms and legs grew substance. They didn't seem quite as transparent. Bella handed Cody over to Kevin. Cody licked Kevin's face and stuck his nose in Kevin's ear like a cotton swab. Kevin smiled and said,

"Sshe aalways ddoes tthat." It was such a sweet moment. There we were, trapped in a terrifying dungeon with a powerful evil monster, yet a small dog was able to muster the love and quiet the fear, if only for a minute or two.

Chapter

EIGHT

Babs, Paul-Anthony Waldron, and Family

Babs and Paul-Anthony Waldron lived down the block. They had a big house and a bigger family. Dakota liked them immediately. They provided many playmates. They had three dog-loving children who showered him with affection. They each rescued their own dog, totaling five people and five furry friends. The six dogs became quick friends, often romping together in the tremendous yard. They delighted in sniffing each others' butts, play-fighting and chasing each other around the trees.

The house was located on a three-acre plot on the cusp of a cul-de-sac. There was a huge living room to the left of the front door. Their furniture was situated against the walls so the children and dogs had plenty of room to play and run around. They didn't care if the carpet was full of dog hair or food crumbs, nightly vacuuming took care of the build-up. The more important issue was everyone had fun, cared for each other and took especially good care of their dog. To the right of the living area was a den full of children and dog toys. Going further in a clockwise circular motion was a kitchen, installed with the usual appliances. A counter, used as the table stood in the center of the kitchen. The floor was black and white tiles, purposely chosen for easy clean up.

To the right of the kitchen completing the circle was a smaller room housing the five dog cages. The cages were equipped with blankets and covered in dark sheets for privacy, sleep and comfort. They remained open, so the dogs were able to use them when needed. They usually choose to sleep in their respective cages, but often used them to escape the noise and excitement when necessary. One bathroom was behind the kitchen, the other behind the den. The bathroom doors had to stay closed or one of the dogs would steal the roll of toilet paper and run around the house. The four dogs followed, snapping at the thin white tissue flowing behind the leader of the pack. The pounding rivaled a 6 or 7 on the Richter Scale.

The wooden staircase was to the left of the front door leading to the four bedrooms and four bathrooms on the second floor. Each child had its own bedroom. Babs and Paul shared the Master Bedroom, although a young human or furry friend was apt to intrude on their privacy.

Babs was a Veterinarian's Assistant. She worked part-time at The Plainledge Animal Shelter while the children attended school. She and Paul saved enough money so she was able to stay at home when the children were home and rescue as many dogs as possible. Her dog's name was Siggy. She chose the name in honor of her favorite psychologist, Sigmund Freud. Babs took an introductory psychology course at St. Katharine's University, where she earned her undergraduate Bachelors of Science degree in Biology. She remembers how passionate Dr. Diedre spoke about the theorists, the Id, the Ego and the Superego. She found it so interesting she minored in psychology.

61

Siggy was a beagle. She was 15 inches and 20 pounds. Babs made sure to keep Siggy's weight under control. As a Veterinarian's Assistant, she was aware that a dog needed to maintain an appropriate weight for a healthy lifestyle, mobility and ease on their joints. Siggy had long floppy brown ears, a white and tan tail that stood erect, and a white stripe around her nose. She had an amusing howl that always produced a smile or laugh from the people nearby.

Babs' only worry was her bad dreams. Since Kyle, her oldest, was born, she had a recurring nightmare. She dreamed she took Kyle for a leisurely walk in her neighborhood, while her dog, Tucker, followed closely behind. Tucker was a Newfoundland. He was tremendous, reaching 27 inches and weighing 160 pounds. Luckily, he was well-behaved or Babs would have difficulty controlling him.

As what often happened in dreams, she was suddenly in an alternate reality, finding herself in a dim, clammy tunnel. It was difficult to see; only a faint light coming from ahead scantly laminated the passageway. She held Kyle with her left arm and held Tucker on his leash with her right arm. Tucker started to whimper. It was a low sound coming from the back of his throat, quickly escalating into a threatening growl, communicating potential threat.

Tucker pulled on the leash with such force that Babs struggled to hold him. She was unable to retain her grip and he ran down the hall. She quickly lost sight of Tucker due to the poor lighting, but heard his cries diminish as he ran further away. She saw a shadow blocking most of the dim light. The shadow was gigantic, about eight feet tall. It was unusual, the arms and legs stretching to unrealistic lengths. The shape appeared to float a few inches above the ground. She yelled for Tucker. It was strange that he wouldn't listen to her calls, but he was too focused on trying to protect her from the hidden danger. His barking became frantic, loud growling and snarling. She saw the shadow lift Tucker off the ground. She heard a dying YELP...

She woke up screaming, shaking and sweating. She was so scared she couldn't move, couldn't even get up to use the bathroom. Paul-Anthony heard her screams and ran in to comfort her. Babs described the dream. Her husband assured her that she was safe and reminded her it was only a dream. She didn't even have a dog named Tucker. Intellectually she knew it was a dream, but she wasn't so sure emotionally. Somehow, it seemed more tangible. She never mentioned her nightmares to anyone except Paul. She was embarrassed admit her fears and night terrors.

Paul-Anthony owned his own successful construction company. It had a very catchy acronym called Paul-Anthony Waldron's Construction Company – PAWs Construction. He was skilled in masonry, HVAC and plumbing. His training allowed him to build exercise equipment, climbing apparatuses and training devices for dogs. The dogs especially liked the agility seesaw showing off their ability to their humans and fellow dogs. He donated many pieces to The Plainledge Animal Shelter. Paul was delighted that his job afforded him the opportunity to support his family and recue multiple dogs.

Paul had his own dog named Vixen. She was a sweet terrier mix weighing 40 pounds, reaching 25 inches tall. She was mostly black with short hair, a long thin tail and ears that stood partially upright then flopped downward. Vixen was an older dog. Paul hoped a tranquil dog would have a calming effect on the children and the other dogs. Of course, he was wrong, but he didn't mind the constant noise and chaos at the Waldron family household. Paul-Anthony always loved dogs and wanted for a big family, maybe three or four children, each having their own dog. His wishes were fulfilled.

Babs and Paul-Anthony had three children, who each had a dog. Kyle was 14. He was in 9th grade. He played the trombone in the Plainledge High School band. He rescued a Cadoodle called Max. This breed was a glorious mix of a Collie and Poodle. Max was 22 inches and 50 pounds. He had a white furry body; long, thin black, tan and white tricolored nose; and black alert ears. His eyes were a coffee brown. Max was intelligent and energetic.

Kyle had night terrors similar to his mother's, but harbored the fear himself. As many 14-year-old boys, he didn't want to show any emotions that may label him a coward. His reputation was important and didn't want anyone to think less of him. He used to experience the nightmares a few times a year, but recently they had been occurring more often, almost weekly.

Kyle dreamed he was in school in the crowded hallway between classes. The rush of students chatting, going to their lockers and running to their next class was typical. Like most dreams, the scene changed without warning. He was in the school building, but there were no other students or teachers. The hallways were deserted. He could hear his own footsteps as he walked around slowly, trying to make sense of the quick change. He suddenly felt a projectile weapon, landing on his chest, knocking the wind out of him. He fell backward to the ground, landing on his back. Before he registered the pain, he felt a wet sloppy tongue sliding across his face.

Max had somehow managed to find the High School and decided to keep Kyle company and protect him from any possible evil dweller. Max was usually able to make Kyle laugh, but Kyle was not amused at the moment. The walls started to bulge and expand. Kyle grabbed Max and tried to run. He couldn't move. The walls turned into crazy glue. His sneakers stuck like a Band-Aid on a fresh wound. Max jumped out of Kyle's grasp, bit down on his shirt and tried to pull him out of the sticky muck. They heard a soft eerie laughter coming from behind the wall a few inches to their right. Max released his hold on Kyle and sprinted to the wall. Kyle cried out for Max, stretching his arms out as far as possible, desperately reaching for him. Kyle was helpless. He couldn't reach Max, nor could he move.

Max jumped through the brick wall. He simply glided through without any difficulty. It was an impossible feat, but Kyle watched Max as he disappeared. He heard a hasty bark; a fleeting whimper and Max was gone. Kyle woke, trembling and sweating. He couldn't differentiate realty from the dream. He heard a low rumbling snore and found Max sleeping at the foot of his bed. Although Kyle felt reassured, Max never slept on his bed. He always slept downstairs in his crate next to the other dogs. Something was amiss.

Maddie was 10. She was big for her age, already 5'4", weighing 130 pounds. She used her size to her advantage, playing goalie on her 5th grade Plainledge Elementary School intramurals team. She rescued Nicklaus, but called him Nick. Nick was a mix of various breeds, unknown to the shelter. He had furry white hair. His black eyes and nose were the only parts of her that were not white. He was 27 inches tall and 100 pounds. Maddie wanted a big, tough dog to match her own size and personality. They were similar in their personalities, as they were assertive to a fault. They were fiery loyal to those they loved and wouldn't stand down to any oppositions. Maddie experienced more opposition than she should have at such a young age.

Maddie observed a lot of bullying behavior in her elementary school. It often happened in the lunchroom. Lucas was the school bully. A fifth grader who was really a coward. He only picked on children smaller and younger than himself. He made certain to have a few friends by his side before tormenting another student. His biggest mistake was when he chose to pick on Daniel.

Daniel was the youngest at 6 years old. Daniel was a quiet child who wasn't relaxed around his 1st grade classmates. In fact, he wasn't at ease in any social situation. He was diagnosed with a mild form of Asperger's Syndrome. He only responded to questions with one-word responses and never initiated a conversation. However, he would speak through his dog. He didn't display any affection, but obsessively stroked his security blanket.

He rescued Chestnut, a Pomchi, a Pomeranian Chihuahua mix. Chestnut was 6 inches and weighed 12 pounds. He had a rich sable coat with pointed ears and cute black button eyes and nose. He looked like a small chubby fox. Daniel was able to substitute Chestnut for his blanket, petting and stroking him throughout the day and evening. Chestnut enjoyed this obsession and never complained. Daniel felt more comfortable with his dog than he did with people. If you looked closely, you could see a small curve form on his lips resembling a smile whenever Chestnut was near.

Daniel brought his own lunch to school, but always kept lunch money in his backpack. His mother gave him money on the first day of school and it stayed in his backpack for months. He felt uncomfortable standing in line to buy a school lunch, so he ate his cold sandwich while the other kids enjoyed a hot lunch. His favorite food was pizza. Every Friday was "Pizza Friday." He longed to walk up to the line, take a tray and pay the lunch lady just like everyone else. Daniel was motivated to make this Friday different. He had a long talk with Chestnut last night.

I had a long talk with Daniel last night. He told me he was afraid to get in line to buy pizza tomorrow. I snuggled him and licked his face. He understood my nonverbal advice. This was how I told him to think of me when he was in school, to pretend I was with him. I advised him to put one of Karen's homemade dog biscuits in his backpack to remind him of me. He could reach in and touch the biscuit whenever he needed my support. It would be just like petting me. I told him it had magic. (Little boys believe in magic.) I was not trying to deceive Daniel, but to offer him the support he needed, even when I could not be present.

Daniel reached into his backpack and grabbed his lunch money. He touched Karen's homemade dog biscuit, felt Chestnut's presence and took a deep breath. He looked around the lunchroom, slowly stood up and walked over to the line. He grabbed a tray, took a slice of pizza from the shelf and paid the cashier. He was elated. His was able to buy a piece of pizza and enjoy a hot lunch like a normal person. He started to walk back to his seat, with his head held a little higher. He felt proud of himself.

Suddenly he was falling. His tray flew across the room causing a loud clatter. His pizza landed cheese-side down. His elbows smashed into the floor, the pain shooting up to his shoulder. Then he heard it. A slow laugh behind him. He turned his head and saw Lucas standing above him, bellowing and pointing at him. Daniel stood up while the hooting escalated. Tears streamed his face, pain coursed through his arms and snot dripped from his nose. Time stopped. As he stood listening to the thunderous laughter, he blanked out. He could no longer hear or see the sneering buffoons around him. His mind took him to Chestnut. They were in his house, sitting on his bed. He stroked Chestnut rhythmically. Back and forth, soothing his fragile state.

He felt someone shaking him and he returned to reality. Maddie escorted him back to his seat. She just finished hockey practice. She heard the commotion as she was heading to the locker room to shower and change. She wore her goalie uniform and padding, her cleats, her helmet and she held her goalie stick.

Lucas saw her and the laughter died. His grin disappeared from his smug face. Maddie walked toward him as if she was defending her goal, her goalie stick threateningly at her side. Lucas had no time to consider his next move. She crouched down and hit him with her shoulder in his midsection. He lost his breath and doubled over. She swung the goalie stick upward, making contact with his chin. He slipped on Daniel's pizza, falling backward, and landed on his spine. The pain hit his tailbone and continued up to his neck. He laid in a fetal position, covering his head for any possible future blows.

The cafeteria went wild. One student began to clap, others followed suit until the applause was deafening. Maddie calmly proceeded to Daniel, took him by the hand and led him out of the lunchroom. Daniel shyly looked up at Maddie with a smile on his face that brightened her heart. She figured she would suffer some consequences, but she chose her own actions and would accept the penalty.

Paul-Anthony was busy working, constructing a student center on at the High School athletics field complex. He received a call from the Junior High/High School Principal, Ms. Blake, who reported the incident in detail. Paul-Anthony loaded his materials onto his van in earnest. The white construction van highlighted blue letters depicting the company name:

Paul-Anthony Waldron's construction.

The initials, P.A.W, were painted cobalt blue to accentuate the anagram he loved. He drove the speed limit to the school. He didn't want to add a speeding ticket to the family crisis. Babs was involved with a dog who swallowed a sock. She administered some ipecac syrup to help him expel the sock and immediately drove to the school.

Paul-Anthony and Babs arrived at the school at the same time. The administrative assistant immediately whisked them into the principal's office. It reminded Paul-Anthony of his high school days when he was summoned to Principal Crowley's office. The students feared Crowley. He would slap their hands with the ruler until red welts surfaced. The welts made designs on his knuckles like bloodshot spiders trying to break through the back of his hands. Fortunately, Crowley no longer occupied The

Principal's Office. Ms. Blake was the acting Principal for both the Junior High and the High School.

Her office was practical and uninviting. She sat behind a tan plywood desk that contained two small drawers on the left. The flat top was 4 feet long and three feet wide. It barely fit an antiquated computer and a black land-based telephone. Two aluminum chairs were situated in front of the meager desk.

Ms. Blake sat behind the desk when Paul-Anthony and Babs walked in. She was built like a bulldog, five feet tall wearing heels, 130 pounds of pure muscle. She was either a Cross-fitter or a weight trainer. Her short-cropped brown hair made her look severe, stern and unfriendly. She was somewhere between fifty and sixty years old.

Suddenly, Paul-Anthony wished Principal Crowley occupied the role.

Although Babs wasn't intimidated, Paul-Anthony shyly sat in one of the wobbly chairs. He was afraid to make eye contact, so he gazed at the floor. Principal Blake snatched a ruler from the draw so quickly it looked like a magic trick. She held it in her right hand while she continued slapping it in her left hand. She blamed Maddie's behavior on poor parenting, accentuating each word with a slap of the ruler. She stared at Paul-Anthony sensing his apprehension. He recoiled in his seat.

When she finally finished her monologue, Paul-Anthony scurried out of her office and managed to get home without further incident. Babs shook Ms. Blake's hand and asked her if the two of them could chat more about Maddie at another time. Paul-Anthony discussed the situation with Babs. They were happy Ms. Blake didn't call child protective services, accusing them of neglect. They decided on an appropriate consequence for Maddie.

Maddie accepted the responsibility for her actions and agreed to the punishment. Her parents required she volunteered at The Plainledge Animal Shelter for five hours per week for five weeks. Babs was aware of the importance of community service. She wanted Maddie to learn to think of others before meeting her own needs, to engage positively in the community and to acquire patience. The dogs would help her gain these skills.

Maddie loved dogs, so this was the best punishment she could receive. She did acquire these skills. She was forced to behave kindly and positively when she ordered dog supplies and food from the various agencies, especially when she requested discounts or free donations. She completed her chores, feeding the dogs, filling their water bowls and cleaning their cages before she ate her own dinner. She had no trouble with patience, as she lovingly cared for each dog's specific dietary needs or mobility assistance. These qualities arose naturally to her when she was caring for the pups. Nick reaped the benefits. He joined Maddie every day at The Shelter.

I loved following Maddie around the store, playing with the other dogs and occasionally stealing an unwrapped homemade dog biscuit from a nose-level shelf. I quickly learned how to hold a biscuit in my mouth. I was so smart, this was not difficult for me, although I did have to repress the urge to gobble it up so I could offer them to the puppies. I would zoom from the shelf to the pup's cages bringing them cookie after cookie. I loved watching their tails wag and delighted in their pleasure. I was so excited; I peed on the floor a few times. The senior dogs were more of a challenge. Some of them were not able to chew the crunchy cookies. I had to find a box of soft-chews, rip it open

71

with my teeth before I could deliver them some treats. I remained in their pens while they ate their cookies. I wanted them to take their time so they didn't hurt their sore gums. Somehow, I would have to figure out a way to deliver a message to Karen asking her to bake soft cookies necessary for the older dogs.

Maddie received additional consequences, however. Lucas's parents sued the Waldron's for his medical bills. Lucas suffered a broken jaw and had to have his mouth wired shut for six months. He was only able to eat a liquid diet. Maddie was responsible for paying his parents for the medical bills. She walked dogs and dog- sat when their humans went out for the evening. She earned quite a bit of money as the dog owners paid well for quality care.

The principal suspended Maddie from school for a week. It would not be included on her permanent record, as she was a minor. However, she would be responsible for completing the assignments, homework and projects she missed, during her own free time. She used the opportunity to work in The Plainledge Animal Shelter for extra money and Maddie used her first paycheck to send Lucas a box of chocolate caramels.

Daniel had ambivalent reactions to Maddie's behavior. He was touched by her loyalty and thought she was so bad-ass for her actions. She was a real superhero. Yet, he was disappointed that his attempt at bravery failed. He felt like a loser. He was afraid he would never again be motivated to buy a hot lunch. The magical dog biscuit didn't help, nor did his false bravado. He felt like an ant carrying food to the anthill, only to be squashed by a shoe. He cradled Chestnut in his arms, buried his face in his fur and sobbed until he was exhausted.

Kyle heard Daniel's cries and knocked on his bedroom door. He and Max entered. Kyle sat next to Daniel and placed his arm around his shoulder, pulling him close. Max jumped up, his hind legs missing the edge of the bed. His front paw catching Kyle's shirt pocket. He lost control and slipped backward, taking Kyle with him. They spun to the floor, Max landing on top of Kyle. Before Kyle had a chance to react, Daniel started laughing. He was crying and laughing, simultaneously. Chestnut wagged his tail and licked Daniels tears. Kyle joined the appreciated change in mood and laughed with Daniel. Max, hesitant to repeat his failed attempt to snag the bed, manically turned in circles in pursuit of his tail.

Kyle explained to Daniel how bad things happen to everyone, even if they don't deserve it. We must keep trying or we can never reach our goals. He told Daniel he was so proud that he mustered the nerve to stand up and buy the pizza. He sympathized how difficult this was, how much courage Daniel must have and how he was able to access the inner strength to act brave in an uncomfortable situation. Some people rejoice in hurting others, but most are kind and caring. The main lesson is, "Don't give up." The bad guys always get what they deserve in the long run. Kyle reminded Daniel how Lucas suffered a broken jaw and dire consequences.

Chapter
NINE
Ms. Blake

Ms. Michelle Blake happily accepted the principal position at both the Plainledge Junior High and High School when Principal Crowley died twenty years ago. Ms. Blake taught history for ten years before taking on the administrative role. She graduated St. Katharine's University with a Bachelor of Arts degree in History/Adolescent Education. Her advisor, Ms. Tricia, was instrumental in her academic success. Ms. Tricia advised Michelle, helped her with her course selections, her student teaching and the interview process. She enthusiastically wrote a stellar recommendation, which landed Michelle her first teaching job.

Michelle married Mike Blake two years later. They purchased a spilt ranch house in walking distant to the schools. The house was large enough for a family, but not big enough to be presumptuous. The master bedroom was located as you enter the front door and walk down the stairs. There was a full bathroom on the lower level and an additional small bedroom. As you stepped up the stairs, a great room occupied most of the floor. They only owned one television. They spent most of their time reading, playing board games and entertaining small groups of friends.

The kitchen was situated to the left of the great room, another full bathroom was further down the hall and an extra room faced the backyard. They used the extra room as a gym. It contained a treadmill, a rowing machine and weights. They believed they would turn it into a third bedroom when they had a second or third child. That never happened.

Four years after they married, Michelle gave birth to Caleb, a nine-pound, nineteen-inch baby boy. They were elated. Michelle took delight in breastfeeding Caleb. She loved to watch him hungrily suckle at her breast and fall asleep in her arms when he was full.

She designed her own nursery. She painted the walls blue and glued a puppy-themed borders around the top of the walls. She purchased a charming wooden rocking chair and tied thick blue-gray cushions on the seat and the back. She furnished the room with a white crib changing table and a three-drawer dresser. She placed a small white lamp on the dresser and hung a zoo-themed musical mobile across the crib. She added a gray and white cloth doggie rocking horse to the back corner of the room.

She delighted in raising her infant son. She returned to work twelve weeks later and understood more about child development, attachment and psychology than she previously learned in school. The years flew by, pleasant, but uneventful, until Caleb turned five years old.

Michelle and Mike planned a fifth birthday party for Caleb. They invited the children and their parents to their home for games and cake. The night before the celebration, Mike took Caleb to choose decorations and party favors at the local Party City, while Michelle cleaned and decorated the house. Caleb decided on a piñata, shaped like the number five, and water guns for his friends. They purchased bags of sweet and chewy candies to fill the piñata.

Mike surprised Caleb with an extra treat. They stopped at the park, filled two water pistols with water from the fountain and chased each other around the park. It started to rain, which increased the fun. Their clothes and hair were dripping wet by the time they returned to the car.

Mike strapped Caleb in his car seat in the back seat on the passenger side; it was the safest spot for the child, and they proceeded home. He didn't realize Caleb still had his water gun, ready to strike. Caleb watched his dad drive and took the opportunity to shoot him when his dad turned his head to the right, keeping his eyes on the curve in the road.

The stream of water struck Mike in the eye. He instinctively cried out and lifted one hand from the steering wheel, protecting the injured eye. The car swerved to the left, hitting an oncoming tractor-trailer. The truck slammed on its breaks, swayed too quickly to the side, slipped on the wet surface and lost control. The truck flipped over, gliding on the slippery highway. It bashed into the passenger side of Mike's car, killing Caleb instantly. Mike banged his head on the left window, breaking the glass. Shards of glass plunged into his left arm, shoulder and his neck. He felt weak and tired as blood rapidly pulsed from the wounds.

He unfastened his seatbelt with his right hand. He felt around for the clasp since he couldn't see clearly. He struggled to breathe. He wrestled with the darn clasp. It hurt to move. He tentatively turned his body to check on Caleb. The boy sat dead in his car seat. The massive force tore off his right arm and it catapulted forward. It landed on the front dashboard.

Blood spurted from the elbow and oozed down the glove compartment. His right foot was almost completely amputated, hanging onto his leg by a strip of skin. It swung like a metronome. Veins and muscles dangled from his son's leg. Caleb's head drooped to his chin. His teeth clamped his tongue on impact. The tip laid on Caleb's lap. A huge dent appeared above his right ear and the dripping blood congealed in his hair. Mike opened his mouth to scream out in horror. He died on the inhale.

Michelle was inconsolable. A child's death may undoubtedly be the worst pain a parent can experience. To add the death of a husband is unimaginable. She absorbed herself in her career. She taught History for ten years. She remained at the High School after hours, tutoring the students, attending their performances and organizing the events. She accepted any task or project the superintendent requested.

Twenty years ago, Ms. Blake interview for the principal position. Principal Crowley died and the administration needed coverage immediately. Her resume was full of teaching experience, athletic competitions and extracurricular activities. Her fellow teachers and colleagues wrote outstanding recommendation letters. The superintendent hired not only for the High School position, but offered her the principal role for Junior High School as well.

Ms. Blake was an effective and admired principal, but never recovered from her family tragedy, until she encountered Babs Waldron. The two women met by chance in the Plainledge Elementary school. After discussing Bab's daughter, they met for coffee, walks, dinner and their friendship evolved. Babs mentioned The Plainledge Animals shelter, her position as their

Veterinarian Assistant and the wonderful dogs. Ms. Blake was curious and was always searching for additional means to occupy her time.

She ventured to the shelter on a day Babs worked. She and Babs had coffee at the counter; Babs gave her the tour of the facility and Ms. Blake visited the dogs while they romped in the yard. Two litter pups, Eddie and Ethan never strayed far from each other. Their last humans abused them and they found comfort in their close proximity. They took a special liking to Michelle. They ran around her in circles, wagged their tails, jumped on her leg and dropped their ball on her feet. Before she realized it, she was running with them, throwing them their ball, playing tug-of-war. She felt comfortable. She was laughing! She purchased the two pups on the spot. She bought them toys, treat, and cushioned beds; everything required to offer them a happy life. Eddie and Ethan offered Ms. Blake everything she required for a happy life.

Two weeks later, Ms. Blake asked the shelter owners, Helmuth and Irmard Weber, if she could tutor her students at the shelter. The dogs could benefit the students in their studying. Children are less stressed when they are in the company of dogs. The children were permitted to play with the dogs when their finished their homework for and additional reward. The students' grades increased and many dogs were adopted.

Chapter
TEN

Cathy, Janet and Yukon

Janet made tea while she listened to Cathy tell her a story. She filled the teakettle with water, took two teacups from the cupboard and set the table. She selected two homemade brownies and placed them on the cake plates. She purposely moved slowly to allow Cathy and Yukon time to decompress.

They sat at the kitchen table drinking chamomile tea. The sun just started to rise and there was a chill in the air. Yukon sat very closely to Cathy with his head on her knee. He calmed down quite a bit, but wouldn't leave Cathy's side.

Janet listened intently. Cathy explains the tale with minute detail as if it was real. Janet broached the subject sympathetically when she asked Cathy if she had another night terror. Cathy didn't talk about her night terrors. They were so frightening she experience panic attacks if she spoke about them. Janet was the only one Cathy confided in.

Cathy experienced night terrors since she was a child. She dreamt she was alone in a cold dark place. She couldn't see very well, only images. The images floated around her and whispered her name. Their camouflage coloring caused them to blend into the walls, and then reappeared; only their outlines and faces were visible. The faces scared her the most.

They looked like frightened ghosts. Their eyes and mouth forever open in a constant plea for help. They slowly swirled around her head while they called her. The voices were stuttering echoes, overlapping each other like a round in a repeated song.

She would wake up screaming and sweating, until her mother ran in from her own bedroom, hugged her and calmed her down. Cathy always remembered the dream, but couldn't figure out if it was a warning or some kind of foreboding.

This was different. Cathy was convinced this was more than a bad dream. Janet was concerned. She had so many questions. If this episode was more than a dream, who were crying for help? Were children involved? Who kept them captive? Most importantly, how could they help them escape?

Janet experienced many instances of child abuse while she worked in the foster care system. She remembers the one mother who locked her daughter in a dark closet for a full week. She opened the door just long enough to throw in a crusty piece of bread and a cup of warm water. She wanted the child to suffer, not die.

Janet and the two other caseworkers found the child when the school district reported her missing and the mother did not respond. They placed the child in a mental health residential program for six months before she was healthy enough to live with a family in a foster care setting. The child claimed this was not the first time the mother locked her in the closet, but she was unable to note how often and how long her mother shut her in.

Janet notified the authorities. The police arrived and took the mother into custody. Janet didn't follow the story afterwards but heard, the mother willingly admitted she was jealous that her husband loved the girl and lavished her with attention. His overt expressions of affection angered her. He didn't treat her as well. Her anger and jealousy increased with each hug, kiss or tickle. She felt justified to seek revenge and the abuse began.

She found comfort in finding suitable homes for many mistreated children, affording them an opportunity to belong in a loving home. Janet's caring nature would not permit her to ignore a child's cries for help. She would have to further explore the possible explanations for Cathy's story. If there was any possibility that children were trapped with a monster, she had an obligation to assist in their escape.

Cathy and Janet discussed their plan. They would recreate the scene, hoping to return to the dark place and figure out a way to help those who cried out for help. They would take some necessities, a couple of flashlights, a shovel and a first aid kit. They contemplated whether to take Yukon, but he made the choice for them. He wouldn't leave their side, following as they gathered their supplies and headed for their bedroom. They put on Yukon's collar and leash and entered the room.

They sat huddled on the floor and waited for any sign, any smell, any sound. Janet was more convinced that Cathy's experience was only a bad dream as the minutes whittled away. They sat for over an hour when Yukon started to whine. The trio sat up more erectly and listened more intently. The heard a rumbling and an unwholesome stench emanating from under the bed. Janet crawl underneath first.

She was trembling, but courageous. She reached her right arm under the bed frame followed by her left arm, ducking her head down to clear the bed frame. She used both arms to scoot her head and body below the center of the bed. Her feet were still sticking our when she felt a rush of wind dragging her downward. She tried to scream, but the pressure made it impossible for her to make a sound. Yukon grabbed Janet's sock with his teeth. Cathy grabbed Yukon's midsection and they both tried to force Janet backward, out of danger. Her sock ripped and Yukon lost his only means of attachment. Cathy and Yukon fell backward while they watched Janet disappear into the abyss. They desperately dug and feverishly scraped the floor hoping to reopen the hole.

She heard Janet calling their names, a distant echo vibrating from afar. Yukon's ears perked up and he started to growl. Cathy quickly flipped the bed over, took the shovel and frantically poked and bashed the shovel into the carpet.

Yukon followed suit using his front paws and sharp claws, obliterating the carpet and the wood planks below. He frantically continuing his manic behavior until his nail beds bled. Cathy stopped him, led him over to the far wall and sat there staring at the ruined space, trying to catch their breath.

I heard Janet calling my name. I could smell her scent. I was aware of her presence but couldn't see her. The last place I wanted to revisit was the Dark Place where the Stretchman lived. I was petrified, but I didn't want to be a coward. I would pretend to be a Super Dog in order to help Janet and Cathy. Dogs are similar in that respect. We are grateful for the love our humans possess, feeding us, playing with us; they spend a lot of time and money to build a happy life for us. We would never back down in times of trouble. I scrambled to grasp Janet's hand, foot or clothing, but she was sucked down too quickly. I took hold of her sock, aware that I didn't have a great grip. I wanted to bite myself when her sock ripped and I lost contact with her. I didn't relent. I scratched and clawed, hoping to open the abyss so I could jump in and save Janet.

I failed.

What kind of dog allows their human to slip from their grip and fall to her death? Cathy will probably return me to the shelter. The other dogs will think me a loser, a failure. I kept scraping and digging until Cathy stopped me. She held me close and led me over to the far wall. We sat there trying to calm down. She checked my paws, cleaned them with some warm soapy water and put some gooey ointment on them. I stopped bleeding; my paws were sore, but less painful. Cathy put one hand on each side of my face, looked me in the eye and told me she was proud of me for my bravery. She was grateful I stayed by her side trying to help her reach Janet. If I was able to cry, I would have. I thought I knew how much I loved them before, but I loved them even twice as much in that minute.

Janet continued to fall through the vacuum. It was both horrifying and exhilarating. She fell without tumbling. The air flowing through her hair, the cool breeze intoxicating her body. It was like a terminal roller coaster ride, only descending, never having to take the initial ride upward. It would have been pleasurable if she wasn't terrified of her destination.

She landed with a soft thump. She would never doubt Cathy again. She landed in an alternate reality where darkness permeated. This was not a bad dream. This was real.

There was a soft glow ahead allowing to glimpse a faint view of her surroundings. It was a cave with tunnels running in multiple directions. She heard miserable cries of anguish. The ground was composed of course sand and crunched with her every step. The murmuring was loudest in the tunnel to her right, so she chose to head in that direction. The cave became increasingly colder as she took further steps into the tunnel. She thought she heard someone whisper her name, so she turned to her right. Then it sounded like someone whispered her name to her left, so she turned again. Repeatedly, her name was called as she continued to spin around. She became dizzy and disoriented; dropped to the ground and cried. She hugged herself, tried to calm down and think. She called for Cathy and Yukon to no avail.

Janet had to move. She headed toward the dim light. She only advanced two steps when she saw it. It was just a shadow of a monster. It was difficult to predict its size, as its shadow grew in the light. It grew as it walked toward her. Its arms stretched at an unrealistic length. Its hands and fingers stretched enough to reach her from a distance. She tried to run, but her feet stuck to the ground like gnats on flypaper.

This Stretchman seized her with both hands. Its arms constricted as she was forced closer and closer to its body. It began to leisurely squeeze her. She didn't feel the pain until it squeezed more ferociously. It smashed her into a condensed round package, a ball of bones. The pain was excruciating as her bones broke and cracked. Her eyes bulged and popped out as her skull was crushed. Blind now, she wriggled, squirmed, and screamed. Her last thought was hoping Cathy and Yukon would not try to find her. She didn't want them to risk their lives and repeat her fate. It was too late for her. Her brain was pummeled into a pulpy mass as she was annihilated.

Chapter
ELEVEN
Shaggy, Helmuth and Irmgard

Shaggy was 18 years old. Her birth name was Shana, but her parents always called her Shaggy due to their special love for dogs. Shaggy liked this nickname until a few years ago. She was an only child. Her parents, Helmuth and Irmgard Weber, owned the Plainledge Animal Shelter.

Helmuth was a dog trainer. He worked at The Plainledge Animal Shelter teaching people how to train their dogs before leaving the shelter, or for those who purchased dogs elsewhere. He rescued a female Collie called Candy. She was nineteen inches tall and weighed 35 pounds. She had a long, slender snout, dark eyes and small perky ears. She had a white and brown coat and a fluffy lengthy tail. Like most Collies, she was highly intelligent. She modeled perfect behavior for the dogs in training.

His motto, "There are no bad dogs, just bad trainers." He was financially stable enough to train and sell the dogs on a sliding scale, enabling many people to purchase and train a dog who may not normally afford to do so. He rescued dogs that people had to give up when they moved or could no longer care for them properly. He captured feral dogs from deserted streets. He housed them at the shelter for adoption. There were times Helmuth broke the law to save a dog.

Ten years ago, Helmuth saw a man abusing his dog while they were walking in the park. The dog was a mixed breed. Helmuth figured it was mostly a mix of a German Shepherd and poodle. She had scruffy black and tan long hair, a black nose and long floppy ears. She was about twenty-three inches tall and appeared emaciated, at forty pounds.

The dog was confused, not listening to the human's commands. The man tugged on the dog's leash and demanded her to sit. The dog wanted to please his human, but had no idea how to behave. The man kicked the dog each time he gave a command that went unanswered.

Helmuth ran over and introduced himself. He told the man he was a dog trainer and may be able to help. The man said his name was Chucky and allowed Helmuth to show him some training techniques. Helmuth demonstrated the appropriate "sit" command, gently tapping the dog's backside while lifting his chin upward. He explained how a positive reinforcement approach was more effective than a punishment tactic. Chucky took back the leash from Helmuth, rolled his eyes and told Helmuth how he disagreed with his ridiculous methods. Chucky said the dog will listen to him, no matter how severe the punishment. To prove his point, Chucky pulled on the choke collar harsh enough to cause the dog to gasp for air. The dog was terrified. He froze in fright and peed on his own back legs. Chucky laughed an evil snicker. Helmuth was concerned for the animal's safety and well-being.

Helmuth followed Chucky and his downhearted dog to their home. He hid outside and waited until nightfall when the house lights were turned down, the glow of the television disappeared and the house fell silent. He slipped into an open basement window, landing with a *whomp* on his knees. He ignored the shooting pain as he was on a mission. He quietly ascended the staircase. He stopped twice when they creaked, making sure he did not wake Chucky.

He found the dog chained to the kitchen table on a hard tile floor. The dog raised her sad little head. She was smart enough not to make a sound and wagged her tail. Helmuth untied her, lifted her gently and carried her down the basement stairs. He continued to stroke the dog gently and speak softly in her floppy ears. He told the dog she was safe and she was going to rest comfortably at The Plainledge Animal Shelter. Of course, the pup did not understand the meaning of Helmuth's words, but the calm reassuring voice calmed her. He lifted the dog over his head and carefully placed her out the window and climbed out afterward. Helmuth named the dog Chance. Helmuth was not aware that he would repeat this vigilante process many times.

Helmuth drove Chance to the shelter. He soaked her in a warm bath. The dog sat in her glory, allowing Helmuth to scrub, rinse and dry her without any fuss. Helmuth set up a cozy crate with a large cotton blanket and laid out a bowl of dog food and a bowl of fresh cool water. He added a squeaky gopher toy that quickly became Chance's favorite item. Helmuth left the shelter and returned to Chuckie's house.

My life was miserable until I met Helmuth. My human, Chucky, took me for a daily walk. It was an awful experience for me, but I think Chucky relished in it. He would yell at me, and then kick me. I couldn't understand what he wanted me to do, or believe me, I would not have hesitated. I would have saved myself a lot of pain and humiliation. When I first glimpsed Helmuth walking toward me, I was hesitant. I was afraid he was going to hurt me, as that was my experience with humans. I was hopeful when I heard him ask Chucky if he could help. Helmuth was kind and gentle. I couldn't believe my luck. Who was this warmhearted soul? I was devastated when he deserted me and left me with Chucky. We returned home to a run-down house. I was fed with minimal proportions; my water stale; tied to a chair. I fell asleep alone, without a blanket or a toy to cuddle.

When Helmuth padded in, I thought I was dreaming. I learned how to be quiet. I never wanted to wake Chucky, there would always be a kick to my side or a tightening of my collar. I did not know Helmuth's intentions, but I was curious. I didn't move my head, but my eyes followed his every move. He untied me and gently me into his arms. He was so warm and soft. My heart jumped into his. I was his forever. I couldn't understand his words, but his voice had a calming effect. I trusted him. He lifted me out of the house of horrors. My mood lifted in synchrony with my body. I looked back, eagerly waiting for Helmuth to join me. After a bath and dinner, I slept contently in a warm cozy bed with a toy gopher at my nose.

Helmuth packed a duffle bag with a few accessories and returned to Chuckie's house. He slipped in the basement window as he did the first time. He climbed to the second floor. It wasn't difficult to find Chuckie; Helmuth followed the snores, grunts and groans. He pointed a meat cleaver to Chuckie's jugular and pressed on the vein until Chuckie woke. He sputtered and kicked until he realized the movement caused more pain and it was better to be still and listen to the maniac with the knife. Helmuth removed the taser gun from his satchel of fun. He purchased it purposely for these special occasions. He squeezed it into Chuckie's fat gut and pressed the trigger for a few seconds. Chuckie seized and fell to the ground. He dribbled a little white foam and his tongue lolled outside of his mouth. Helmuth thought he might have held the trigger a little bit too long.

No use crying over spilt dog abusers. He reached in his pack for a dog-training collar and a 12-inch wooden pole. He never used this on a dog; it would be inhumane. The collar was silver-plated surrounded with J-shaped hooks. He slipped it over Chuckie's head and secured it close to his neck. He attached the leash to the collar and pulled Chuckie over to the kitchen table. He tied Chuckie to the same kitchen table where Chance recently lay. The taser wore off and Chuckie returned to his normal state, except a fraction more terrified, angry and hurting. He tried to move. The contraption forced him backward and tightened the hold on his neck. He heard his esophagus crunch, felt the collar constrict. He grabbed the collar, desperately trying to loosen the grip. He reached his hand out for Helmuth. Helmuth took a step forward, jerked the table toward him and watched Chuckie take his last breath.

Irmgard, Helmuth's wife, was an adjunct instructor at St. Katharine's University. She wrote and taught a course called, "The Dog and Human Connection." The students were quick to register for the course. It was soon the most popular course at the university. The students were required to donate dog supplies to The Plainledge Animal Shelter and write a term paper on the importance of the Dog-Human bond. The topic mandated a thorough discussion about domestication of dogs and the ethical considerations on how humans are responsible to treat them with kindness. Many of the students took their dogs to class when giving their oral presentation. The dogs were permitted to roam freely around the classroom, sniffing each other and looking for the dog treats. Irmgard hid various goodies around the room before they entered. The period was full of interesting information, humorous experiences and a special kind of bonding between the students and the dogs.

Irmgard rescued a Standard Poodle mix. Curly was twenty inches and fifty pounds. She had curly golden hair and a long thick tail. She was sociable and loyal. She joined Irmgard when she taught the dog class, at The Plainledge Animal Shelter and the dog park.

Irmgard's goal was to teach the importance of the human dog relationship, the unconditional love only available from our pups and a desire to donate goods or volunteer time to dogs in need. She coordinated trip to The Plainledge Animal shelter every semester, giving the students a chance to see how a rescue center operates. She showed them the daily feeding, walking and exercise schedules and how important it is to maintain it and keep it running. The students had the opportunity to go out to the fenced in area in the back yard to watch the dogs during their exercise period. Most of the students joined the dogs, tossing Frisbees and playing tug-of-war. This was the most enjoyable day of the semester. The experiential learning and ability to apply what they learned to real life situations was just as important as learning the theories and course content.

Helmuth would demonstrate a brief training session and Shaggy would make limited ingredient dog biscuits with the students. She used a special recipe from Karen. The students could take the treats home to their own dogs, or donate them to those at the shelter.

Shaggy appeared disinterested, but she wasn't really uncaring. When Shaggy was eleven years old, she rescued her first dog. She grew up with dogs, but this was the first one she named and chose herself. She purchased Tanya to ease her anxiety. Tanya was Shaggy's emotional support dog. Shaggy suffered from Generalized Anxiety Disorder (GAD) she was very young. GAD is a mental illness causing unprovoked anxiety and worry for no apparent reason. Shaggy had difficulty concentrating, sleeping and performing routine tasks that other people could do without any conflict. It prevented her from succeeding in school and going out with her friends. She happened upon an article about emotional support dogs (ESD) when she was researching anxiety disorders. ESD are not service dogs, so they have limited rights and may not always permitted in restaurants, schools or air travel. An ESD provides security, helping those cope with anxiety and neglect, abandonment issues, depression and many others issues. Shaggy used Tanya for emotional support, feeling less stressed and better able to cope when her pup was nearby.

Tanya was three or four years old when Shaggy rescued her. She looked like a Vizsla, but was probably mixed with a German Shepherd, as she had the physical characteristics of both. She was 24 inches tall and weighed 80 pounds. She was mostly chestnut colored except for her muzzle, which was black. Her ears were party erect, but flopped downward. She had the sweetest disposition, quiet and loyal. Shaggy took Tanya everywhere. She felt comfortable and relaxed for the first time since her adolescent years. They went food shopping and clothes shopping. They went together when Shaggy got a haircut or a mani-pedi. There was no problem working since Tanya was welcomed at The Plainledge Animal Shelter. Shaggy took great care of the dogs. She feed them, filled their water bowls and played with them. She allowed them to run free in the fenced in yard behind the shelter. Tanya would romp around with the other dogs, entertaining each other all afternoon. However, dogs are not immortal and Tanya was getting old.

Tanya died two years ago, when she was sixteen years old. She lived a great life and loved Shaggy until her last dying breath. Shaggy was unable to cope with the loss. She walked around her bedroom aimlessly for weeks. She couldn't eat or sleep. She refused to go to work. She couldn't fathom returning to the Plainledge Animal Shelter filled with loving memories of Tanya. Her anxiety returned with a severe episode of depression. Depression is a consistent feeling of sadness, emptiness and grief. A person loses interest in activities they once enjoyed; they feel hopeless. Shaggy felt the loss as physical pain. She often found herself lying on the floor in a fetal position, hands around her knees, sobbing like a child. Her stomach ached, her head pounded and her eyes itched. She would cry until she was depleted, lacking enough energy to produce one more tear and she'd fall asleep where she lay.

After three months, she denied these painful emotions. She decided it was easier not to care, not to offer or accept love. The consequences were extreme and intolerable. Her parents forced her to work at the shelter to earn enough to support herself and pay them a token monthly rent. She was a certified dog groomer, but wouldn't even brush or pet a dog. They allowed her the few months to grieve, but insisted she return to work. Shaggy returned to work stoically. She fed the dogs and gave them fresh water on a limited bases, only enough to ensure their survival. She never played with them nor spoke to them. She could barely look at their cute faces and sad eyes. She was petrified to love any of them. They all reminded her of Tanya. Her behavior wasn't limited to dogs. She lost contact with her friends, didn't eat her meals with her parents and was not friendly to the customers.

Her denial worked. She didn't feel any more pain, in fact, she felt nothing at all. The nothingness was a reprieve. She vowed never again to feel a loss as she did with Tanya. She struggled through each day like a battery-operated toy running low on power.

Chapter
TWELVE
Seth and Trista

Trista lost her identity after the rape. She gave birth to Samael and felt nothing for him. How could she love a baby created by such violence and hate? She didn't condone Seth's treatment of the child, but she didn't care enough to stop it. On the few occasions she tried, she was rewarded with a harsh and unusual punishment.

She was not able to divorce Seth. She had no job, no money, nor any family to sustain her. She threatened to leave once and Seth exploded. He backhanded her jaw with such force; she was thrown into the wall. She hit, headfirst. The pain was excruciating. She put her hand to her mouth and found a handful of blood combined with two teeth. Her gums swelled immediately. She ran to get some ice in the bottom freezer. Seth was immediately behind her, dunking her head into the container of ice cubes and held her underneath. She struggled to free herself, kicking and jumping. She could hear him laugh as he tightened his hold on her neck. The ice-cold air filled her lungs. It was difficult to breathe. Her lungs felt like they were on fire, burning her from the inside out. He finally pulled her out by her hair, throwing her to the far side of the kitchen. She slammed into the wall and agonizingly gulped in full breathes of air.

She never mentioned divorce again.

Trista didn't feel sad or depressed, just displayed a blunted affect because she didn't have the energy to care. She lost faith in her friends and family after her attack. They offered no support. Her mother told Trista the rape was her own fault; she shouldn't have trusted a stranger. How stupid she was to take a drive with a young man she hardly knew! Her mother found fault in every aspect of the rape. Why was she wearing skimpy clothing and why did she drink alcohol? The most hurtful remark was when her mother implied that it was not a rape at all, that Trista consented to sex and only blamed Seth when she found out she was pregnant. Although she was never popular, her reputation plummeted. The girls who despised her before the attack were relentless in their bullying.

The one person she still had feelings for was Seth. Instead of a disinterest, she hated him. The hateful feeling consumed her. She hated every part of him, his physical features, his behavior, his attitude; even his perverted sense of humor. She initially married him for the baby and now found herself trapped in a worthless marriage.

Seth discovered one great benefit in the sacrament of matrimony. He had the ability and power to rape his wife at his whim. He would take delight in the unique ways he abused her. Sometimes he would tie her to the bed. He would sneak up on her when she was sleeping and tie one arm to the bedframe before she woke up. When she struggled to fight him off, he would grab the other arm and secure that one to the bedpost. He wouldn't tie her legs down because he liked when she provided some fight. It excited him.

She would kick frantically which would only increase his fuel. It gave him another reason to brutalize her. He would clutch her thigh on the soft skin and dig his nails in the muscle until she bled. The pain was awful; she was immobile with fear and simply lied still. When he finished, he would punch her in the stomach as a cool down.

On other occasions, he would hold her facing the wall while he sodomized her. He wielded a knife for this sport, forcing her to face the wall, demanding she pull down her own pants. She had no escape. She tried to wriggle free, but the knife was close to her body. When she moved, the knife would nick her. Even when she acquiesced, he sliced her lower torso while he forced himself inside her. He never cut her enough to warrant an emergency room visit, just enough to bleed and sting.

His favorite pastime was tackling Trista when she picked up the crying baby. It reminded him of playing football. Trista heard the baby screaming. He laid on the floor next to them, while Seth raped Trista repeatedly. Samael's face turned beet red from the prolonged crying, mucus slipped from his nose, his hands flailed up and down. Trista couldn't help him and Seth had no desire to interrupt his fun to console the miserable wretch. Samael continued to sob until he exhausted himself and fell asleep on the hard floor.

Seth received an extra reward when he was able to watch himself attacking his wife in the floor mirror. He never ceased to amaze himself. After all these years, he was still such a skillful lover, an attractive spectacle, the envy of all ordinary men.

As Seth continued to gaze into the mirror, he noticed the reflection changed. Slowly the human figure decomposed. Arms and legs became hazy, unclear, stretching to abnormal lengths. The head elongated. The skin covering the eyes tore and cut leaving strands of blood like a giant claw ripping the face apart. Empty back sockets replaced the place the eyes once rested. The white teeth and rosy lips turned into an empty hole, opening widely like a snake unhinging its jaw ready to eat its prey. He was surprised at his revolting reaction to the image. He was slightly alarmed. He stood up, swiftly donning his pants, and left the room rapidly.

Trista was relieved when Seth finished, even more so when she saw him scurry out of the room. If she didn't know any better, she would have thought he was spooked.

She grabbed the mirror for support and gingerly hoisted herself up. It hurt to move. She felt pain in every part of her body. Her arms and legs were bruised from Seth's rough handling. Her head was aching from crying, screaming and rocking back and forth. The delicate place between her legs was swollen and throbbing. Blood was trickling down her legs, her arms and from her mouth. The baby cried himself to sleep. Trista left him on the floor while she slowly managed to reach the bathroom where she took a scalding shower. She tried to wash away the scum and the filth. The tangible squalor was much easier to rinse away. The emotional and mental anguish remained a blemish forever. She remained in the shower for more than thirty minutes, scrubbing and scouring, screaming in anger and weeping over her miserable life.

Chapter
THIRTEEN
Samael

Sam's single positive relationship was with his paternal grandfather, Aaron. When the kids in elementary school bullied him, Aaron would listen quietly while Sam shared his story and cried. He wasn't permitted to cry in front of his father or he would receive a beating for not being a man, for admitting weakness. His grandpa explained how some people are unkind and cruel, but most are friendly and considerate. The trick is to find the people who make you happy.

Samael loved spending time with Aaron, but it wasn't easy. Seth was not fond of their relationship. He hated the fact that his son and his father had a special bond. Sam didn't deserve to be treated like a prince, like he was special. He wasn't special at all. He was a loser, an idiot. He should be more independent, manlier. How could such a stud like himself create such a weak creature? He was embarrassed. He despised how his father encouraged Sam's meek qualities. Aaron treated Sam just as he treated Sarah before she killed herself. It was intolerable and impermissible. Seth vowed to put an end to this relationship, or to sabotage it.

Aaron would pick up Sam from Plainledge Elementary School when he had the opportunity to sneak away from Seth at the auto-body shop. Ms. Blake allowed Aaron to collect Sam, even though he wasn't listed on the parental approval sheet. She was aware of his unlovable home life and wanted to help him out in any way she could. Aaron would take Sam for a drive so Sam could talk in private, or they would stop at the ice-cream shop and buy a chocolate ice-cream cone with rainbow sprinkles.

Sam's favorite outing was The Plainledge Park. This special day they decided to stop at the park. The park was beautiful. Aaron and Sam would take a hike through the paths, admiring the scenery and nature. The trees were full of green leaves, swishing in the mild wind. The birds whistled happily. Sam spied a robin redbreast, a blue jay and an abundance of pigeons. He wanted to learn more about the different birds and wildlife. Aaron promised they would take some books out of the library and read about the animals and trees native to Plainledge.

Aaron always brought a bag of peanuts with him and they would feed the squirrels. Sam loved how the little guys would approach him and take the nuts right from his hands. Since he wasn't allowed to own a dog, he treated the squirrels as if they were his own. The gray furry animals nibbled on each peanut as if they were starving. They appreciated every bite. Sam wondered why most people did not eat as slowly and gratefully as the squirrels.

One day when Sam and Aaron fed the squirrels, Seth happened to speed passed the park in his Mustang. He was a reckless driver, never paying proper attention to the road. He would light a cigarette, change the stations on the radio or watch the young girls pass by. He licked his lips while he watched a young mother bend down to pick up her baby from the stroller. Her skirt blew in the wind and Seth was delighted at the view. He happened to glimpse beyond the skirt and noticed a familiar sight. He screeched to a stop as he spotted Aaron's car parked on the curb. He suspected Aaron secretly visited Sam without his permission. He flew into a rage. He found the two of them sitting together feeding the dirty disgusting rodents.

He stormed over, ripped the bag of peanuts from Sam and chucked them into the trash bin. He picked up Sam by his collar and yanked him to the Mustang. Sam's feet dragged on the ground; he couldn't gain his balance. One of his shoes tore from his foot and his foot grinded on the cement. His sock ripped and the blood from the wound made its own trail in the park.

Seth punched Sam on the top of his head and said, "You just ruined a good sock."

Sam screamed out in pain.

Aaron rose from his seat and ran to defend Sam. Seth punched his father in the gut with one hand without releasing his grip on Sam. Aaron slipped on Sam's bloody trail, fell backward and banged his head on the park bench.

Seth yelled, "I'll come back for you after I take care of the boy."

Seth launched Sam into the back seat of the car before Aaron was able to catch his breath.

Seth locked Sam in his bedroom for the night without dinner. He wasn't even allowed to come out of his room to wash up or use the bathroom. Trista inquired about the punishment. Seth replied with a backhand to her right cheek. The stinging sensation caused her eyes to tear and her rage to flourish. A spittle of blood formed around her bottom teeth as she continued to seethe with controlled anger. She decided to end the conversation rather than accept additional lashings.

Sam sat in the corner, his knees bent upward and his arms around his knees. He wanted to squeeze himself as small as he could, to make himself invisible. His scalp was sore and he worried about his grandpa. He was happy when Aaron stood up to defend him, he thought it may prevent a situation with his father, but the feeling turned sour when his father punched his grandpa. Sam's body tipped to the side as he drifted off to sleep. He remained on the floor, cold, hungry and alone, until morning. He was embarrassed to find he peed his pants during the nighttime, but he was locked in his room and couldn't leave to use the bathroom. He changed into some clean, dry clothes, threw the dirty clothes in the corner and brushed his hair. He heard the door click. His father finally unlocked it. He stepped out to take a shower before heading to the bus stop and noticed a huge box with his name scrawled on top with fancy black lettering.

Sam was excited to receive a present. He figured it was either from his grandpa, who sent him a gift to raise his spirits, or his father who felt guilty over his abusive treatment and tried to make amends. He needed two hands to pick up the cumbersome package. It wasn't too heavy, but it was big and difficult to finagle. It smelled weird, so he dipped his head to the side while he carried the box to his bed. He laid it on top of his comforter. It wasn't sealed shut, he only had to flip over the cardboard cover.

He leaned in to peek and gasped. He jumped away and bumped his legs on his dresser. He felt like he was going to vomit. Fear and anger coursed through his body. He was sad and enraged. He didn't realize he could feel worse than he did yesterday, or two minutes ago. He couldn't understand the depths of evil his father could reach.

Inside the box laid three dead squirrels. They were decapitated, their blood still oozing from their necks. Their poor little bodies were broken and bent at odd angles. He couldn't comprehend the suffering they endured and it was all his fault. He should have known better than to sneak away with his grandpa. He vowed never to play with an animal again. He left the gruesome present on his bed and dashed to the bus stop. He was shading so badly he had to stop twice to bend down and gulp some air. He forgot to shower or take his lunch or backpack.

He sat on the school bus by himself. The bullies threw spitballs at him while others laughed. He hugged himself, hung his head and starred at his lap. He didn't care about the bus tormentors. Tears rolled down his eyes for the squirrels and himself.

He didn't attend his classes. He sat behind the school building by himself. He was cold, tired and hungry. He wanted to punish himself. His poor little gray furry friends; they only ate their peanuts and made him laugh. They didn't deserve Seth's abuse. The school day was agonizing, but not half as torturous as the Ravana household.

Chapter
FOURTEEN
Samael Meets Shaggy

Samael progressed through elementary school without any close friends. He was tirelessly bullied and learned to accept his fate. He's walked through the years with his head down accepting any punishment, mockery or flying objects thrown in his direction.

He entered Plainledge High School without any change, and without the dog he always wanted. His father resented dogs after they caused his injury, preventing him from reaching his football stardom and wealth. His mother had no choice but to agree with Seth's decision. She wouldn't want a dog living with them anyway. The extra cost for the food, toys and miscellaneous expenses would be a financial burden.

Samael wanted to earn his own money, maybe enough to buy some new clothes for High School. Perhaps the bullying would decrease if he wore clean, stylish clothing. He may decide to try out for the football team. He wasn't as big as his father, but he could run fast. He could try out for a wide receiver position. Either way, he would need money to spend on clothing, equipment and training.

Samael avoided the school bus and walked to school daily. He passed through town and the quaint shops that weren't yet opened. He always checked out

The Plainledge Animal Shelter, looking through the window, peeking in at the dogs and puppies. They were always happy to see him, jumping on the glass, wagging their tails. He never ventured in after school due to the clerk standing behind the cash register. She reminded him of an eerie character in a book he'd read. The fictitious person was exceptionally tall and emaciated. Samael wasn't concerned about her physical appearance; it was her penetrating gaze. He was certain she was suspicious of him. She probably hoped he wouldn't enter the shop. She thought he was ugly, mistrustful. She watched his every move and would definitely prevent him from touching any of her precious dogs.

He was walking home on Friday wondering how he would survive another weekend with Seth and Trista. He found the courage to speak to his father about football. He broached the subject while Seth drank his morning coffee and scoffed down half-dozen jelly donuts. Sam wondered how many donuts Seth actually digested, as his mouth and chin were full of sticky red jam and syrupy sugar. He occasionally wiped his face, starting at his elbow, sliding it over his chin, until he reached his wrist. The glutinous mess clung to his arm like a maggot on bacteria.

Samael explained how he decided to try out for the Plainledge High School football team. He explained how he might excel at the wide receiver position, as he had the speed to outrun any player and the ability to catch a football better than those currently playing in his chosen position. He hoped his father would respect his desire to play the game as he once enjoyed. He didn't expect the immediate response he received.

His father roared. He laughed so violently he doubled over, pounding his knee with his monstrous hand. His coffee and donuts skyrocketed out of his mouth, making a trail of muddy gunk on the kitchen floor. He said he would embarrass him and ruin the great Ravana reputation. He had no regard for Samael and his own feelings or potential abilities.

He forbade Samael from playing football. Just for additional fun, Seth forced Samael to clean the mess on the floor. Sam stared at Seth, standing his ground. Seth swooped his right leg across Sam's ankles with such impact, Sam fell to the ground with a thump, slipping on the wet debris, cracking his right elbow. The physical pain did not rival the emotional anguish. Sam pushed himself to his knees with his left arm, placed his left arm on him left knee to return to a standing position.

He ignored his father's humiliating cackling in the background. He promised himself to take revenge in the near future. He found a bucket and sponge under the sink, filled it with warm soapy water. He scrubbed the floor, taking precautions to protect his injured arm. Seth poured himself another cup of coffee, plunked on the stool and watched the show. He occasionally experienced a jolly urge to splash half his coffee in the muck Samael was not able to clean up in a fast enough pace. This torture lasted for forty-five minutes, until Seth grew bored, dropped his remaining coffee on the floor and exited the room.

Samael finished scrubbing the spewed puke and exited the house. He wandered the neighborhood and found himself directly outside The Plainledge Animal Shelter. That unfriendly girl was unlocking the door for business. He could hear the dogs barking, excited for the company.

The girl turned, suddenly aware of his presence and jumped back, startled. Sam apologized and asked if he could enter and check out the dogs. The girl was apprehensive, but nodded her consent. She ignored him as he adoringly stared at the cages, hoping one day to own a dog of his own. He turned to leave and almost bumped into the girl. Seth was certain she was watching him. ensuring the dogs' safety, checking his movements for thievery or disturbance. She probably assumed he was a derelict, a troublemaker or even a criminal. He would have thought similarly. His clothes were dirty, he smelled like vomit, his arm was swollen and he was still quivering from his recent ordeal.

Samael was shocked when the girl asked him if he would like to hold a dog. He froze, unable to speak. The girl picked up a timid dog and gently placed her in Sam's arm, the one that wasn't swollen.

Shaggy said the dog's name is Chance. Her father rescued him from an abusive home. He was afraid of people, but needed love and affection. San cuddled the dog and buried his head in the soft furry body. He felt a warmth like never before. His eyes filled with tears as he silently cried. This lovely creature allowed Sam to touch her, to cuddle her and cry on her without any judgement. The dog didn't squirm or try to break free from his hold. San felt a sense of relief and a calmness spread through his body. He sensed the creature cared for him. Sam reciprocated the feeling. However, he understood he could not take this puppy home. He would not risk the abusive treatment Seth would dole out. He lingered a while longer, soaking in the pleasant unfamiliar feeling, then tenderly handed the dog back to the girl.

The girl said her name was Shaggy and asked Sam if he would like to help her feed the dogs. Sam nodded shyly, introduced himself and followed Shaggy to the dog food aisle. Sam pointed out the feeding instructions on the various dog food bags. She explained how the puppies ate a special puppy food and the older dogs received special older fog formula. There were specific foods for dogs with allergies, diseases and ailments. She handed Sam a one-cup scooper and pointed the last set of cages where he should begin the feeding process. A label on each cage listed the dog's name, their age, their weight and various issues that my effect their diet. Sam was careful to read each label, ensuring each dog received the proper meal. Shaggy left him to his task while she started the chore at the beginning of the cages.

Sam was so excited and felt truly happy for the first time. He strolled gaily from one cage to the next, talking to the dogs, petting them and laughing at their humorous antics. He loved the way they eagerly awaited his visit, thumping their tails as he reached their cages. As an extra surprise, Shaggy allowed him to open the pens. Sam found himself sitting on the floor surrounded by friendly, rambunctious dogs. After they inhaled their food, they jumped on him, licked his face and zoomed around him. Chance was not as energetic, but did not leave Sam's side. She sat near his legs while the other dogs bounced around. Sam laughed until he fell backward as the dogs and puppies cheerfully assaulted him. He considered Chance's hesitancy and gave her a quick pat on her head every now and again.

Shaggy met Samael at the halfway point. She saw Sam lavishing in delight. She tried to ignore deep-rooted old feelings, tried to suppress them to protect herself from future grief. However, Sam's laughter was contagious. A smile appeared on her lip, then an ear-to-ear grin. Before she realized it, she was giggling. Sam invited her to join him. She hesitantly entered the cage area. She initially froze when the first puppy pranced about, leaping on her leg. She glanced at Sam, looked down at the pup, finally deciding to pick him up.

Shaggy was taken back by her own reaction. She was flooded with past emotions; tenderness, attachment, primal love. Her reaction was similar to Sam's. They both longed for this unequivocal love. One who never had it; the other afraid take a risk. Shaggy unlocked the back door and walked into the fenced in field. Sam and the puppies eagerly followed. It was a beautiful cool sunny day. They remained outside for hours throwing Frisbees, playing catch, dancing all over the grassy yard like carefree merrymakers.

As the sun set, they cleaned up the dog poop and returned to the shelter. The animals were tired and thirsty. The humans were contently exhausted. Sam and Shaggy filled each dog bowl with cool fresh water, dimmed the lighting to induce a well-deserved nap and proceeded to the front of the store. Shaggy took two bottles of cold water from the store refrigerator and offered one to Sam. They drank for a few minutes in silence, silently reminiscing of the lovely day they shared.

Chapter
FIFTEEN
Lucy and Dakota

Kevin handed Cody back to Bella. The children huddled next to me. They wanted me to help them excavate their parents. We tackled the enormous task, wildly scooping considerable amounts of dirt from the ground. The dogs helped considerably. We heard faint sounds arising from beneath. We were finally able to see a tip of a finger. We scrambled over to uncover the remaining fingers, hand and person attached to the finger.

We were gravely disappointed. The thing we unearthed was a remnant of the once substantial human body. The facial features were mere outlines of a former well-defined face. The eyes were black with large pupils. She appeared scared to death. The nose smooshed into the face and the mouth spread into the chin. The body was cloudy, not yet totally transparent. The fingers were useless, unable to grip or aid in the digging mission. Her legs and feet were scrawny; they deteriorated faster than the rest of her body. However, to my amazement, the children were able to discern this figure was their mother. She had difficulty rising from her dwelling, as her ghostly legs couldn't even support her minimal weight.

We finally dislodged her from the pit. Kevin wafted over to her. He positioned his arms around her shoulders, but they hung just above them, as she did not have sufficient mass for a solid connection. He didn't give up. He kept his arms around his mother. She gained substance from his support. Connor stood firmly in place. He was ambivalent, both relieved at her recovery and disturbed at her appearance. Bella glimpsed at the figure quickly, her eyes wide with terror, and hugged Cody more closely. The dog wiggled from Bella's arms, heading directly toward the mother. He joyfully pounced on her without hesitation. Miraculously, she caught him, suddenly having an ability to grasp him. Her arms gained some solidity immediately after the dog made contact. It seemed as though the dog and her love for her family helped authenticate the mother's substance.

Bella launched into full-blown hysterics. She was traumatized when the dog squirmed away from her. She grabbed my hand and called for her dog. Cody was loyal to the entire family, but Bella was his human. He sprang from the mother's grip and hurried over to Bella. Bella calmed promptly, her sobbing diminishing to soft mewling.

The mother didn't fare as well once Cody leapt from her. Her body reversed its solidification and began to deteriorate. She reached for Cody as he leapt from her grip. Her arms trembled, and began their painful path of degeneration. Her mouth opened wide, trying to communicate with us, but we only heard a loud perturbing moan. Her head rolled back and she descended into her dwelling. It was a dramatic display of anguish. Her hand reached toward us, the last part of her to disappeared from our view. The scene looked like the opening of the Chiller movies. Her crusty wedding band managed to catch a reflection in the dim light, striking a faint glimmer on our retinas.

I felt dizzy and touched the wall to gain my balance. I felt a few inconsistencies in the wall, small protrusions. I tried to ignore both those and the horrors surrounding us. I ankle-rolled onto a crevice and I started to slip. Before I even reached the ground, a hand slipped out from the wall. It tried to grab me. I wasn't sure if it was benevolent or malicious, but I quickly pulled away, stumbling to the sandy floor, scraping my arms and elbows. The children screamed. They retreated into the hole.

I tried to stand up. Dakota helped me. She pushed against my back while I struggled to maintain my balance. Between the new pain in my ankle and the dark halls of the tunnel, I felt off-balance and nauseous. As she helped me to regain my position, the hand grabbed her hind leg. The hand tried to pull Dakota into the wall. I wasn't sure if the hand wanted Dakota to help it, keep it company, or if it wanted to hurt her. She yelped and kicked, turning side to side trying to bite the hand to release its hold.

The poor dog was terrified. She stared at me with her eyes wide open, searching for help. I grabbed her around her midsection, pulling her toward me, away from the hand. I was able to dislodge her. I held her close while her body shook and her hairs stood on end. We remained there until she calmed down. I kept repeating that she was a good girl and she was safe. Neither believed the latter.

I was overwhelmed with emotions. I saw the hand reach out to steal my human. I recently lost one human and did not intend to lose another. Thankfully, Lucy was able to slip from the hand's grip. I sensed she was hurt, so I help her up, pushing on her body to give her leverage. No sooner was she upright when a different hand grabbed my leg. I looked at Lucy; I looked back at my attacker. I didn't know where to turn first. Danger surrounded us. I was afraid for my own safety, but more concerned for Lucy. I didn't want to leave her alone to face these demons. She needed me and I needed her. We were a team and together could defeat any obstacles. She grabbed me, releasing my attacker's hold.

Dakota started to growl again, that alarming noise that indicated danger. I cautiously looked around. I saw a furry little paw sticking out of the ground, digging itself out. We helped the dog out of the hole. He was a small black dog covered in filth. He was fully formed, but very weak. He couldn't stand securely on his four paws. He must have been traumatized, as he was no longer shaking, just perfectly still. I brushed him off and slowly stroked him. Dakota sniffed his butt, then came around and licked his face. I picked him up and started walking. He wasn't very heavy, only weighing a few pounds. We saw a brighter light ahead so I followed in that direction.

The image in front of us was impossible. There sat The Plainledge Animal Shelter. However, it looked like it was 100 years old and abandoned for decades. The walls were crumbling; the roof was decayed, not even able to protect the building from the elements. The door hung to one side on its hinges, the front window was shattered and the sign fell off its post, laying nearby.

We couldn't reach the building. A gap in the floor widened like a slow-moving earthquake. We stood there while the gap expanded and filled with water. It looked like a mote surrounding a haunted castle. We would have to jump over it to get to the shelter. I am not sure why I thought this was a necessity, but I had to follow my instincts. I explained my plan to Dakota, who probably understood more than I thought. I signaled with my arms, indicated we would have to jump. She growled lightly. We were hesitant, but had no other options. I walked back about 30 yards so I could get a running start. Dakota followed my lead. I held the dog securely and started to run. Although I was in fairly good cardiovascular shape, the dog now seemed to weigh a hundred pounds. My ankle was throbbing, my arms were sore and I was worried about Dakota.

We ran, building up as much speed as we could muster. Dakota was a bit faster and took off before me. Time slowed down and accelerated simultaneously. I saw Dakota suspended in the air and land with speed and grace. All the while, I was running toward the newly-formed crater. I hurdled, up and over.

I made the mistake of glancing down. I saw more horrors below. Drowning in the green mucky water were figures of people and their dogs, all sizes and ages. They were reaching up to the heavens, struggling to breathe, thrashing and panicking. Some stepped on others trying to gain an advantage, keeping themselves emerged for a few brief seconds only to be swallowed down by the evil forces lurking in the slime.

We landed safety on the other side of the water. Dakota was relieved to see us. She wagged her tail and danced around a bit before reality hit her like a punch to her stomach. She strode over to us and settled at my side. I wouldn't dare put the little the dog down. He cried while I ran and he howled in despair as we took flight. At least he came out of his stupor. I hoped that was a good sign.

113

The Plainledge Animal Shelter was as decrepit inside as outside. It was cold and damp. The walls were riddles with peeled plaster, enormous spider webs and grime. The massive webs were full of giant bugs, some still alive, wiggling for their freedom. My curiosity was detrimental in this case; I was drawn to inspect further.

The abnormal insects were 5 inches long and probably weighed a full pound. It sported the usual six legs, maniacally fighting against the sticky silk. The brown lower body looked like it may have included wings, but they were disabled. The upper body, shaped like an onion, boasted black and white stripes. Its head was the most disturbing. A human face occupied this colossal cockroach. It stared at me, opened its mouth and tried to shout. No sound emerged. Its mouth was full of thick strands of the white webbing. I turned to look behind the atrocity and observed rows of bug-men caught in giant spider webs, struggling to dislodge themselves. I held the little dog closer to me. I grabbed Dakota's collar. She barked threateningly and I was afraid she may jump at the bug-man and stumble into the fibrous prison. I moved away quickly. I had no desire to wait for the spider to return for its dinner.

The wind screamed as it swept through the slits in the walls and torn parts of the roof. I wanted to reward Dakota for her bravery and good behavior, when I remembered I had Karen's homemade dog biscuits in my pocket. I took a one out of the bag and gave it to Dakota. Something startled her and she dropped the cookie. The cookie was sucked into the ground. Dakota sniffed for the vanishing cookie and looked at me questioningly. I shrugged my shoulders and reached in the bag for another cookie when we noticed another strange occurrence. The place where the cookie landed and disappeared started to change. It morphed into a more realistic floor, slowly resembling the shelter back home. I purposely placed another cookie on the ground. Dakota looked at me questioningly. I told her to leave it. She understood the command, but...

Really Mom? I already missed the first vanishing cookie when it suddenly disappeared like a Houdini magic trick. Now, I have to leave this one alone? Sometime you humans expect too much from us dogs. However, I also witnessed the strange occurrence. When the dog biscuit disappeared, the bizarre looking shelter appeared brighter, more like the one we visited at home. I decided to listen to Lucy and wait to see what happens...

Once again, the structure shifted and creaked. The grime slid off the wall, the holes filled themselves. It sounded like it was in pain, but I realized it was the monster crying out in rage from somewhere behind the walls. I dropped a few more biscuits and the transformation resumed. The wind accelerated, capturing us in its spinning motion. We circled upward, through the hollow roof and landed back at home. I no longer held the little dog in my arms. Dakota and I escarped the stretch-thing, but it managed to snatch the dog we tried to save.

We will return to rescue those we can. I managed to leave with an insightful piece of important information. The symbolic love from the homemade dog biscuits and the human-dog bond may be a significant force to conquer the Stretchman.

Chapter
SIXTEEN
Helmuth Strikes Again

Helmuth continued to train the dogs who arrived at the shelter. He wanted them to have the best opportunity to connect with a customer. If a dog is well behaved, their relationship with their human is stronger. The dog wishes to please their human and the human is delighted. The human-dog bond increases and the chance of returning the dog decreases.

Helmuth and Irmgard Weber earned a great reputation in the community. People in the church, the school and surrounding neighborhoods were aware of their good deeds and dedication to the dogs.

Helmuth received a call from Gail, a woman at the local pharmacy, describing a situation where a customer left his dog in their car. The windows were tightly shut. The dog was lying down in the front passenger seat panting. Gail said she called to the dog, but he would not move. The dog didn't even lift his head. The woman was concerned and angry.

Helmuth left Shaggy and Samael in charge of the shelter and he headed for the pharmacy. He packed a crowbar, a bowl, cold water bottles, wet towels and some of Karen's homemade dog biscuits. Gail waited for him at the old yellow Volkswagen Beetle where the dog was trapped. She said she found the dog at

116

least a-half an hour ago. Helmuth brazenly smashed the window on the front driver's side seat, furthest from the dog. He laid a cold towel on the ground, gingerly lifted the dog and placed him on the towel. The dog was barely breathing. He was a cute little black Dachshund, about 15 pounds. His soulful black eyes looked at Helmuth gratefully.

He wrapped the dog with the additional cool cloths. He and Gail remained with the dog until the dog recovered. Gail felt comfortable in leaving the pup with Helmuth and headed home. The dog drank a full bowl of water and gobbled down a number of Karen's biscuits. Helmuth placed the dog in his own car, started the engine and the air-conditioner and waited for the customer to return to the parking lot.

The man arrived a half hour later, carrying only a bottle of iced tea, chugging it as he sauntered to his car. His felt his feet crunch upon window glass, looked up and noticed that his windshield was shattered. His dog was gone.

Helmuth pulled his car over and told the man what he observed, "Excuse me sir. I saw a man smash your window and take your dog out of the car. He left your little Dachshund on the ground and took off. I kept the dog in my car until you returned. I can drive you and your dog home if you would like."

The man accepted the offer, stepped into Helmuth's olive-green Jeep Cherokee, and fastened his seatbelt. He turned his head to look at his dog, and huffed, "Shannon." He didn't thank Helmuth or reach to pet the animal. Regardless, Helmuth introduced himself. The man hesitated, and then responded in an unfriendly manner, stating his name was Jeremy.

They arrived at Jeremy's house. It was a small unkempt house on the corner of a decrepit neighborhood. They heard babies crying, parents yelling and dogs barking. Jeremy opened the Jeep's back door and called for Shannon. The dog wouldn't budge. Jeremy grabbed her collar and yelled louder. Helmuth swiftly clutched Jeremy's arm, but calmly said,

"I'll carry her into the house for you." Jeremy shrugged his shoulders and led the way.

The house was filthy. Empty beer cans, pizza boxes and cereal cartons scattered the counters. You couldn't see through the grimy windows and the place smelled like the garbage truck dumped its load in the kitchen. Helmuth walked into the den area, pushed away some trash with his foot and placed Shannon on the floor with the blanket. He patted her and told her to stay.

Helmuth returned to Jeremy. He asked Jeremy if he could have a beer before he left. Jeremey gave Helmuth a dirty look.

Helmuth said, "Just one for the road? I won't stay." Jeremy exhaled deeply, rolled his eyes and opened the refrigerator door. It was empty but for a case of beer on the bottom shelf. Jeremy bent down, stuck his arm inside and reached for a beer can. Before he was able to stand and exit the fridge, Helmuth slammed the door on his head. Jeremy was startled and dazed.

He said, "What the..." and the door struck his head again. He tried to retaliate, but he felt dizzy and couldn't regain his balance. He cursed and screamed, threatening to kill Helmuth. After five or six blows he was rendered unconscious.

Helmuth whistled happily as he unloaded the beer cans, unhinged the selves and threw them behind him. He lifted Jeremy's body and tucked it into the cold machine. He remembered a riddle Shaggy used to tell him when she was younger. She would ask him if the refrigerator was running. He would say, "Of course it's running."

She would reply, "Well, you better go catch it."

For some reason Helmuth found this joke apropos and more humorous than usual. He laughed as he leaned the kitchen table against the refrigerator and stacked it with three of the four chairs. He went into the den to check on Shannon. He caught a glimpse of the battered couch and decided to slide it next to the kitchen table to reinforce the barrier.

Helmuth carried Shannon into the kitchen, cuddling her in his lap. He sat on the one remaining chair, sipped his beer and waited for Jeremy to regain consciousness. He snatched another beer from those spewed around the floor. He smiled at himself. What a great idea he had to take the beers from the fridge. He may be waiting a while. Shannon snored quietly while Helmuth polished off three beers.

Helmuth was delighted when Jeremy finally recovered from most of his head injuries and realized his predicament. He banged on the doors, yelling obscenities, threatening Helmuth. He had no luck with his antics, so he tried the Mr. Nice Guy approach, begging for release and offering money. He heard Shannon bark and resorted back to screaming and ranting. He realized why Helmuth locked him in an enclosed space with no means to escape. He didn't feel guilty for leaving Shannon in the car, she was just a dog. However, he would use his knowledge to his advantage. He tried another tactic, confessing for his wrongdoing and accepting responsibility. He said it was a stupid, thoughtless act and learned a valuable lesson.

Helmuth was thrilled that Jeremy apologized and confessed. He stood up, placed Shannon on the floor and the two of them exited the house.

Helmuth drove Shannon to The Plainledge Animal Shelter and called Babs. Shaggy cleaned her tenderly, cuddled with her and found her a comfortable dog bed. Babs examined her. She found not serious injuries. Shannon acquired some cuts and bruises. Babs assumed her owner did more than lock her in a hot car. Shaggy and Samael slept in the shelter to keep the new dog company throughout the night.

Chapter
SEVENTEEN
The Memorial Service

The days passed with no indication that Janet was alive. Yukon and I missed Janet very much. We waited in the bedroom for any noises or possible sign. Yukon did not hear or smell anything unusual. We exhausted our prospects. We could not find a way in the Dark Place.

We had a Memorial Service for Janet one week after her disappearance. Co-workers from the Foster Care Agency and The Plainledge Animal Shelter attended, as well as family and close friends. We made sure the Funeral Parlor welcomed pets. All of the people who worked at the shelter arrived with their dogs. Yukon felt comforted. Although he grieved for Janet, his furry friends improved his mood. Dakota laid next to Yukon with her chin on his back. The Veterinarian's Assistant, Babs, showed up with her husband, their three children and their five dogs. Four of the dogs entered silently and took their places near Yukon. They huddled closely together sharing their love and support. Daniel carried Chestnut in his arms and sat in the seats next to his parents.

The church was a quaint building residing on the main street in town, sharing its time with the town hall. Folding chairs were set in rows, so the inside of the church looked more like an auditorium. The stage substituted for the altar, the parishioners for the audience and the priest for the main role. The heavy curtains were rolled securely to the sides of the stage with beautiful thick burgundy ropes. The residence of the town attended weekly services and engaged in community affairs and service. A basement area was converted into a recreation room where marriages, new babies and parties were celebrated. Every Sunday after-service get-togethers were scheduled. Churchgoers baked cakes and cookies, percolated coffee and poured juice in carafes for the children.

Cathy and Yukon arrived first. They were beyond tired. The last week's happenings stole all of her energy and positive thoughts. Yukon was more resilient, as most dogs. They had a gifted soul, able to absorb negativity and rinse it clean, using the additional energies to provide support and comfort to their human friends. Cathy grieved for Janet, but tried to remain strong for Yukon. She hoped to return to the Dark Place and rescue Janet. The fatigue, mixed with the inability to rest caused a deep despair, a weariness that sapped her spirit as she sat and listened to the eulogy.

She felt the floor shift slightly. She looked around, but no one else seemed to notice the disturbance. She was not aware of Daniel, holding Chestnut tightly to his chest. The young boy was trembling, looking to his parents for support. They sat intently listening to the priest speak and did not notice anything out of the ordinary. Chestnut allowed Daniel to hold him closely without fussing. He was smart enough to remain motionless, to give Daniel a sense of peace in an unnerving situation. He did not want to stress Daniel, but he smelled a wicked stench and felt the building shudder. He was aware of impending danger, but acted like a true emotional support dog. Daniel's safety was his priority.

Cathy clutched her chair as it began to vibrate. The chair bounced off the floor, returning to its original position, again and again. No one paid any mind to the commotion. The dogs focused on Yukon. Although they felt the quaking and smelled the funk, they remained composed on the floor next to Yukon. They watched for any additional signs, ready to attack and protect their humans, each other and Yukon.

Cathy saw the next few minutes in slow motion in a trance-like state, but noticed the other attendees did not share the same perception. They chatted silently, while the priest continued the service. She thought the dogs were oblivious to the intrusion, simply lying on the floor respecting Yukon's grief. However, they were aware of the disturbance.

The priest raised his wooden crucifix for a final prayer. The crucifix shuddered. The priest held on with all his might, but the crucifix shot out of his hand and flew across the altar. The priest jumped to catch it but the cross surpassed him and wedged itself upside down in the closed coffin.

The priest appeared horizontally suspended in the air, reaching for the crucifix. The Christ figure dismantled from the wood, lodging itself in the priest's chest. He fell to the floor, landing on his left side, clutching his chest. He stifled his cries to maintain control of the services, but the pain was unbearable. He took hold of the Christ figure with both hands. He inhaled deeply and heard his lungs crackle. He agonizingly wrenched Christ from his chest. Blood spewed rapidly from the wound, oozing down his robe and streaking down his side. It spurted in gobs, like tennis balls pumping out of the ball machine.

He fell to the alter floor seizing, his arms and legs pounding on the floor, trying to force air into his lungs. The sound of his thrashing vibrated like the choir organ. The blood continued to flow and pooled around his head like a halo. White foam poured from his mouth, like heavenly clouds. His pants reeked of excrement and stank of urine as he relieved his bowels and his bladder in his final throes.

Yukon started to whine. The other dogs stood up and followed suit, sounding like the church choir. He placed his two paws on Cathy's lap. Dakota sensed something was amiss. She pushed her nose under Cathy's chair, and lifted it up and back. Yukon jumped off and bent to check on Cathy. He patted her arm and licked her face. Max, Nick and Vixen circled the chair, examining the area for additional risks: barking to ward off potential evils. Kyle, Paul-Anthony and Maddie attempted to restrain and silence their dogs. The usually obedient pups were so determined to rid the church of the evil forces; they paid no attention to their humans.

The dogs continued to run around the chair, weaving between the chairs, knocking those over, which were not occupied. The people panicked, clutched their children, found paths between the crazed dogs and fled the church. It was complete chaos, people yelling, children crying, dogs circling and barking, and a priest, dying on the altar.

Cathy fell to the floor, breaking her trance. She woke from her hypnotized state and looked around. She felt embarrassed by her behavior, relieved to return to reality and petrified of the scenes she observed. She was even more troubled that she was obviously the only one who witnessed the upheaval. Lucy and Babs assured her she was safe. They reminded her how grief presents itself in various ways, some benign, others, bizarre. She wasn't convinced that this was manifestation of grief, but something more sinister.

The two women escorted Cathy from the church. The dogs stayed inside until all of the guests departed. They calmed down but continued to sniff the altar area.

The church began to tremble once again. A fetid smell wafted from the empty coffin, causing the dogs to return to their anxious mood. A shadow emanated from the right side of the coffin, growing rapidly. A form emerged from the shadow. Spindly legs, no feet, a large head, hollow eyes. Yukon recognized the Stretchman at once.

The dogs gathered like a pack. Yukon retreated for a brief second, and then courageously joined his friends. They heard the coffin creak. A few scrawny degenerated fingers slipped out from the side of the enclosure. They gripped the lid and flung it open. A right leg circled up and over the side followed by a head and a torso. The left arm was missing. The uninvited church guest resembled the Stretchman, yet different. The form was visible but fading. It seemed confused. Its eyes and mouth were wide open. It stared at its own hand, moving it side to side, trying to process the image it controlled. The thing spotted Yukon. Its lipless mouth spread upward, while what remained of its eyebrows relaxed their tense pose.

Yukon recognized Janet, or whatever part of her existed. His tail wagged slowly, hesitant to approach.

The Stretchman called, "J a n e t." A slow echoing filled the church, bouncing off the walls. The Janet-

Thing turned toward the monster. She began walking toward him, forgetting about Yukon. She no longer heard Yukon's barks or pleas for acknowledgement.

The Stretchman had gained control of her mind and body. She no sooner reached him than he clutched her hand. The touch created a powerful spark. The menacing particles flew like fireworks on the Fourth of July in Hell. The elements reacted like flint on the altar cloth, igniting a flame. The heavy curtains caught fire. The booms and explosions resonated inside the church and in the outer courtyard. Those outside heard the blasts, turned to the church and saw flames climbing up the walls. The children ran toward the church to rescue their dogs. Their parents held them back. Paul-Anthony called the fire department.

I heard the rumbling but I was too tired and full of grief to move. My friends comforted me for a while. I felt good lying next to Dakota and the other dogs. Cathy's chair began to tremble and I knew I had to help her. She sat on that chair, staring straight ahead, oblivious of her surroundings. Dakota and I managed to turn over the chair, bumping Cathy's head on the floor, jarring her out of her altered state.

Max, Vixen and Nick ran around her looking for any impending danger. We barked and yelped loudly to ward off the evil presence. Since we didn't find any danger near Cathy, we expanded our search to the entire church. Many children were sitting on the chairs. We had to make sure they were safe. My friends chased me around the church, barking and seeking out the evil spirits. I felt like a detective on my favorite Private Eye show.

The children wanted to play too. They bolted off their chairs and joined in the game. They ran after us shouting and laughing. It was like follow-the-leader and I was the leader. We knocked over many chairs in our wake. This was just what I needed to raise my mood. The parents however, did not find this amusing. They were concerned. They couldn't understand the recent events. Humans don't have the ability to hear or smell as well as dogs can. They can't feel invisible danger. Their lack of sensory perception makes them unequal to dogs. Therefore, it is required that we stay close to them and prevent any negative consequences.

I watched the crucifix kill the priest. I was nervous about what may follow, but my loyalty remained on Cathy. We were successful in our attempt to release Cathy from her possession and relieved when she left the church. We stayed back and checked out the altar. I saw the Janet-thing creep out of the casket. I was petrified and disgusted. We dogs stuck together, willing to fight, but the curtains caught fire and spread quickly. We dashed out of the church into the arms of our humans.

The parents were relieved to see the dogs exiting the church. The children stopped in their tracks, no longer needing to enter the building to rescue them.

__Chapter__
EIGHTEEN
The Waldron Family

Daniel was an amazing little boy. Because he had difficulty interacting with humans, he focused on dogs. He had a remarkable ability to sense their needs. He communicated with them on a strange telepathic level. He frequently dreamed of dogs in obscure locations. Like his mother and brother, he avoided sharing these dreams. The Asperger's Syndrome produced an additional difficulty with his ability to share his thoughts, fears and dreams. Daniel did not find this much of a burden. His dreams had a certain theme and he was often the hero.

Daniel found himself in the familiar Dark Place. It was cold and damp. He was alone in a tunnel-like structure. At the start of the dream, he was frightened. It was dark; he didn't know where he was, yet knew he visited this place before. He was immediately relieved when he heard the faint barking of a dog or, more than one dog.

He followed the sound. The barking was easy for him to follow, as the sound increased as he walked forward. He thought the dogs would comfort him when he found them, but he was terribly mistaken.

He discovered two big dogs in the clutches of a monster. The monster was three times Daniel's height and had an impossible-looking head that reached

128

from its own waist to the ceiling. It stretched its fingers wide enough to circle each dog around their waist, like they were cotton swabs. Daniel reached into his back pocket and located his slingshot. He had not played with it in months. He didn't remember placing it in his pocket, but used it to his advantage. He withdrew an unfamiliar object from his side pocket. He had no time to identify the object, it fit into the palm of his hand, had a rough surface and an odd hour-glass shape.

He carefully loaded his slingshot, aimed at the monster's hollow left eye and blasted the object into the Stretchman's mouth. He didn't hit the eye as planned, but was satisfied with making contact. Although the monster was big enough not to miss, Daniel's hands were shaking so badly, he was surprised he was able to load and shoot the slingshot in the proper direction.

The Stretchman hurled backward as the object launched in its throat. The monster swallowed the object and sneered briefly. The sneer swiftly turned into a frown as the object worked its magic. The monster's arms and legs reversed their course, becoming smaller and less powerful. It continued to shrink. Its legs compressed, the bones crunching under the pressure. Its mouth opened wider until it encompassed its entire head. Its eyes merged into its mouth, assembling into one vacant black hole. The creature's head, just an empty nothingness, melted into its chest.

The Stretchman bellowed out a last roar, flexing its constricted arms, and slunk into the ground beneath its footless legs. The monster released its hold on the dogs as it cried out in shock and disbelief.

The dogs landed with a thud. Daniel was relieved and exhausted. He was so concerned for the dogs' safety; he didn't realize how frightened he was. He stopped to absorb the recent events and had difficulty standing on his own two feet. The dogs regained a portion of their strength and traipsed over to Daniel. He strained to climb on top of the bigger dog, like a jockey on his horse. Both dogs floated into the air. Daniel's heart soared with the elevation. The dog's warm fur and the slight breeze in his hair caused a feeling of well-being. They shepherded him to a soft landing where his head lightly touched a fluffy surface. He felt his slingshot fall from his hand, startling him. He opened his eyes to familiar surroundings. He landed in his own bedroom.

He realized it was a dream. He had these types of dreams many times. They seemed so real. He rolled over to check his clock on his nightstand when something fell off his bed. He reached for the object. It was his old slingshot. He remembered using it to annoy Maddie. He used to place some crumpled paper in it, draw it back and watch it hit Maddie on her head. He never hurt her. He only used soft paper or tissues. Yet, he had not used this toy in quite a while. He wasn't sure how it materialized on his bed.

*His dream…*he used the slingshot *in his dream*. It was the weapon that destroyed the Stretchman.

He sensed he might meet this monster face-to-face in the near future. He was motivated to be prepared and ready for the fight. He packed his backpack with his slingshot, some rocks, his marbles; any items he could blast from slingshot. He added a water bottle and some chewy fruit snacks for himself and a bag of Karen's dog biscuits for Chestnut. He also decided to include a few extra collars and leashes in case he needed to rescue and maintain the dogs he envisioned in his nightmare. He needed Chestnut at his side for any important mission. His furry friend was consistently able to uncover Daniel's suppressed bravery and courage.

Maddie didn't fuss when Daniel teased her, it was harmless and he loved her. She didn't have the night terrors like most of her family. However, she possessed a hostile temper. She was involved in an incident before she attacked Lucas. She never felt guilty about her behavior; she was just curious why she was the only one in her family who reacted viciously.

Maddie remembered a year ago, when she was in 4th grade, before she attacked Lucas in the cafeteria. She was in the middle of physical education period. The class played hockey, Maddie's favorite sport. It was the school championship game. Her team was winning when her friend Jackie received the ball and ran for the goal. She had a clear shot, but missed. Her team lost the game. The other girls on her team booed her. They threw the ball at her and cackled her. Jackie cried her way to the locker room, where the girls continued their jeering and taunting. They wouldn't stop. They told her she was ugly, uncoordinated and a loser. Mean girls don't need much ammunition to ruin a classmate's day, or school year.

Maddie had a lot of patience where revenge was concerned. Her instinct was to immediately attack, but she was certain she may be hurt in the process. Four bullies against one vigilante.

The girls continued to tease Jackie all week. They laughed at her, gossiped about her lack of athleticism. They even posted goofy pictures of her on social media. Jackie wasn't very popular before the missed goal attempt, but found herself with less friends and more isolated after the social media affects. Most of the students found it humorous to pick on a scapegoat rather than sympathize with her. They were afraid if they didn't join the crowd, they would be the next victim.

Lyndsay was the female version of Lucas. Her claim to fame was to embarrass and humiliate others.

Maddie remained in the locker room during Friday's gym class. The dressing area consisted of ten lockers in a row with a long bench in between. There was only two feet in between the lockers and the bench. She was aware of the potential consequences, but took the risk. Her plan would be enjoyable even if she had to miss one gym class. She waited for the class to exit the room and she took out her goalie stick. She remembered how to crush the combination lock and pop open the locker as she did to Lucas's locker. She bashed open the four mean girls' lockers. She hesitated to confirm no one heard the ruckus. She poured glue on the girls' clothing, jewelry, shoes and books. She was fortunate her father kept his construction van full of tools and items useful in these types of situations. His toolbox contained a large tub of strong adhesive.

Maddie took pictures of the banged-up open locker for future use. She set up a superior plan for Lyndsay. She filled a bucket with the glue and leaned it precariously on the top shelf of the locker. She closed the door gently as the container leaned against it.

Maddie was excited to hear the bell signaling the period was almost over. The class was on their way to the locker room to change from their gym clothing for the next class. The three girls followed their leader. They passed by their own lockers first and gasped in shock, then started screaming for the physical education teacher.

One stupid girl reached in to grab her shoe, not realizing that the white goop was glue. Her hand touched the shoe, which immediately stuck to her. She shook her hand furiously, trying to shake it off. She banged it against the bench. Her shoe broke and dripped wet glue; it drained all over the top of the seat. A second bully grabbed the glue-covered shoe and struggled to yank it off her friend. Stupid Girl cried out in anguish as the tugging pulled her skin from the adhesive. Second bully's hand stuck to Stupid Girl and her shoe. The third friend sat on the bench exhausted. She looked to Lyndsay for help and realized her rear end was stuck to the bench.

Lyndsay was no longer concerned for her friends. She had to change her clothes and fix her hair to look nice for the next class. She opened her own locker. The pail tipped over, the glue covered her head and slid down her face. She swiftly wiped it from her eyes and her hair. The glue took hold of her hand and she couldn't remove it from her hair. She froze in embarrassment with her hand clutching her head. Maddie recorded the entire episode and posted it on social media. Jackie was terrified of the on-goings, but found humor in their humiliation. She signaled a thumbs-up when she saw Maddie recording the incident.

Ms. Blake charged in after hearing the commotion from her office down the hall. She called The Career and Technical Education Department and asked them to carry over as much WD-40 as they had in stock, some towels and cloths. Stupid Girl and Second Bully cried uncontrollably as they waited for the chemicals to loosen the bond. Ms. Blake tenderly separated the shoe from the girls' hands, but it tore their skin leaving welts and bruising their palms and fingers. Ms. Blake was able to pry Bench Girl off the seat. She also sustained bruising and cuts on the back of her legs.

Lyndsay would have to procure a short haircut after the glue was cut out of her hair. Maddie laughed at the irony. Lyndsay prided herself on her physical beauty and long curly blond hair. The short unfashionable hair was an extra delight in the revenge plot. Ms. Blake demanded Maddie hand over her phone, but Maddie refused. She turned on her heals and exited the building. Instead of walking home to greet and take care of Nick, she headed toward Trista's house.

Trista was pleased with my plan and the results. We were both excited that the bullies endured pain and humiliation. Lyndsay's fall from grace was our prized accomplishment.

I sat near my cage for a long time. I was home alone, waiting for Maddie to barge in and play with me. However, she didn't come home after school again today. The Waldron's and my doggie friends often kept me company but I missed Maddie. I was so sad I couldn't even eat. My food didn't taste good, neither did the dog biscuits or treats. I obsessed over being a bad dog. I wondered what I did to disappoint my human. I will wait forever for Maddie to love me again. I promise to be a good dog.

I heard a rattling on the front door. I stood up, perked my ears and wagged my tail. I must have been wrong; Maddie did come home for me after all. She was just a bit late. But the door didn't open A rush of smoke streamed in through the bottom on the door. It made a bee-line to my cage. It whipped around me and tossed me up and down. I was caught in some malevolent force. I couldn't find my bearings. It lifted me up. I couldn't reach the ground nor make a run for it. I was frightened, I yelled for Maddie. No one answered my cries. I drifted downward, bumping into unyielding walls as I fell. I heard my head and body collide painfully against the walls and heard my rear leg snap.

I landed roughly on a solid surface. I was unable to stand up or move due to the ache in my leg and the injuries to my body. I remained immobile on the cold ground crying for Maddie.

Trista and I proceeded to her bedroom. I sat on and old beat-up chair, in front of an extraordinary antique mirror. My reflection looked unfamiliar, strange but powerful like a superhero. Trista brushed my hair and told me how she always dreamed of having a strong beautiful daughter. She played a weird song on her old record player. It repeated the same mysterious words, "Be careful what looks back at you."

The music was slow and eerie. The echo resonated louder than the song. The speed accelerated and I felt dizzy, my head rotating as fast as the disc. I heard Trista's voice. It wasn't louder than the music, I heard it in my head. She instructed me to move closer to the mirror. It was mesmerizing. I took a few steps and noticed my eyes were red, my smile reflected a grimace. Two of my front teeth were missing and my gums were bleeding, filling my mouth with thick red goop.

Trista snatched my hand, leading me close enough to touch the glass. She bent her head down and gently placed it on the mirror. She positioned her other hand on the back of my neck and set my forehead on the reflector. I felt a vibration course through my body. It started in my head and traveled down my legs and arms. I observed my reflection. I stood straight, my right foot stepped through the glass and the rest of me followed. Trista refused to release my hand and force her way through the portal with me.

It was dark and damp. I was surrounded in cold dirt, yet I was able to breathe. I was both exhilarated and terrified. I watched Trista push the dirt aside and I followed. We arrived in an oval-shaped room in an underground cave. I had limited sight but could hear moaning from my sides and above me. It sounded as though ailing people were stuck in the walls yearning for assistance. I wasn't concerned for them. I didn't care. I figured they probably deserved their fate, as if they were in Hell suffering for their sins. I glanced at Trista. She was smiling at me. We understood each other. We would not help these people

A figure emerged from my right side. First, a hand struggled to free itself from the compacted dirt, and then an arm emerged. The arm wasn't fully formed, it was partly transparent. The half-human continued its plight to join us. We watched without assisting. She looked pleased and powerful. I mimicked her behavior.

The figure, probably a woman, toppled over and landed on her stomach. She wasn't strong enough to pull herself up, but she managed to balance on her knees. She reached her hand out to me. I saw Trista shake her head, so I did not offer any help. Trista walked over to the figure, put her hands on the shoulders and pressed down. The woman easily sank into the ground, disappearing from our sight. I heard her diminished cries as she vanished. Trista clapped her hands and jumped up and down like a child who won a race. I copied her once again and felt a similar feeling of victory.

The triumphant feeling suddenly stopped when I heard a different kind of crying. It sounded more like a dog whimpering. It was very familiar. I recognized it immediately. I ran toward the noise. My legs felt heavy in this Dark Place. It was as I was moving in quick sand. It was difficult to pick my legs up and move them forward. I was compelled to find the dog, *my* dog. It was Nick calling for me. I ran faster as the grip on my legs increased making it more difficult to advance. However, I continued to push forward.

I heard Trista laughing in the distance. I stopped to assess the situation. I closed my eyes and listened for Nick. I felt an inner sadness. Memories of recent events flooded me. I neglected him. I left him without fresh water I chose to stay at school and fill up glue traps instead of going home to play with Nick. I walked to Trista's house rather than my own. He was my loyal companion, my best friend and I let him down. I was so focused on revenge; I forgot what was most important.

I stood in The Dark Place thinking about the monster I turned into, abandoning those who loved me most. Nick's whimpering jolted me from my memories. I trekked slowly toward the cries, my eyes closed, and my heart open. The quicksand melted away; the obstacles faded. My boy was lying on the ground, his body crumpled. His leg was bent at an unnatural angle. His eyes, just slits. His coat was matted with dirt and grime. He was badly hurt. His tail wagged slightly when he noticed me. I slumped down next to him. I stroked him and assured him I would forever take care of him, but he had to hold on, he couldn't leave me. I wept over him, repeating the same four words, "I am so sorry, I am so sorry."

I remembered something important. Trista had enough evil power to push that woman figure under the cave, out of the lobby. Her anger fed her strength in This Dark Place. What if my love for Nick could save him and help us escape? I could relinquish my own hateful feelings and muster the positive feelings I used to have, those buried inside.

I leaned my hands onto Nick's body. I thought of the great times we shared; when I rescued him from the shelter, when he took up more space on the bed than I did, when I finished in the bathroom and he greeted me as I was gone for weeks. I talked, I laughed and I cried. I pushed down delicately on his body and we started to rise. I refused to let go of him as we reached the ceiling and floated through without incident.

We tenderly landed on a soft carpet. I looked around and blinked. We were home.

Nick remained immobile. His cries became shallow, less frequent. I called my mother at The Plainledge Animal Shelter where she was working and hurriedly explained how badly Nick was hurt. She grabbed her medical supplies and flew out the door. I called my father and asked him to drive to our house with his company van so we could transport Nick to the Animal Emergency Hospital. I stayed at Nick's side, calmly talking to him and telling him how much I love him. I promised him we would play catch with his favorite ball as soon as he healed. I promised to brush him and give him fresh water daily and that I would never again neglect him. He stopped whimpering. He was so still. I yelled his name over and over until my parents dashed through the front door.

Mom started an IV and splinted Nick's rear leg. Dad carried a dog stretcher. He and Mom gingerly lifted Nick onto the carrier while I held the IV bag. We stepped into the van and sped to the Animal

Hospital at the edge of town. Mom was able to convince the vet to allow me into the recovery room after the surgery.

Nick had a cast on his broken leg, his body was wrapped with medical tape and he was hooked up to an IV. I approached him and said, "Hi buddy." He tried to pick up his head but didn't have enough energy. I received a slight tail wag. I'll never forget the sound of that faint tail-thump. It was the best sound I ever heard. It was in synchronicity with my own heartbeat, strong and happy.

I sat at Nick's side and patted his head while he rested. He remained in the hospital for two full days. When he arrived home, the other dogs surrounded him with doggie love. They licked his nose, and sniffed his wounds. Their instincts prevented them from playing roughly, they moved around him cautiously.

Ms. Blake allowed me to complete my schoolwork at home so I could nurse Nick back to health. I stayed with Nick and finished my assignments. I forgot all about Lucas, Lyndsay, and my need for revenge.

I didn't forget Trista however. I had a feeling I would have to confront her in the near future.

Chapter
NINETEEN
Shaggy and Samael

Shaggy spoke to her parents the night before and explained Samael's predicament. She told them how he helped at the shelter the entire day, loving the moments with the dogs. She mentioned how he always wanted a dog, but his parents forbade it. She wondered if they would offer him a part-time position at the shelter. Shaggy agreed to train and supervise him. Her parents hesitantly agreed with the condition that they meet and interviewed Samael the next day.

Lucy arranged to work that Monday morning to manage the shelter while Shaggy trained Samael. She and Paul-Anthony agreed she would work on Monday morning at the shelter and Monday afternoon at the construction company. Lucy rang up the sales and handled the register while Dakota greeted the customers. She romped to the door when she heard the bells clang. She grabbed a homemade dog biscuit from the shelf and dropped it in front of the incoming dogs. The customers were delighted with the display of affection and Dakota's intelligence. She happily received caresses and smiles all day.

Samael arrived at The Plainledge Animal Shelter early that morning. He felt like a new man, happy and motivated to do something worthwhile. Cleaning the cages, exercising the dogs, cuddling with the puppies, he had purpose in his otherwise useless life.

Shaggy discussed the job opportunity with Sam as soon as she arrived. He was elated. He smiled broadly, grabbed her and hugged her. He stepped away from her quickly when he realized he overstepped the bounds. Shaggy playfully laughed and assured him everything was just fine.

Shaggy showed Sam how to log the inventory, order supplies and discard the expired items. She allowed him to order additional toys or treats he thought the dogs may enjoy and would benefit sales. He took the initiative to clean the counters, the aisles and the floors whenever a dog did their business in the store. He grabbed the mop and bucket before Shaggy had a chance to ask. The two of them ate lunch at the register every day. Sam decided to start each day with bagels, cream cheese and coffee. He would stop at the local deli on his way to work and buy breakfast for both of them. Sam gained some well-needed weight and muscle. His strength and stamina increased as he lifted and stocked the heavy cartons and boxes off the delivery trucks. He found the incentive to shower, wear clean clothing and style his hair before leaving for work. He wasn't sure his enthusiasm stemmed solely from the dogs, but it may have been partially the reason.

Samael headed for the puppy room. A woman found the puppies abandoned after she picked up her medication from the pharmacy. She exited the store and headed to her car when she heard soft mewling sounds coming from around the building. The five black puppies were in a box without food, only an empty water bowl remained. The woman called for and looked around for their mother, but couldn't find her anywhere in the vicinity.

This is not an unusual situation. People dump their unwanted dogs wherever they think someone may find them and take care of them. Others abandoned them without concern. Helmuth was aware of these atrocities and accepted any stray or unwanted dog into his shelter. Fortunately, the women tentatively carried the box of puppies to her car and drove them to The Plainledge Animal Shelter. They kept the puppies in the box for comfort and warmth. Sam was ready to bottle-feed each puppy. He picked up the smallest one first. He loved the soft feel of their fur in his arms, the loving nature of the pup and the famous puppy breath his detected as he reached it up to his face for a lick on his nose.

Sam suddenly felt the ground shake beneath him. Shaggy noticed it also and ran over to ask Sam if he thought it was an earthquake rumble. He placed the puppy in the box for safety and the rocking increased. He grabbed Shaggy's hand. They looked at each other, without saying a word, wondering what was causing the rumbling and what should they do.

They watched as an arm sliced through the floor next to the puppy box. It stretched from the right side, up and over the box. The arm was battered. It appeared as if the skin was torn from its flesh. They could see the exposed muscles, veins and bones. The muscles contracted as it picked up a puppy. The arm slowly retracted with the pup in its grip and slunk back into the Earth. The pup emitted a painful whimpered. Sam moved to help it, but Shaggy pulled him back.

She said, "Did you see…?"

Sam nodded, his pupils dilated, his mouth hung open in disbelief. They were terrified and trembling. They couldn't believe what they just witnessed.

Shaggy started to cry and Sam pulled her in for a hug. She willingly accepted the display of affection and sobbed for quite a while. When she felt better, she told Sam she was going to call her father and walked to the counter to retrieve her phone.

At that exact moment, Samael turned and bumped into his father who was suddenly standing behind him.

Seth took a walk to purchase a coffee and half-dozen donuts before travelling to work. He scarfed down a few jelly donuts, wiped his mouth with his sleeve and washed them down with a few gulps of sugar induced java. He passed the awful animal rescue place. For some strange reason, he casually glimpsed in the window. Since his attack and subsequent injury, he despised every animal, especially the loathsome dogs.

He blinked twice and shook his head. He couldn't comprehend what he observed. Samael was holding a revolting mini-mongrel up to his face. The disgusting animal licked his face as Sam laughed outwardly. Seth charged in, like an express train, straight for Sam. He saw the dreaded look in Sam's eyes immediately before he grabbed the mutt and threw it, like a football bullet pass, into the cement wall. She emitted a soft *humpf* as her last breath was forced from her body on impact. They all heard the sound as her body connected to the wall and slid down to the floor. The blood splatted on the wall and dripped down to the floor.

Sam was stunned and horrified. He cowered back, afraid to retaliate. Shaggy heard the commotion. The

143

man did not look familiar. She dropped her phone, grabbed the goalie stick Maddie left under the counter and sprinted toward Seth. She hooked his foot with the stick, turned it in a clockwise direction and watched him fall on his hindquarters. She held the weapon securely in her hand, mustered up an authoritarian tone and told him to get the hell out of the shelter. Seth stood us, brushed himself off and motioned to leave. His turned at the last minute, warning them that he would return when they least expected him. He promised them they would be regret their actions.

Shaggy shrugged her shoulders and held out her hands, as if to ask Sam to explain. Sam admitted the man was his father. He described some of the ways his father had abused him and his mother throughout the years, how he feared the man tremendously and the evils his father could inflict on others.

They both turned to the wall covered with blood. The puppy lay crumbled upon her side, like a deflated ball. They looked at each other and without any self-consciousness, began to cry. They stepped toward each other, sharing this intimate moment of grief and sob uncontrollably. Tears streamed down their faces as their bodies trembled. They yelled, screamed and cursed at the fate of the poor little creature, the cruel ending of a life just beginning, the injustice of it all.

They couldn't bear to clean up the broken carcass. Shaggy called her father. She cried and screamed so loudly; he couldn't make sense of what she was trying to communicate. He understood that she wanted him to come to the shelter immediately. She said it was an emergency, but wasn't able to explain or offer any details over the phone.

Helmuth arrived moments later. He was furious, angry and inconsolable. He was unable to speak. Shaggy and Samael retrieved a bucket, a mop and cleaning supplies and quietly set them next to Helmuth. No one uttered a word.

Helmuth placed the puppy's remains in a plastic bag and scrubbed until his fingers bled. Tears silently streamed down his face. He used his sleeve to wipe his face and continued with the grueling task at hand. When he finished, he carried the bag to the field behind the shelter, fetched a shovel from the supply room and dug a hole. Shaggy and Samael trailed behind Helmuth, understood his actions and picked up a couple of shovels to assist in the traumatic but necessary task.

They dug a hole five feet deep, three feet long and two feet wide. They gently lowered the puppy into her final resting place, covered her with the dirt and bowed their heads in silent prayer. They were hot, sweating and thoroughly fatigued. Shaggy and Samael dismally stored the shovels in the supply room. Helmut exited the shelter shovel in hand, without a single word. Shaggy and Sam decided to sleep in the store with the dogs, as they were still whimpering from the disturbance. They washed themselves with the bathtubs and soaps they use for the dog grooming. They made a makeshift mattress with blankets and towels and hunkered down with the dogs for a fitful night's sleep.

Helmuth did not go directly home. He walked to The Ravana's Auto Shop. He didn't want anyone to spot his car in the vicinity. He heard several bangs and commotion as he neared the shop. He slowed down and strolled through the trees so he wasn't detected. He didn't want to raise any suspicion.

Chapter
TWENTY
Lucy, Dakota and The Lane Family

I decided to research the house due to the mysterious and disturbing events. I went to the local library and began digging for information. Dakota stayed in the car. I left the window open for her and equipped her with some squeaky toys, a blanket and a bowl of water. I secured a baby monitor to the dashboard so I could keep track of her. I didn't want to leave her alone in the vehicle for an extended amount of time, so I set my watch alarm to chime in a half-hour. She loved the car and usually curled up and slept on her blanket.

Cathy and Janet previously informed me of the Lane family who lived there before me. They were close friends and spent a lot of time together. They were a family of five who suddenly disappeared without a trace. The police organized search teams including law enforcers and community volunteers. Cathy and Janet were devastated and were the first to volunteer to assist in the search. They looked for weeks without a clue. A few close friends continued combing the area, hanging missing persons' flyers and offered a reward for any information leading to their safe return.

The mother, Yanna, was a veterinarian and a veteran. She worked at The Veterinary Hospital and volunteer at The Plainledge Animal Shelter. I thought that was a strange coincidence, as I found Dakota at the shelter. The father, Walter, was a Suffolk County Police Officer. This was an advantage in setting up the search parties. Most of the local and State cops assisted in the search and rescue attempts. Unfortunately, their attempts did not come to fruition. Their children, Kevin, Connor and Bella were ten years old, seven years old and four years old, respectively. The family never had any issues with the law, school system or their neighbors. They lived in the house for ten years.

Yanna and Walter moved into my house ten years before I did. They were hesitant at first, as the neighborhood lacked diversity. They were a black couple in a white community. They were pleasantly surprised when two women knocked on their door with a homemade banana nut bread, a package of herbal tea and a beautiful, gigantic dog named Morgan.

They found the unpacked box containing the teakettle, set the table with the handy paper plates they used until they unpacked, and chatted about each other and the neighbors. They found comfort in each other's differences that caused various roadblocks along their paths. Cathy mentioned her bullying experiences while Walter and Yanna shared some issues with prejudices and stereotyping. Janet explained how she and Cathy were also uncertain when they moved into the block, but assured them that the people in the community were open-minded and welcomed diversity.

The couple had trouble conceiving so they decided to rescue a few dogs to love and care for while they waited for their miracle baby. Cathy and Janet recommended The Plainledge Animal Shelter. Yanna and Walter thought it was a great place to start, as they adored Morgan.

The four friends planned a trip to the shelter the following day. The woman named Babs unlocked the fenced area for them and allowed them to visit and play with the dogs. She told them to take their time and make their selection at their leisure.

The dogs jumped and wiggled, wagged and barked. They were always so excited to meet people, sniff their butts and lick their faces. They were all enjoying their tie when Yanna noticed three dogs huddled in the back of the area. The Doberman was the biggest of the three. The other two smaller dogs squeezed closely next to him. The three appeared frightened, but the Doberman looked ready to protect them regardless.

Yanna inquired about the three dogs. Babs informed them that the dogs were recently found in an alley. They were about seven years old and apparently previously abused They found them dehydrated, starving and frightened. The Doberman had dried blood on his jowls and his chest.

Babs explained how her husband, Helmuth, an experienced dog trainer, had a difficult time capturing the dogs. They did not trust him and repeatedly ran from his advances. It took him a few days to convince the poor pups to enter the cages he set up for them. When they finally stepped inside, he took them to the shelter. He cleaned them and fed them, but they retreated to the back of the pen whenever he or customers approached. They named the Doberman

Loki. The two little brown dogs were called Cody and Jenna. Cody's right ear was clipped, probably due to abuse. Helmuth used this mark to distinguish between the two.

Yanna remembered Babs. Babs taught the class on dogs and communication years ago when Yanna attended St. Katharine's University. She used the knowledge she gained from the course. She grabbed a few sample cookies from a container and proceeded to the three dogs slowly without making eye contact. She sat about 15 feet away from them and spoke calmly. Her voice was friendly and non-threatening.

Her three human friends walked away to give them space. They checked out the rest of the store and bought a unique dog biscuit labeled, "Limited Ingredient Dog Biscuits." Babs mentioned Karen, a local resident who created these homemade treats for dogs who have digestion issues. She donated boxes of them every month. Karen previously recued a dog with colitis and found it difficult to find treats that didn't cause him pain and discomfort, so she manufactured her own. Janet bought a few for Morgan and Walter purchased a box well aware that he would be leaving the shelter with a furbaby. Less than one hour later, they heard Yanna laughing loudly and calling the dogs' names.

Yanna patiently sat and waited. She took a peek over and noticed one of the smaller dogs glanced her way. She must have been Cody, as a piece of her right ear was missing. She tapped the floor with her finger and simply said, "It's OK."

The pup looked at the Doberman, then back to Yanna. She took a step forward, hesitantly took another step toward Yanna, then leaped over and landed on Yanna's lap. Yanna remained in her position and continued to speak tenderly. Jenna, Cody's sister, watched with keen interest. She also took one tentative step at a time, moving slowly toward Cody. When she realized the woman had no intention of hurting her, she jumped on her lap next to Cody. Loki cautiously observed the woman's behavior. He produced a subtle warning growl to announce his presence and to let her know he would protect and defend his friends if warranted.

After he surveyed the situation and checked out Yanna's behavior, he decided she was safe and had good intentions. He stood up, stared at the woman then sat down with his head held high, eyes fixated on her. He waited. She gently put the pups down and tapped the floor again. She dipped her head down, opened her palm and laid it flat on the floor facing toward the ceiling.

Loki took a few steps, gingerly scratched her hand and backed away quickly. He couldn't believe the woman remained still. He repeated this antic ten times and yet the woman did not react cruelly. She accepted his apprehension, his need for reassurance and his hesitant nature. He mustered the courage to continue on as he stuck his nose on the woman's check and licked her nose.

She smiled and said, "Yes boy, that's good."

Loki was hooked. He dropped down near her leg, put his head on her knee and soulfully gazed at her. She stroked his head until her friends approached.

I saw the two couples walk into the shelter. I was not about to let them come near Cody, Jenna or me. The woman called Yanna approached. She smelled friendly, but I was cautious. I like how she sat their patiently so we could check her out. Cody trusted her more quickly than Jenna and I did. I watched Yanna's interaction with Cody. I was ready to attack for any reason. Jenna noticed the woman's gentle nature, and she also approached Yanna. They both sat on Yanna's lap. She spoke quietly as she pet them. They licked her hands and face, yet she didn't get angry or strike them. Instead, she laughed, accepting their affection.

I figured she was safe, so I hesitantly walked over, backed up and moved forward again. She didn't yell at me. I licked her, then jumped back quickly so she couldn't hit me. She said I was a good boy! I liked being a good boy. I felt good with this lady. I allowed her to take us home.

Yanna and Walter decided to adopt the three dogs. They didn't want to separate them. They understood that the dogs needed to feel safe and secure and how important it was for them to remain together.

Kevin was born on a beautiful sunny day in the middle of May, two years later. Since the couple had no close relatives, they asked Cathy and Janet if they would be Kevin's Godparents. They accepted instantly.

The Baptism ceremony was scheduled three weeks later at ten o'clock on June 6th at 6 pm. Walter looked dapper in his white suit and matching shoes. He was in great physical condition, as his career on the police force warranted weight training and cardiovascular drills. He was six feet tall and 180 pounds. His dark hair and short-cut hair matched his dark skin. Yanna worked out with Walter to maintain her svelte figure. She was five feet eight inches tall and weighed 140 pounds. She looked awesome in her knee-length snow-colored dress. Cathy and Janet both decided to wear light-blue dresses to give the Lanes the spotlight in their ivory clothing. The baby wore a beautiful lace Christening gown and bonnet. He donned the shimmering gold cross Cathy and Janet gifted him for the occasion. The priest wore a white vestment a clerical collar and a large silver crucifix.

They walked into an empty church. They were surprised there were no other families who planned their baby's Christening on the same day. Since they were the only attendees, the priest allowed the four dogs to join the ceremony. The dogs wore a white bandana for the Holy day. Father John blessed four small sliver crosses and attached them to each dog collar. He handed Janet a book of psalms and instructed Cathy to hold Kevin.

The priest motioned Cathy to the fountain. The others followed closely behind. Loki, Cody and Jenna squashed themselves between Yanna and Walter. Morgan scooted close enough to position herself on Janet's feet. Cathy held the baby over the Baptismal font with his head close to the Holy water. The priest scooped the holy water into the scalloped shell and poured it over the baby's head, saying, "In the name of the Father...."

Before he filled the ladle for the second time, he noticed a ripple in the font. He was confused at the disturbance. He bent down to get a closer look and felt a tug on his crucifix. He tried to stand upright, but the pressure was too strong. His head plunged into the holy water. He reached his arms on the font and tried to wrench himself free. He was able to suck in a breath of air before he was forced under again. He felt his parishioners' hands on his arms struggling to help free him.

He detected an evil force lurking below. He found himself in a Dark corridor beneath the water. Dark shadows seemed stuck in the walls, unable to escape. Hands materialized from the dark sides and ceiling. Cries echoed all around him. He extended his arms as he tumbled, desperately trying to grasp those in need. He was unable to reach them. He couldn't breathe and slowly lost consciousness, descended into an ungodly oblivion. The pleas, the misery, the chaos caused him to lose focus. It was maddening. An enormous inhuman form emerged, stretched its arms and seized Father John. The water bubbled violently covering him and dragging him into the earth.

He said the *Our Father* in his head, for the last time.

Cathy stepped back with the baby. Janet, Walter and Yanna desperately tried to free Father John. His head emerged once, but a malformed hand ascended from the water, grabbed his crucifix and continued to submerge him. Father John fought to gain control. His head bobbed in and out, he inhaled as much air as possible until his head no longer surfaced.

The baby started crying, startled by all the noise. His tears were red, dripping down and staining his christening gown. The holy water rose and overflowed over the font. It sizzled as it dripped on the altar, burning the wooden floorboards. The dogs barked frantically. They ran in circles around the font, sensing danger but unable to help. Their instincts told them to avoid the holy water damaged planks.

The house was found in good condition after the Lanes disappeared. There was no indication of a burglary attempt or foul play. Most of their personal items remained. Their car, cell phones, wallets and money remained. The only weird piece of evidence was a massive sized burn mark underneath the bed in the master bedroom. The forensic team analyzed the stain for clues, but found none. The report indicated that the stain was twenty years old or more. This was a contraindication, as the article also stated the house was built fifteen years ago. It appeared as if they rushed out with no regard to their important possessions, or perhaps the spot beneath the bed was more sinister than expected. I heard Dakota bark the same moment my watch alarm sounded, that annoying beep and foreboding bark. I ended my search abruptly and hurried to my car.

I loved waiting in the car. It was the next best thing to being with Lucy. She kept the window open so I could smell all the interesting odors from the library parking lot. The children stuck their little hands through the window and patted my nose. Their parents probably should not have allowed them to stroke an unknown dog, but I was irresistible and calm mannered and I found joy in the children.

I dozed off for a minute and heard a peculiar moaning. It sounded like a miserable plea for help. I wasn't sure if I was dreaming. I opened one eye to scope the area and saw a shadow of a hand on the window. I sat up and looked around. There were small handprints scattered all over the car. Some were faded more than others. The moaning was soft but agonizing. I tried to touch the inkblots, but they disappeared as I made contact. My first instinct was to cover my face with my paws, which I did at once. However, I quickly remembered what a brave dog I was and how I was obligated to protect Lucy.

I sat up straight on my haunches, took a deep growl and squished my nose into the window. I heard a brief childlike laugh. It stopped too quickly, replaced by a sad cry. I was no psychologist, but my intuition told me a child was nearby who needed help. I couldn't unlock the car doors; nor would I leave Lucy. I twirled in circles a few times to release my anxiety. We dogs behave in this manner when we are anxious, confused or bored. They are called displaced behaviors. They are similar to humans who wring their hands, pace back and forth or yell when they feel strong emotions.

Debra Zaech

I knew Lucy could hear me through the baby-monitor, so I started howling. It was my, "beware of danger" bark and Lucy recognized it immediately. I saw her scramble out the library and rush to the car.

Chapter

TWENTY-ONE

Seth and Trista

Trista was convinced the mirror frightened Seth. She would have been afraid to see her own reflection if she were ugly on the outside as well as the inside. She would have laughed at the irony; Seth was like a vampire, afraid to observe his own self.

The mirror was strangely beautiful. The stand looked like an antique three-legged coat rack. The glass was dark with age, throwing back an odd fuzzy reflection. It was oval-shaped, extending from the floor to six feet high. The sides were flanked with cast iron handles resembling parenthesis brackets. The head of the mirror was adorned with a triangular shaped silver crown. Two black stars sat in the center of the fixture. The stars watched those who watched themselves. Trista was convinced the oval shape tilted to gain a better view of the current happenings.

Seth purchased the mirror for Trista as a wedding gift. He found it in some out-of-the-way antique shop. It was partially covered. He glimpsed it through a slit in the casing from the corner of his eye and was attracted to it immediately. He found it strangely beautiful and figured Trista would absolutely love any gift he purchased for her. She would think he cared enough for her to buy her a present. He didn't care for her at all, but she was convenient and she offered

him a nice body he could take advantage of whenever
he pleased.

He had no desire to spend much money on Trista,
but felt obligated to buy her a token gift of
appreciation. The owner of the shop, Smitty, said the
mirror was not for sale. He was certain it was haunted.
Seth did not believe in such ridiculous superstitions,
but Smitty relayed the story. His grandmother
inherited the mirror when her mother died. His
grandmother, Amelia, was accused of sorcery. The
townsfolk believed she used the mirror to cast spells.
She supposedly cast a love spell on the priest, who
couldn't control his burning desire. He fell for her
charms and they began a torrid affair.

The town rumor was Amelia asked Father Gabe
to deliver her Holy Communion one weekend when
she was not feeling well and couldn't attend Mass.
When he arrived, she called him to her bedroom
where she lay seductively in her undergarments. He
asked her to cover herself and explained how
inappropriately she dressed. She smiled wickedly.

The priest caught a glimpse of himself in the
antique mirror standing in the corner. His reflection
looked like a demonic version of himself. His blue
eyes turned eerily red. Small tufts of long, silver gray
hairs stuck out in random areas on his head, where a
thick mane of blond hair usually sat. He stared at his
own lustful, evil grin. He reached up and touched his
own face. It didn't seem like his reflection matched
reality. He felt his thick hair, but observed otherwise.
He glanced at the mirror again and viewed the demon.

His longing for Amelia boiled inside him. It
bubbled over like a filthy caldron. He moved closer to
her. Her scent increased his desire. He kissed her
passionately. They made love for hours. He bent

down to pick up his clothes when they were finished. His reflection deteriorated. He looked larger, more powerful, more *evil.*

He sensed an attraction to the mirror, an unholy force calling him. It promised unlimited power, strength and mastery. The priest understood the devil's presence. He fought against the urge. He dressed as quickly as possible, only tripping once as he lifted his leg to put on his pants.

Father Gabe returned for repeated engagements. He continued to fight against his urges, but he was weak. He prayed, he fasted and he flagellated himself. His Sunday lectures focused on sin and atonement, and then to the parishioner's dismay, he discussed the immoralities of sex. His homilies deteriorated. He talked about mirrors, reflections and the beast who resides in all of us.

His followers complained to the bishop in their diocese. Father Gabe broke down and confessed his sins to the bishop. He admitted his affair, his desires and attempted to explain the mirror.

The church excommunicated him. He suffered extreme guilt. He couldn't sleep. He dreamed of spending eternity in Hell, burning to death every day, never able to meet his God. He was aware of the devil lurking nearby. He woke to find his sheets scorched at the corners. His crucifix was hidden underneath his pillow. His clock stopped, blinking at 12:00 am. He lost his appetite. He dwindled to a mere skeletal figure, his skinny bones protruded from his arms, legs and torso. His face, gaunt, his checks sunk like a constant puckered face. His eyes encompassed most of his face, appeared like two half-dollar coins, gawking mesmerizingly at an unknown attraction. His inner pain increased to an intolerable level.

Father Gabe took a rope and a chair from the storage room. He walked zombie-like to the back of the church, dragging the chair behind him. He placed the chair in front of his favorite oak tree. It was so beautiful this time of year, full of rich green leaves, baby birds chirped in their nests and squirrels scampered from one tree to the next, playing chase with their fellow squirrels.

Tears rolled down his transparent checks as he stood on the chair and looped the rope over the branch. He fashioned a hangman's knot at the end of the rope, tied it tightly around his neck and pushed the chair from underneath him. He didn't die instantly. He heard the chair thump to the ground. He swung from side to side, clutching the rope with both hands. He thought, perhaps he chose the wrong course of action. However, it was too late. His body weight added pressure to his spinal cord and carotid arteries, cutting off his oxygen supply. He swayed for a very long ten minutes before he expired.

The villagers also accused Amelia of starting a fire that destroyed her neighbor's house. She had argued with the neighbor the night before. The house burnt to the ground the following morning. The neighbor was found lying on the floor against the front door. Deep, red scratch marks were visible, running vertically down the door. Her frantic digging wrenched the fingernails right off her nail beds. She died wearing her flannel nightgown and fuzzy pink slippers with pink pom-poms.

They also blamed Amelia for the drought that damaged their crops and left them to starve all winter long. They sentenced her to a horrifying death by drowning. The crowd crept into her bedroom and tied her up while she slept. She wasn't able to fight them

159

all off. They placed her in a burlap sack and dumped her in the lake behind her house. It floated before it filled with water. They shouted in glee as they hit her with broomsticks, oars and shovels. They watched as the water engulfed the bag. They waited; afraid she had the ability to resurface. Some of the elders spent the night at the shore, confirming her demise.

Her daughter, Smitty's mother, Lynn, was completely devastated with the news. She vowed revenge. She would not allow her mother's brutal death to go unpunished.

Lynn loved the antique mirror. She took it from her mother's bedroom before the neighbors torched the house and the rest of Amelia's belongings.

Lynn had good fortune with the mirror. She noticed bad things happened to people who weren't nice to her, who slighted her or simply to anyone she didn't like. Lynn was obsessed with the mirror. She admired her reflection for hours, changing clothes, posing like a model and talking to it as if it were her ally. She told it how her best friend flirted with her boyfriend. The next day, the friend disappeared and her boyfriend was struck by a car. The girl was never found. The boy remained in a coma for weeks. He woke up in a vegetative state and remained in that condition until he died years later.

Lynn became angry when she failed her math class. She complained to the mirror about the teacher. Lynn thought the teacher purposely failed her, even though Lynn tried her best to earn passing grades. The teacher had a sudden heart attack and died that night. She was only 25 years old. Lynn noticed her reflection changed each time the mirror sought revenge on her behalf. She appeared older, her nose grew longer and pointier. She accumulated wrinkles on her face and neck. Her brown eyes displayed a red glow. Her teeth looked crooked and stained. Her body shifted into a monster type image, tall and gaunt with a pasty colored hue. Lynn wasn't concerned.

Her family and the few friends she still encountered did not notice these changes, except for Smitty. He was her only child and observed her personality deteriorate from a once loving mother and person to a mean-spirited angry woman. Smitty was never superstitious until he heard his mother talking to the mirror and he noticed unpleasant incidences started to happen to those who disturbed her.

Smitty's mother died two months ago. She aged rapidly. He body shrunk and dried up like an old prune. Her physical appearance morphed into the likeness of her reflection.

Smitty inherited the house and all of Lynn's possessions. He covered the mirror and placed it on the curb for garbage pick-up. The trash collectors refused to pick it up. They claimed it burnt their hands when they tried to touch it. It exuded a negative vibration. They were afraid to move it or touch it. Smitty tried to smash it and crush it. He even used a chain saw to dismantle it, but he couldn't make a dent. He finally decided to store it in the antique shop. He covered it and ignored it.

Seth was fascinated with the story, although he didn't believe a single word. Smitty was glad to be rid of the ugly artifact and gave it to Seth for no charge. It must have been a match made in Heaven because Seth lifted it with no further ado and drove it to his adoring wife.

He was grateful for Trista and all the wonderful perversions she allowed him to inflict on her. As per Seth's true nature, the present was a useful selfish object. He experienced double the pleasure when he watched himself rape and abuse Trista. It was if he was raping two women at the same time. He was able to view his own actions; he adored his own body and was able to see it in motion.

Although Trista despised the mirror, she didn't notice the appalling deformed figures developing inside. Every instance of rape, abuse, sodomy and other despicable stunts from Seth, the reflection grew increasingly sinister. Trista felt a powerful evil being waiting in the mirror as Seth violated her time after time. She was terrified of Seth, but dreaded the potential malevolent forces of the antique wedding gift.

Seth had a great day after all. He thought the spooky mirror would have dampened his entire day, but he was lucky yet again. After he found his son in The Plainledge Animal Shelter and he threw that ugly mutt to its death, he felt light-hearted. He drove his Mustang to the auto shop. He didn't mind working at the auto body shop, especially after his father's death. It was about time he inherited the business.

The damn old man lived well into his sixties. It was an unfortunate accident, but no loss to the business.

Chapter
TWENTY-TWO
Lucy and Dakota

I heard Dakota from the baby monitor. She notified me with her distinctive emergency whine. It sounded like a mix of a bark and a cry. I immediately stopped my research and headed for my van.

Dakota squished her nose against the window. Her breath covered it with moisture and fog. I detected small handprints seeping through the fog. I know the children who pass the van love the stick their hands in the window and pet Dakota, but these handprints covered all of the windows. There was no consistency. Some were upside down, some backward; many overlapped each other. They were not signs of happy children reaching in to pet a dog. They appeared to be trying to enter the van, in a hurry.

I clicked my key fob to open the door, but nothing happened. I tried again. I heard the clinking sound, but the door would not unlock. I fumbled with the fob. There was a metal key inside, but my hands were shaking and I couldn't open it.

Fog filled the car. It began to swing violently. Dakota cried out. I screamed at my inability to retrieve the key. It slipped from my hand. It broke when it crashed to the ground. Smoke hissed from the fob. It soared upward, encasing the van. I saw two arms appeared in the fog. They stretched above and

163

around the vehicle. It clasped its hands underneath the van like they were hugging it. The arms picked up the car. It hovered about six inches from the ground. The arms shook the van as if it was weightless.

Dakota furiously scratched at the windows with her paws. I could see her struggling to get free. I no longer had the key to get in and help her. She started to cough. It sounded as if she was choking. Her cries lessened in frequency and volume. I bent to pick up the key, regardless of its effect. My hand burnt at the touch. I didn't release my grip. The heat became unbearable as it seared through my palm. I couldn't hear Dakota anymore.

More small handprints materialized. They smashed against the glass from the inside and the outside. They slipped under the top of the driver's side window and pulled it down with an invisible force. Dakota lied motionless on the passenger side seat. The little hands yanked down the other three windows allowing fresh air to waft through the van.

The fog subsided. I heard an angry moan and the arms retreated. My key fob returned to its normal working condition. I pulled on the door and it opened with ease. I carried Dakota out and laid her on the floor. She lay motionless. I placed my hands on her body. She was not breathing.

I yelled out, "No, please, not my baby." I dropped down next to her and stroked her head. I told her what a good girl she was, how much I loved her. I begged her to come back to me. I needed her. I sobbed.

The images of the children's hands reappeared. The formed indentations on Dakota's body. Little ghost-like fingers, scratching behind her ears, patting her head and caressing her torso. Dakota moved her paw. I heard gleeful giggles surrounding us. Dakota slowly opened her eyes and lifted her head.

I waited while Dakota rested for a while. I massaged her body, calmly stroking her from head to tail. The cute little handprints appeared again, tracing my own movements. Before they vanished, I heard a whisper in the wind,

"Thank you, Dakota, for always letting us pet you." And they were gone.

Dakota was hesitant to jump into the van. I sat in the driver's seat, with the all the doors ajar, talking to her, assuring her she was safe. I wasn't sure I believed it myself, but I had some faith in our spiritual friends.

I love my Lucy, but she certainly put me in some uncompromising situations. I saw her clumsily struggling to unlock the van. She even dropped the car fob, what a goofball. I panicked when the van filled up with fog. I tried to claw my way out of the windows, but they wouldn't break. I found it difficult to breathe. I inhaled the poorly oxygenated smoke. I felt myself becoming weaker.

I remember lying on the ground. I could hear Lucy call my name, but I was unable to respond. It hurt to breathe. I was afraid I would remain in this state forever, never licking Lucy's face or sniffing another dog's butt.

Then I felt the children's hands. The physical massaging sensation, mixed with the tenderness and affection, revived me. A rushed of warm joy coursed through my body. I felt rejuvenated and hopeful. I opened my eyes. Lucy laid by my side, crying. I licked her nose and thumped my tail.

I rested a while and listened to Lucy before I dared venture into the van. Lucy expected me to sit into the back seat, as per usual. However, I took full advantage and jumped into the passenger seat. She smiled at me and I woofed back at her.

I decided a treat was in order. I drove to Starbucks's, bought myself an herbal tea. The Mint

Tranquility usually soothed me. I purchased a puppucino for Dakota. We sat outside on a rock sipping our beverages. I was pleased to know we had a group of positive energies on our side. A rush of wind blew through my hair and I thanked the children.

Chapter
TWENTY-
THREE
The Waldron Family

Maddie continued to volunteer at The Plainledge Animal Shelter after she completed her mandates. Kyle and Chestnut helped Daniel recover from the pizza incident. It took Daniel weeks to feel safe enough to attend school without crying or panicking.

Lucas recovered from Maddie's assault and sought revenge. He created a plan and asked his brother Gino to assist him. Lucas and Gino watched Daniel's movements for a few days. They observed him leaving his classes before the period ended. Because Daniel had had an emotional support dog, he was permitted to check out of class a few minutes early when the halls were empty to decrease his anxiety.

One Friday before the last period bell rang, both Lucas and Gino asked for a pass to use the restroom. They timed their stroll down the hall perfectly. They reached Daniel's classroom as soon as he and Chestnut exited. They followed him from the classrooms to the front lobby. Gino approached Daniel and asked if he could hold the dog. Daniel refused. Lucas kicked the back of Daniel's knees, forcing Daniel forward He lost his balance and released his hold on Chestnut.

Gino snatched the dog.

He and Lucas hurried out of the front door laughing and hooting all the way to their house. Their mother exited the house to run errands and demanded they join her. Gino stuffed the Chihuahua into his jacket. Chestnut was silent, as he was trained to remain calm and quiet at all times. However, the dog decided to pee on Gino's leg before he was stuffed into the jacket. The urine dribbled down Gino's pant legs. He cursed without alerting his mother.

They entered their SUV and stopped at the gas station up the block. While the mother filled up the tank on the driver's side, Gino opened the passenger side door and placed the ugly mutt down to finish his business. He didn't want to have another spray of urine drip down his shirt as well as soak through his pants. The scrawny mutt, determined to cause him misery, pooped a load of uncontrolled diarrhea. The stench was nauseating. They couldn't even clean it up, not that they wanted to; they had no wipes, plastic gloves or bag to contain it.

The two boys shopped in the sporting goods store while their mother bought groceries in the market. After an hour, they shoved the dog in the car while they walked around to find their mother. They left the windows closed and the doors locked.

I was trained to behave and stay silent. I was also smarter than these two clowns were. I was well aware that they wouldn't have the ability nor intelligence to carrying out any ridiculous plan they contrived. I knew the Waldron's would be searching for me. I had to leave a trail so they could find me quickly I purposely peed on the boy called Gino, I knew he'd give me the opportunity to relieve myself instead of dumping on him again.

His brother wouldn't even touch me, he was afraid I would urinate on him also. The idiot gave me the change to mark my territory. My dog friends would have no trouble finding me. Since I was already worried and anxious about Daniel, I had a bout of diarrhea, which served as an extra advantage. The stink was intolerable. It was hard to breath cooped up in this car without ventilation. I was alone and missed Daniel. I hoped they found me soon.

Daniel ran to the principal's office in a panic. Ms. Blake phoned his parents and called for Maddie and Kyle to report to the main office at once. Paul-Anthony was already in his PAWs construction van heading home from work when he received the call. He arrived at the elementary school within minutes.

Ms. Blake gave Paul-Anthony Lucas's address. She was aware of the ethical implications but decided it the morally correct choice. The children jumped in the van and stopped home to fetch the dogs. The dogs would be better able to track Chestnut. Babs was working at The Plainledge Animal Shelter. She signaled for Siggy and they drove off to meet their family at Anthony's address.

The dogs barked furiously as they neared Lucas's house. Paul-Anthony opened the side door. The dogs bounded out so quickly, he was knocked down and the dogs tumbled over each other. He didn't mind. He realized they caught Chestnut's scent as the sniffed frantically.

The dogs followed the scent by foot and the humans followed the dog via the van straight to the gas station. Vixen remained in the van with the humans. She was too old to keep pace with the younger dogs, but she was always willing to help and wanted to be included. Nick discovered the nice loose load of crap that Chestnut dumped to assist in their search and he barked to notify the others. Maddie and Kyle rewarded them with "Good boy," but they didn't need the reinforcement, they were on a mission and continued onward. Their ears perked when the heard a familiar bark. The proceeded to the strip mall in the direction of the barking. The dogs and the van arrived in the parking area within seconds of each other. They spotted Chestnut trapped alone in a car with the windows closed and the doors locked.

Paul-Anthony found a window breaker in his construction company toolbox. Kyle phoned Babs to notify her of their location. Paul-Anthony broke the window, reached in for Chestnut and handed him to Daniel. Daniel withdrew a water bottle from his backpack, scooped some water into his palm and offered it to Chestnut. The dog lapped it up gratefully.

Babs arrived with Siggy, who started howling for no apparent reason, as beagles often do. She and Paul-Anthony chatted briefly. They switched vehicles; Babs loaded the kids and the dogs into the PAWs company van while Paul-Anthony lingered behind with the family car. He waited for Lucas and his family to finish their shopping and explained the situation to their mother.

Paul-Anthony was shocked by her reaction. She didn't blame her sons for their behavior. She blamed their behavior on Maddie who had injured Lucas severely. She though a small prank such as this was painless and quite necessary for her son's treatment. They probably felt better with a little harmless revenge. She added how she would notify her insurance and lodge a claim against Paul-Anthony for the damage to her vehicle.

If that wasn't enough, she would file a restraining order against him preventing him from close proximity to her and her family.

Paul-Anthony was angry but tried to understand her reaction. He was a gentle man who did not like conflict. He described the incident with his family. He encouraged them to stay away from Lucas and Gino and to ignore their antics. Chestnut was fine, no one was hurt and the dispute between the two families should end now. The dogs seemed to understand and cuddled on the floor together. Babs, Kyle and Daniel nodded in agreement. Maddie marched upstairs with Nick to plan her next move.

Chapter
TWENTY-FOUR
Seth and Aaron

Two days ago, after father and son worked a ten-hour shift, Aaron allowed Seth to clock out. His father enforced Seth to punch in the stupid time clock on his arrival to and departure from work each day. Aaron refused to pay Seth any more than he deserved. Seth was annoyed at the pathetic control his father held over him. It angered him a great deal. He loathed his weak, greedy, selfish father. The money issues didn't affect him terribly, as he stole the money from his father's wallet and the cash register. However, he hated the man who pretended to be nice and caring, while he was actually a hateful, unloving person.

Seth was not grateful when Aaron permitted him to leave after ten hours. Was he supposed to appreciate the fact that his friends were already partying without him and his wife was enthusiastically waiting for him to return home?

He slipped on a pair of mechanic gloves, slid into one of the cars parked in the shop waiting for repair-work. He quietly closed the door just enough so the light went out but it did not produce a sound. He remained in the car and watched his father clean up the shop.

Seth was very patient. His determination allowed him to sit still calmly until the moment was perfect.

172

He perked up when Aaron headed for the bathroom. He snaked around the garage, selected a lovely oilcan and poured a substantial amount all around the bathroom door. He danced to the music his father had not yet turned off, sprinkling extra oil on the walls, the tools and the unfortunate cars blocking his path. He felt like Tiny Tim tiptoeing through the tulips.

He stood a few feet back from the restroom until, at last, the door opened. His father smiled awkwardly when he spotted Seth, wondering why he had not left the shop. Aaron took a step out of the bathroom. His smile faded as he lost control and slipped backward. He bumped violently on his tailbone, and then landed on his back. His hand flailed at his sides, as he tried to break his own fall. His eyes widened in disbelief as the pain soared up his neck His head cracked on the cement floor and blood pooled out rapidly. He continued to gaze at his son as tears streams down his face. He envisioned his happy times in the park with Samael as he lost consciousness. He smiled briefly and then he expired.

Seth felt miserable. Now he had to clean up the mess. He despised cleaning. He had no choice but to scrub the floor, scrape up the blood and discard the body. He figured it would take hours and would ruin his entire evening. Seth was an optimist, so while he wiped, mopped, scoured, and shoved the body into the trunk a car, he thought about the fantastic day he experiences. He killed a puppy and rid the world of a dirty beast. He watched his clumsy father fall to his death while he inherited a business, or so he thought. It was certainly one of his most exciting days.

Helmuth entered the garage and hid behind a car on his right. He witnessed an older man falling while a younger man, holding an oilcan, leaned against a table full of tools. He identified these men as Aaron and Seth. Aaron and his auto body store had a stellar reputation, unlike the son who was known to be a greedy, abusive alcoholic. Helmuth watched Seth pick up and heave Aaron's lifeless body into the trunk of a car. He included "murderer" to the list of Seth's despicable qualities.

Helmuth waited until the killer meticulously cleaned up his mess. He selected a crowbar from the tool-table, hit Seth on the back of his neck with a solid blow enough to deliver him unconscious, but not enough to kill him.

He dragged Seth's limp body across the shop where Seth previously parked his prestigious Mustang. He wrapped a greasy, grimy cloth around Seth's mouth to muffle any future screams. He tied Seth's hand behind his back with another slimy discarded cloth. He tied his feet together with copper aluminum wire he found sitting on the workstation bench. The auto repair shop was a convenient place to find what you need to complete a chore.

He dumped Seth inside the Mustang.

It was an arduous task.

Fortunately, the shop had helpful devices specifically designed for these occasions. Helmuth found a battery-operated lifting device and slammed Seth's body on to the platform. He heard a grunt escape Seth's lip, but Seth remained semiconscious. Helmuth powered up the machine. When the body reached trunk level, Helmuth tossed Seth inside. He closed and locked the trunk. Seth had left the keys in the ignition for a quick get-a-way. Helmuth deposited the crowbar on the passenger seat and drove the car to The Plainledge Animal Shelter. He swung the

Mustang around beyond the fields where the dogs played. He parked the car. He rested, stretched his legs, listened to music and took a brief nap until Seth woke up.

Seth regained consciousness a few hours later. He realized he was gagged, and his hands and feet were tied. He felt the wire cutting through his socks, digging into his ankles. When he struggled to free himself, the wire zigzagged slicing deeper into the lacerations. Yet, if he didn't move, there was no change to escape.

He attempted to figure out where he was and how he arrived in this coffin-like trunk. He remembered watching his old man slip and crack his skull. He vaguely remembered a sharp pain on the side of his head, but nothing else. The realization hit him like his father's head hit the concrete, suddenly and shockingly. His own trunk, he was stuck in his loving Mustang.

Seth was furious. He wiggled and squirmed without any headway. He heard a loud thud and jumped, as any man could while he was bound and gagged in tight quarters. The pounding continued, creating dents in the trunk's lid. Initially he thought whoever was responsible for this would endure a well-deserved beating. After a few damaging blows to the trunk, he reevaluated his position.

He dismissed the revenge tactic and focused on his breakout. The lid was bending toward him; each strike offered him less room. He was forced to lay as flat as possible. He began to hyperventilate as the lid curved toward him, a full-blown panic attack seized his body as he shook and quivered similar to his wife's reaction when he raped her. He sobbed as his infant son did when Seth purposely forgot to feed him a bottle. His fear and sniveling clogged his nose with snot and mucus making it almost impossible to breathe.

The unidentified weapon hit his left knee with such force, he was surprised he didn't black out. He heard the bone crack and felt excruciating agony. The pain traveled from his kneecap up through his waist. He rolled on his left side, as best as he could, to protect his knee when another blow hit the right hip bone. Seth was beyond bewilderment. He whimpered like a neglected puppy. He curled into a ball and received the attacks, landing on his arms and shoulders, one after the next without hesitancy, without any concern for his welfare. His thought was, "Who could act in such a manner?"

When Helmuth finished the assault, he opened the passenger side door, rested the crowbar on the seat and drove to Aaron's Auto-Body shop. It was fortunate that the crowbar only destroyed the truck. The vehicle was not damaged in any other way, it remained drivable. It was unfortunate that a classic Mustang was doomed for scrap metal. He drove the Mustang in the rear of the shop where they crushed the cars. He left Seth trapped in the trunk and trekked home.

Seth heard the attacker curse under his breath while he walked away. He could barely move. Every move caused a jarring pain through his arms and legs. He fell in and out of consciousness waiting for someone to rescue him like a dog waiting in a kennel.

Chapter
TWENTY-FIVE
Maddie Meets Trista

As Maddie's revenge tactics increased, so did her anger. She felt enraged over the slightest injustices. She felt completely satisfied after she attacked Lucas. She looked forward to finding other ways to make his life miserable. Paul-Anthony told his children to ignore Lucas and his family, the feud was over, but not to Maddie.

She left Nick at The Plainledge Animal Shelter the next day. She didn't want Nick with her. She was too angry to talk to him, play with him or watch over him. She walked back to school carrying her backpack and goalie stick.

She was fuming. Her face was flushed, her fists clenched and her brows angled downward. She located Lucas's locker and broke the lock with the goalie stick. She felt exhilarated. She gave a few extra blows to the locker watching it crunch and break. She dumped his textbook, his notebooks and his personal items into her backpack and took a detour through the park. She emptied his belongings into the trashcan and stomped home. She realized she forgot to pick up Nick and had to walk back to the shelter.

Nick was happy to see her and greeted her with his usual tail wag and excited bark. Maddie was annoyed she had to make another round trip to pick up the dog, so she didn't respond to his affections.

I was confused and hurt. I always accompanied Maddie on her after-school excursions. Although I loved playing with my friends at the shelter, I preferred to keep Maddie company. I wondered if I behaved badly. Was I a bad dog? The last thing I remembered was tracking and finding Chestnut. Maddie was thrilled we found him. She said I was a good boy. She stormed to her room that night without filling my bowl with fresh water, nor did she pat my head with the traditional, "Good night good boy." I was devastated. I curled up in my cage, snuggled with my blanket and fell asleep feeling so alone.

Lucas arrived at school the next morning to an unusable locker. His belongings were gone. His school supplies, stolen. He immediately suspected Maddie. Ms. Blake was monitoring the hallway and Lucas called for her. He demanded Maddie pay the consequences for destroying his locker and return the confiscated items. Ms. Blake said she couldn't prove Maddie was the culprit, but promised to have a talk with her.

Maddie denied the accusations. She told Ms. Blake she had forgave Lucas for embarrassing her brother. She acknowledged her extreme behavior. She admitted she felt guilty about attacking Lucas. She also mentioned how her father forbade them to have any contact with Lucas and his family. However, they were all lies. Ms. Blake sensed something strange about Maddie. Her voice was monitored, her expressions were flat and she didn't make eye contact. If Ms. Blake hadn't known Maddie for years, she would have thought she was lying.

Maddie attended her classes for the rest of the day. She was no longer interested in learning; she didn't pay attention. She focused on her next attack.

178

How dare Lucas accuse her of breaking his locker and stealing his junk? Tattletales warrant punishments. He needs a lesson on loyalty and respect for his fellow classmates.

Samael dressed for work when he heard a knock on the door. Seth wasn't home and Trista was sleeping. Officer Rivera asked if he could come in to talk. Sam woke his mother and waited for her to saunter downstairs. Sam felt a terrible foreboding. He had a strong feeling Officer Rivera was going to give him bad news about either his grandfather or Shaggy.

The news pertained to Aaron. He had a terrible accident last night. He slipped and fell while exiting the restroom. He hit his head hard enough to damage his brain and he died a few minutes later. Officer Rivera said they have not ruled out homicide due to the oilcan lying near the bathroom door.

Aaron's body was at the morgue. One of them needed to go with Officer Rivera to make a positive identification. He drove the two Ravanas to the morgue and escorted them to the gurney.

Four gurneys filled the room. It smelled like death and disinfectant. Tools to cut, scrape and gouge, laid on small table next to each gurney. Weight bowls hung from the ceiling over each table. Sam cringed, thinking of the mortician removing his grandfather's organs one at a time, dropping them on the scale, placing them in separate plastic bags and returning them to Aaron's dead body.

The mortician pulled down the sheet, exposing Aaron's' crushed skull. The left side of his face was smashed, his left eye socket was empty and dried blood remained on his hairline. Sam was horrified. He couldn't imagine anyone hating his grandfather enough to brutalize him in this manner. He struggled to hold back the tears. He didn't want his mother to see him break down. Trista stared blankly at Aaron's deformed head, turned and walked away. Officer Rivera and the mortician followed Trista, offering Sam time alone with Aaron.

Sam held his grandfather's hand and cried softly. He told him how much he loved him, how much he appreciated the times they spent together at the park and the auto-body shop. He mentioned how much he will miss him. Most importantly, he will help the detectives investigate the crime and assist in finding the culprit.

Aaron's body jerked; his hand constricted on Sam's hand. His left eye remained hollow, but his right eye pivoted toward Sam. They gazed at each other. Aaron opened his mouth purposefully. His jaw cracked and blood sputtered out from the side. His teeth were covered in dirt. Those on the left were broken and loose from the impact. Aaron's voice was muffled as if he was choking on the liquefied brains streaming down his throat.

He squeezed Sam's hand and uttered one word, "Seth."

Sam ran toward the door, bumped into a second gurney. A dead arm fell from its resting place and hung limp from the side. The body jolted and said, "Seth."

Sam looked around as the other two bodies rose from their tables and whispered, "Seth." Sam darted to the exit door and heard a quartet of "Seths" echoing through the chamber. He bumped into a corpse-like man as he backed out of the room who grabbed him by his shoulder and whispered, "Seth" into his ear.

The mortician yelled, "Sam, Sam, are you OK?" Sam blinked, looking directly at the mortician who appeared normal. He left, traumatized, found the police car and sat dumbfounded until they reached his house.

Maddie walked home instead of taking the school bus. She needed to devise future assaults on Lucas and other bullies. She passed the Ravana house and noticed Samael sitting on the porch with his head lowered to his knees. His body was trembling. She met Sam at The Plainledge Animal Shelter when she served her punishment. He was always friendly and caring. He did not gossip; he wasn't a bully and he minded his own business.

Maddie walked over to Sam and asked him if he needed a friend. He immediately started to talk about his grandfather. Suddenly an older woman appeared. She was disheveled and unkempt. Maddie assumed this was Seth's mother. Maddie never met Ms. Ravana and felt a bit uncomfortable.

Ms. Ravana remained standing there while Sam described his grandfather's death. He told Maddie how the police found Aaron, lying dead, in a pool of his own blood at the auto-body shop. The forensic team concluded he was probably alive for a while as the blood drained from his skull, his nose and his eyes. They suspected a probable homicide, as they found oil spewed all over the area near the rest room and an empty oil can hidden underneath one of the cars in the shop.

Sam asked Maddie if she would inform Shaggy of the accident and let her know he won't be coming into work for the next couple of days.

Sam's mom listened as Sam spoke. She appeared angry rather than sad. She leaned toward Maddie and

181

said, "I'll find out who did this. They will regret it for the rest of their life, which won't be long."

Maddie was surprised that this small, meek looing woman spoke with such assertiveness, such anger, such revenge. Maddie was impressed. She promised herself to contact this woman in the near future.

Chapter

TWENTY-SIX

Cathy and Yukan, Lucy and Dakota

Cathy and Yukon missed Janet terribly. Cathy cried a lot and Yukon whimpered. The days passed slowly. Cathy worked more hours grooming the dogs at The Plainledge Animal Shelter. Yukon joined her. He spent his time playing with the humans and their dogs. He was especially fond of Siggy and Nick.

I missed Janet every day. I spent time with my friends at The Plainledge Animal Shelter while Cathy worked grooming the dogs. Cathy played with me between her grooming appointments. We played catch with my favorite blue rubber ball. I liked how it bounced half-hazard. I would try to figure out where it would land and get there before the ball landed. These activities were a great divergence, but we continued to grieve for Janet. Our threesome dwindled to a twosome. A third of us was missing. One week after the memorial service, we arrived home from the shelter to a house full of fog.

Cathay opened the windows and I checked each room for potential danger. I looked in the bedroom last. It held painful memories. Cathy and I no longer slept there. We kept the door closed and locked. I noticed black smoke drifted from the sides and bottom of the door. I barked for Cathy, who joined me immediately.

She unlocked the door. We were blasted with thick smoke and a putrid odor. Cathy gagged. She covered her hand over her mouth and pinched her nose. She breathed shallowly through her hand until she was able to tolerate the stench. She entered the room before I did and she opened the windows. I sat near the doorjamb and waited for her to signal me.

The fog did not drift out through the windows. It lingered, surrounding us. I saw an object form in the thickness. I whimpered a warning to Cathy, but she did not hear me. She faced the bed and froze. I didn't have time to step inside when the object stretched from under the bed.

The shape was nondescript, but I observed a morbid, featureless hand. I stepped in front of Cathy to prevent the thing from reaching her. Talons extended from the palm. It crawled toward me like Thing on The Adam's Family, except it wasn't friendly. Slowly, the talons dug into the floor, leaving mud filled scrapes in the wood planks. The claws clutched my leg and I yelped. It lifted me up. I desperately dog-paddled the air, but I was no match for the demonic force. I hung in midair until it sucked me downward. Cathy continued to stare blindly in my direction. She remained immobile as the thing dragged me into the fog and I disappeared from the bedroom.

Cathy was conscious of her environment but couldn't move. Fear built up inside her; her heart rate increased. She could hear her blood pump into her heart, pounding and hammering, as she stood immobile. She screamed for Yukon, but no sound emerged. She felt like she was losing him the same way she lost Janet. She was powerless. She saw Yukon scramble to free himself, but the force of the entity was strong and pulled him down. Her beloved Yukon was swept away, vanished with the fog.

She tipped the bed over and looked for the portal. The small circle was smoking but impenetrable. She punched, stomped and jumped on it, but made no progress. She sat and festered for a few minutes, and then she called Lucy.

I plummeted down a well. The walls were composed of packed wet dirt. I clawed and dug my sharp nails in, trying to get a solid grip and stop my fall, to no avail. The hand clung to my hind legs tight enough to cause a stabbing pain from my hips to my paws. I had no choice but to endure the plunge and the agony. We landed in a place similar to The Dark Place I unwillingly visited before. I thumped to the ground further hurting my legs. I was afraid. I needed my humans. I had to remain calm and in control of my emotions so I could think. I noticed the cave was brighter than before. I used the opportunity to explore. Perhaps Janet was stuck in this realm.

The room was oblong. Two tunnels faced in front of me one to the right, at a 45-degree angle, and one to the left. Two additional tunnels sat to each side. The last two stood behind me, one to my left and one to my right. The shape reminded me of a spider. I would chase and eat them when I found them in our house. Both Cathy and Janet were afraid of any crawling insect, so I would help them out and get rid of them in the usual doggie manner. I decided to investigate each tunnel to look for Janet. Each structure was similar. They were four feet wide, dark and clammy. The right front tunnel curved slightly to the left at its peak, while the left tunnel slanted toward the right. The side right and rear tunnels curved backward to the right while the side left and rear left tunnels slanted to the left. They all stopped at dead ends.

My paws slopped in inches of murky water as I explored the Dark Place. I heard frantic human whispers and helpless doggie whimpers. I was compelled to find Janet before I attended to the other captors. The lights dimmed when I finished mapping out The Dark Place. Either an evil force prevented my ability to see clearly or a virtuous force was able to assist me for a limited time.

I saw a huge shape emerge from the wall.

185

It was the Stretchman.

I cried out for my humans, but no one came. I was so frightened I lost my courage. I cowered on the ground and curled my tail around my body, hoping the monster wouldn't see me. I detected a round object ahead but couldn't figure out what it was due to the poor lighting. It exuded a familiar scent. Dogs have a keen sense of smell. I used this to my advantage, as I couldn't rely on my vision. I approached the object tentatively. It was an odd rendition of my favorite blue rubber ball. It was mostly round, but well-worn and dented. Little sticks or twigs protruded from the soft rubber. I couldn't see clear enough to make the distinction, but the lovely aroma was strikingly familiar. It smelled like Janet.

The Stretchman looked alarmed when it saw me recognize the ball on some unconscious level. It stopped in its tracks, bent its head backwards, raised its arms over its head and screamed. It was an angry scream which shook the entire area. It fearfully slinked back into the cave wall.

Cathy called Lucy in distress. Lucy immediately ran over with Dakota. She asked Cathy to repeat everything that transpired. Lucy wasn't holding Dakota's leash tightly but Dakota managed to sprint into the bedroom. She barked rapidly before Cathy had a change to utter a single word. Lucy took hold of Dakota's leash and led her from the bedroom. Cathy locked the door.

They sat at the kitchen table, Dakota sat at Lucy's feet and Cathy boiled water for tea. Dakota was on alert. Her head and ears propped up. She waited for any unusual sound. Cathy slowly explained the recent events. Every time she mentioned Yukon, Dakota growled. Lucy had difficulty containing Dakota. She was aware of the apprehension and lurking peril. Cathy reached the part of the story when the fog seized Yukon and he struggled to break free. Dakota couldn't contain herself anymore. She broke free from Lucy's grasp, almost toppling her off the chair as she bolted to the bedroom. She balanced on her back legs and violently scratched on the door. They decided to enter and investigate.

The room swiftly filled with the black fog Cathy mentioned. The warm dry air transformed into a humid and damp condition. Dakota stuck her nose under the bed. She was relentless in her pursuit to topple the bed and examine what lay beneath. Cathy and Lucy had to use both hands to flip the bed over. It seemed heavier than usual. The tropical air began to swirl around them, picking up speed, developing into a terrornado. The portal returned to its original position under the bed. The same portal that took Janet and Yukon. The wind blew at their hair; it howled angrily; it smelled like molded cheese. Dakota struggle to hold her ground. Lucy grabbed her leash with one hand, and Cathy's hand in my other. The force of the horrorcane and the portal dragged them down.

A very familiar and terrifying wind toppled them up and down. Lucy felt like a diver in the Olympics, performing her most complicated dive. Fingers stuck out of the cold dark walls. They plucked at them, pinching their skin, desperately trying to snag them as they plummeted. They did not land like divers. They hit the ground heavily. Dakota yelped and gazed at Lucy, confused and frightened. Cathy was already dusting herself off, ready for an encounter. Her two loves were trapped here and she was determined to find them. Lucy patted Dakota and held onto her leash.

I was fed up with this Dark Place. We needed to figure out how to kill the monster and save our friends. I always felt stronger and braver when I was beside Lucy. However, I realized I felt even more courageous when Cathy, Janet and Yukon joined me. I missed Janet, I felt sad for Cathy and I longed to play with Yukon. The simple pat on my head gave me the motivation to continue our plight. I heard it first, a low growl coming from the wall. It was Yukon. His odor was fleeting, but I detected it. I stared at the wall, wagging my tail. I tried to alert Lucy. If she approached the wall, I was certain she would notice the sound.

Dakota froze, unmoving, facing the wall. Lucy was attuned to her alert calls. She moved closer to the wall and understood what she was communicating. She heard a faint dog growl.

The Stretchman must have imprisoned Yukon inside the wall.

Dakota jumped up and down on her front paws. She was excited that Lucy heard Yukon. Cathy smiled when she picked up the sound. Dakota pressed her nose against the wall. She sniffed a few times following Yukon's scent with her nose. She jumped back quickly when they heard a wicked, raspy giggle.

The monster's face protruded through the wall. Its nose appeared first, forcing a pinpoint opening, extending wider as its head poked through. Its chin fell to the ground and its mouth hung down, a huge gaping black hole. The monster chuckled once and yelled, "GO AWAY." It did not want them in its home. Somehow, they threatened the monster's power. Its breath knocked them off their feet and they slipped on their buttocks. They continued falling into the ground and beyond. Lucy was able to grasp Cathy's hand. They heard Dakota howling, but she couldn't make contact with her.

The trip back to Cathy's bedroom wasn't as treacherous. They landed softly on the portal, now impenetrable. Dakota thumped in a few seconds later. They huddled together, speaking quietly about a plan. A rescue plan warranted assistance. They decided to ask their human and dog friends at The Plainledge Animal Shelter for assistance.

Chapter
TWENTY-SEVEN
The Inheritance

Samael inherited Aaron's auto body shop. He was ambivalent. He felt honored that his grandfather trusted him to maintain the business, but held some guilt, He didn't want to continue the auto-body lifestyle. He found he finally found his place in life; he was happy when he was with Shaggy and the dogs at The Plainledge Animal Shelter. He wanted to create something that would make his grandfather proud and Sam happy. He had an idea and wanted to discuss his plan with Shaggy and her parents.

They met at the shelter. They set up a table and chairs at the grooming station while they considered the plan and ate lunch. Sam would like to open a dog park on the grounds of the auto-body shop. He would reorganize the interior of the garage and the exterior grounds. He would set up an indoor area, for inclement days, in the huge space where the mechanics used to work on the cars. He would reconstruct the fields full of crushed cars, cart them off to a landfill and create an outdoor facility for dogs and their humans.

Irmgard thought it would be a great addition to include the Waldron's. Babs was a Veterinarian's Assistant and her husband Paul-Anthony owned a construction company. They would be a useful resource. Irmgard called Babs, explained their idea and asked if she and Paul-Anthony were available to meet them at the shelter. Irmgard was excited about the project and said they'd come right over. They would bring Vixen and Siggy so they could play with the dogs while the humans talked without any disturbance.

The four of them attended to the dogs, ate lunch and chatted while they waited for Paul-Anthony and Babs. Kyle and Daniel wanted to be included in the mission and joined the small party with Chestnut and Max. Maddie said she wasn't interested, she already had plans for the day. She was elusive and unfriendly, not like she usually behaved. She asked them to take Nick with them, which concerned her family, but they gave her space and complied with her request. Nick was forlorn, but obeyed Maddie's wishes.

I don't know what's going on with my human. She doesn't want me around her anymore. I brood over what I may have done wrong, if I caused her any distress or angered her in any way. I can't think of anything I did, but I must have done something to offend her. I will do my best to make her happy. I love my human.

The eight of them all had unique talents to offer for the project. Sam would use the inheritance money to finance the construction and materials. Paul-Anthony volunteered his time. He would build the agility and climbing apparatus and create additional toys the dogs may enjoy.

Helmuth would observe the humans, ensuring they behave appropriately with their dogs. He

191

remembers a situation with a man named Chuckie and would rather he didn't have to resort to those means again (but he would if warranted). Shaggy and Sam would oversee the functions of the park, order supplies, maintain the grounds and handle any customer issues.

Kyle asked if they could set up a donation box, for either money or dog food. There wouldn't be a cost to enter the park, but a donation for those who needed a little help with the cost of owning a dog would be appreciated. Samael loved the idea. Daniel smiled at these ideas and felt comfortable enough to place Chestnut down and allow him to play with the other dogs. He was surrounded by people he trusted. He took a risk and it paid off. No one bullied him or mocked him. He was free to eat lunch without incident.

I was surprised when Daniel placed me on the floor. I would be content on his lap or playing with the other pups. But I felt so relieved when he was confident enough to sit with the humans by himself. I stayed by his side for a few minutes in case he needed to pick me up. I took a step forward and glance back at him. He smiled at me. I knew that was a signal allowing me to move away from him. I took another few steps and peeked back again. He was eating lunch quietly and contently. I was overjoyed. This was a big step for Daniel. I played with the dogs with gusto, free to romp around knowing Daniel was safe without me. I didn't overstay my welcome. My place was with Daniel. I returned to him after a little while and laid under his chair for when he needed me.

The first step was to remove the equipment from the garage and the crushed cars from the field. Paul-Anthony was able to fit most of the tools, car parts, paint supplies and other accessories into his PAWs construction van. They hired a moving van to remove the larger items and a flatbed truck for the crushed cars.

When the shop was emptied, Samael and Shaggy researched and ordered necessary supplies, Helmuth started on the climbing equipment and the rest of the group began the arduous task of scrubbing and sanitizing the indoor facility. Daniel was happy sweeping. The repetitive task induced a hypnotic relaxed state for him. Chestnut was never far behind, taking small steps as Daniel moved in each direction.

Sam accompanied the men to the far end of the property where the cars were stacked. Sam's heart skipped a beat. A red, two-door convertible Mustang sat mangled in the compilation. It was a classic, a 1965 like his father's. He noticed the consistent deep dents that demolished the trunk, but the rest of the car was intact. This Mustang was not placed in the car crusher. Someone purposely ruined it.

He took a closer look and observed blood splattered only in the trunk. Someone was attacked while they were locked inside. Although he hated his father, he was concerned. He wouldn't wish Seth any harm.

Sam heard a faint groan coming from the direction of the car. He attempted to pop the trunk. It creaked and screeched in opposition. It took a lot of force to lift it up as it was bashed closed. The moaning inside increased as the person realized someone discovered him.

Sam was horrified at his discovery. He phoned the police, and instructed his father to stay still. Seth must have retained a number of broken bones and severe bruising. The cops and ambulance arrived. They carefully raised him onto the gurney. He screamed in agony with every move. He cursed the field where he laid broken. His breathing was shallow, his blood pressure and pulse rate were threateningly low. They rushed him to the hospital. Helmuth offered to drive Sam. They followed the ambulance in Helmuth's car.

The back field required a landscaping company. They moved, clipped and fertilized their way through the acreage. It took a full week to finish the job. It looked magnificent, just like Sam imagined. The small dog area was to the left of the outdoor field, the large dog area to the right. Dog toys and equipment were placed around randomly. Humans were permitted to bring their own dog toys and snacks. Water fountains and bowls were situated throughout the indoor and outdoor facility.

Chestnut, Max, and Siggy explored the new park. They tried out the agility equipment, the climbing apparatus; they drank the water in the bowls and dug for some hidden limited ingredient dog biscuits Karen made for the new Dog Park. Vixen was content watching them as he relaxed under a shady tree. It was going to be a tremendous success.

Sam called the park Aaron's Dog Park. Tomorrow was opening day.

Chapter
TWENTY-
EIGHT
Maddie

Maddie heard about Seth' attack. He remained in the hospital. His doctor figured he would need another week to heal before they could discharge him. Maddie thought this was a great opportunity to meet with Trista. She thought it would be a nice gesture to bring a cake with her, so she took a cake from her house and walked over to the Ravanas. She knocked on the door tentatively holding the box in front of her as a greeting. She was nervous and excited.

Trista opened the door and smiled. She remembered Maddie from the other day and had a great feeling about her. Trist invited Maddie in and they sat at the kitchen table. The place was a mess. The kitchen set was old and worn. The table sustained chip marks and cigarette burns. The curtains were threadbare and dirty. There were no decorative objects, only the necessities. Trista added water to a rusty teapot and set two chipped cups and a couple of napkins on the tabletop. Maddie sat on a wobbly chair. She didn't mind the disarray; she had an ulterior motive.

She asked Trista how she planned to seek revenge on Seth's assailant. She shared her feelings with Trista regarding her own need for revenge. She was never comfortable talking to her mother or father about these dark feelings. They surfaced when she noticed the abundance of bullying, teasing and gossiping in school. She observed it when she was just in kindergarten. One group of students wouldn't allow a fellow classmate to play ball with them. They kept it away from her, forcing her to run in circles around them. She cried as she ran. Maddie figured the girl would rather play with them in some fashion, than not at all. It bothered Maddie, but she dismissed the abuse.

The school bus was a haven for bullies. They would steal other students' lunches, snacks or money. Last year, Maddie watched as a big kid sat on a smaller boy the entire bus ride. The younger boy cried, but no one came to his rescue. The mean kids were cowards. They always worked in groups, never alone. Maddie's anger increased, but she continued to dismiss the issues.

Maddie noticed more aggressiveness on the roads. She spoke to her mother regarding other drivers. She heard more horn honking and saw more tailgating and more road rage than ever before. Babs explained how people rushed from work to home, running errands, cooking dinner, taking their children to practices and games. They were stressed and impatient. Babs told Maddie to sympathize with them instead of getting angry with them.

Maddie considered these words of advice while her mom drove her to hockey practice. Suddenly, another driver cut them off, so he could enter their lane at the last minute. Babs slammed on the brakes.

Maddie slumped forward; her seatbelt locked, preventing her from catapulting from the car. However, her goalie stick rammed into her stomach. She screamed out in pain. Babs instinctively turned toward Maddie's cries, taking her eyes off the road.

Their car skidded off the highway onto the shoulder, barely missing a massive tree. Fortunately, neither was hurt. Babs was shaken up. She checked Maddie for injuries, called the police and waited for them to arrive. Maddie was furious. Her face glowered beet red, her fists clenched; she trembled with rage. She unbuckled her seat belt, stormed out of the car and bashed the tree with her goalie stick. Babs allowed her to release her anger; however, she was concerned with Maddie's lack of coping skills.

The lunchroom incident with Daniel and the road rage occurrence was the last straw. Maddie used to be more tolerant and less angry, but the viciousness increased and she couldn't sit back and ignore it anymore.

She didn't want her parents to offer her advice or try to change her views. She wanted someone to understand the desire, the burning flame deep inside her soul. It was a sentiment she couldn't deny. Trista smiled, listened. She drank her tea slowly while Maddie explained.

Maddie was relieved to vent. She sensed Trista understood her. Trista dumped the cups in the sink and discarded the napkins in the trashcan. She took Maddie's hand and guided her to the bedroom. She positioned a chair in front of and facing the mirror. She pointed, signaling for Maddie to sit. Maddie obeyed and stared into the mirror. Trista pointed to the mirror and said, "Look closely, take your time."

Trista concentrated, she focused. She said, "Think of the anger, the revenge, and the bullies."

Maddie dug deep inside herself, remembering when Lucas bullied Daniel and when Lucas and his brother stole Chestnut. She recalled the time in gym class when Lyndsay and her two friends teased her friend Jackie until she broke down and cried. As she reminisced, she noticed her reflection change. She looked unattractive, almost nasty. Her skin turned pale; her brown eyes appeared slate gray. The young girl looking back at her looked empty, angry and dangerous. Her teeth decayed. They appeared black and dirty. Some fell out as she opened her mouth wide. Blood dripped from the empty cavities. Thick re ooze dribbled down the corner of her mouth. She smiled a happy, evil grin.

Although her physical attributes declined, her prowess increased. She touched the mirror. A powerful volt of energy streamed through her body. She felt energized, strong and prepared to win whatever battles she faced in the future, wherever she felt the need to ensure justice. She hoisted herself off the chair, ready to inflict pain. She would start with Lucas.

Trista forced her back on the chair. She told her how revenge takes time. She advised Maddie to stay away from her own family and home as often as possible,

"They don't understand you. They will get in your way. They are weak with sympathy and liberal views. People must be punished for their wrongdoings, not rewarded...and your dog, he is useless. He will interfere with your goals. Let someone else worry about him."

Maddie listened. She was hesitant with some of the advice. One part of her felt love for her family and especially for Nick. She didn't want to avoid them. It saddened her to think of Nick without her. The other part of her was excited to plan revenge with Trista. She felt an immense power surge through her. It diminished the negative aspects of Trista's advice. They needed to arrange a plan of action, gather any necessary equipment and proceed cleverly.

She had a lot to prepare.

Chapter
TWENTY-NINE
The Lanes

We lived in Plainledge for a total of ten years. We moved into our home with our three rescue dogs, Loki, Cody and Jenna. The three-bedroom house was perfect for us and our plans for future children. The yard was large enough for our dogs to run around and exercise.

Yanna and I met our neighbors, Cathy and Janet the day we moved into our new home. The walked over with their dog Morgan and welcomed us into the neighborhood. We chatted on the kitchen while the dogs romped in the yard.

We recently recued our dogs from The Plainledge Animal Shelter. They were about four or five years old. They were found in an alleyway scavenging for food.

Yanna and I had our first child, Kevin a year later. He had gorgeous black eyes; a full head of black hair and his brown skin was flawless. Within six years, we completed our family of five humans and three dogs. We had a pleasant but uneventful life until Kevin was baptized. Unexplained malevolent events sporadically took place afterward.

Connor blessed our family three years after Kevin. He looked similar to Kevin with his dark features, except he was bigger. He weighed eleven pounds and was 19 inches long. We supplemented breast milk with formula because he loved to eat and he grew quickly. He slept through the night after one week. Three months later, we experienced another evil occurrence.

Yanna finished nursing Connor, then carried him to his bedroom and gently lowered him into the basinet. I propped the baby monitor on my side of the bed so Yanna could sleep without disturbance. I woke to a crackling sound two hours later. It was loud enough to wake me but not enough to cause alarm. I listened for a minute to the silence and rolled over to go back to sleep. No sooner did I close my eyes when I heard a voice.

It mumbled, repeating itself rapidly, "Be careful, I'm coming for you."

I sprinted to Connor's room without waking Yanna. He was sleeping peacefully. I searched his room for a possible intruder. I checked the closet, in Kevin's room and throughout the entire house. There were no uninvited guests.

I poured myself a glass of water in the kitchen and moved on toward the den. I strolled to the storage room in front of the den and glanced out the window into the front yard. I thought I saw a shadow. I squinted to clear my vision. The shadow grew more distinct as I stared. I watched as the figure developed; stretchable arms and legs, a face that continued to grow and eyes big enough to swallow me. I was both terrified and mesmerized. I turned to leave the room. I wasn't sure how to proceed. Should I call the police, wake my wife or grab the children? I reached for the doorknob when the door slammed shut, locking me in. I hit my head and fell to the floor.

The dark entity stepped through the wall and sat on my chest. Its head was so long, it reached both the ceiling and my torso. It leaned its face to mine, opened its mouth and sucked my head inside. I couldn't breathe. It was pitch dark and smelled like a trashcan left out in the hot sun. I kicked my feet and thrashed my arms. My water glass crashed to the floor as I struggled to push myself out of the monster's jaws. I grasped onto something, probably the leg of a desk. Items stacked on top smashed to the floor landing on my body causing a ruckus.

I heard muffled banging on the door. Yanna yelled for me. She used her military training to kick open the door. She looked down at me quizzically as I lay on the floor, stored objects strewn around. The figure disappeared. I was dumbfounded. I didn't know what to say. I stood up and took a few deep breaths. Then we heard the baby scream. Yanna reached his room first and shrieked. Connor was not in the basinet. Kevin woke and started crying.

The dogs dashed into my bedroom, ignoring us. They stuck their noses under the bed and barked frantically. Yanna and I tipped the bed over. The dogs stopped barking and whined softly.

A circular-shaped marking appeared under the bed. The circumference was ablaze, flames as high as three inches. I stomped on the flames, distinguishing the fire. The dogs rushed out of the bedroom into Connor's room. I went to comfort Kevin while Yanna followed the dogs. I met her back in Connor's room where the baby was sleeping comfortably. Jenna dropped to the floor refusing to leave Connor's room.

From that day on, Jenna was Connor's dog. She stayed with him wherever he slept, crawled or ate. We talked about the mystery many times. It was a traumatic experience. Luckily, the dogs were able to point us in the right direction and alert us to the danger.

Our third and last child, Bella, was born three years later. She had similar physical characteristics as her brothers, except she was smaller at five pounds, and sixteen inches long. She cried often and nursed as frequently. One evening, we found Cody curled up with her in the basinet. It was a humorous site, an infant and a small dog cuddled together. We had no idea how Cody managed to jump into the cradle, but we allowed her to remain with Bella. Every time Bella fussed, Cody succeeded in calming her. Her soft furry presence comforted Bella consistently. We all considered Cody, Bella's dog.

One Sunday morning, Yanna and I were chatting over a cup of coffee at the kitchen table. The boys were playing video games in the den with Loki and Jenna by their sides. Bella was four years old now. She was in her bedroom playing with Cody and her stuffed animals. Bella loved to scamper from her bedroom, down the hallway to our bedroom. Cody learned to take Bella's toys in her mouth, one at a time and follow Bella to our room. After five or six trips up and down the hall, they were set in their new location.

We hadn't experienced an unusual event for years, so we were stunned when we heard Cody bark that distinctive foreboding sound indicating peril. Loki and Jenna sprinted passed us, joining Cody in the maddening cacophony. Cody yelped one last booming bark, the other two howled in return.

We couldn't find Bella or Cody. Kevin and Connor helped us look in her favorite hiding places, to no avail. Yanna and I stared at each other, thinking the same thoughts. We gripped the edge of the bed and tipped it over without exchanged a word. Once again, the dreaded smoke circle appeared in our lives with an ominous presence.

I stomped out the fire. The boys returned to our bedroom. Kevin clutched my hand; Connor took hold of Yanna's. Both boys were shaking. We were all spooked. Loki and Jenna refused to obey our commands to "heal." They continued to sniff the burnt circle, glancing back at us for support. They started digging and the site. Dust and smut whirled out of the circle. I bent down to help hoping we can find our way to Bella. Yanna and the boys followed suit. We were making progress. We plowed out at least six inches of soot when we heard Bella. She was talking to Cody. We placed our ears on the ground and heard her whisper to Cody:

"It's ok. Mommy and Daddy will be here soon. Don't worry. I will take good care of you." Then either her voice changed or something else was with her. A few deep, vibrating words echoed through the portal, "Be careful, I'm coming for you."

We remembered hearing these words during a previous fiendish event. I thrust my arm into the portal as far as I could. Yanna held on to me for support. The dogs carried on with their mission. Kevin and Connor waited beside us, looking into the hole for any signs of Bella or Cody.

I felt an object. It felt like a piece of wood. I was able to wrench it up to take a peek. It was an antique mirror crusted with the same slimy substance as the sludge in this hole. The dogs backed up and snarled. The four of us looked into the mirror. Our smiling faces reflected our images, but the aura changed. The room darkened like the foreshadowing of a horrorcane. The mirror glowed. We investigated closer.

Connor said, "How cool" and touched the glass. He was sucked in.

Yanna and I seized hold of his pants and Kevin hooked his arms around Yanna's waist. The dogs, loyal to the end, jumped through the mirror behind us.

Bella was sitting on the ground waist-deep in mud and filth. She calmly stroked Cody and said, "See Cody, I knew they would come to get us."

We landed in an underground structure. It was dreary, a wet cave, like a beach in a bizarre world. There were tunnels ahead and to our sides. The creepy mirror leaned against a wall, content to have accomplished part of its mission. It seemed it wanted to steal our reflection. It had the ability to transport us, but not to absorb our strength, our beings. We gathered around Bella to help lift her up when the mirror started to shake. Connor picked up Cody for comfort, when the glass in the mirror glowed red. Loki growled, Kevin patted his head, and we noticed a reflection appeared in the mirror in addition to the five of us. A vague image morphed into a demon. It had long arms and legs and a monstrous head. It was the exact monster that previously slid through the wall in my house and tried to swallow me.

I grabbed Yanna's hand and guided the children and the dogs behind us where I could better protect them. The mirror clanged with anger. The monster's arms and legs emerged from the mirror. Its fists balled in anger, its feet stomping up and down as if having a tantrum. The glowing red light illuminated exponentially, creating an explosion of fireworks. The antique reflector sucked itself into the wall and disappearing from our view.

We were trapped in this Dark Place. I needed to find a way out of these tunnels. I investigated our immediate vicinity and found nothing but hard sandy grounds. I tapped the side wall.

The entire structure was contrived with similar substance. I hesitated with my hand on the wall. I felt a small vibration, then I heard a weak moaning. Something touched my hand. I jumped back but stared at the spot. Two fingers emerged from the wall, followed by a hand and an outstretched arm. I didn't want my family to observe this horror, so I turned my back in haste. Yanna detected my strange behavior and shrugged her shoulders, as if to ask me what transpired near the wall without using any words. I took her hand, pointed in the direction of the materialized arm. The arm was no longer visible, but three fingertips wiggled in our sight.

Yanna squeezed my hand tightly, her eyes opened wide. She tried desperately not to scream and alert the children to the horrors inside the cave.

Loki, who was always vocal, started growling louder than usual. He sat up and sniffed the air. Jenna also detected an odor, stuck her nose upward and inhaled deeply. We all discerned a young girl's voice crying for help shortly after the dogs picked up the scent.

I yelled out, "I'm here, keep talking, I'll follow your voice." Loki and Jenna led the way, as their sense of smell was more accurate than my sense of sound.

Chapter
THIRTY
The Séance

The dog park was a huge success. People deposited toys, food and money into the donations bin. Ms. Blake showed up with her two French Bulldogs, Eddie and Ethan. They were built like Ms. Blake, short and strong. They were approximately the same size, reaching 12 inches tall and weighing 30 pounds. They were a bit overweight for bulldogs, but Ms. Blake took them for daily one-mile jogs keeping them in decent physical condition.

Ms. Blake was a career woman who dedicated her life to her education, her students and her dogs. She was thrilled with the dog park, the organization and creativity involved. She wanted to add to the advancement and success of the park. She spoke to Sam regarding her ideas. She offered a sizable donation for equipment, maintenance and for part-time employees. She wanted the Plainledge High School students to learn about the business, dogs and responsibility.

Ms. Blake met a woman at The Plainledge Animal shelter where she rescued her dogs. Irmgard taught a class about dogs and human bond at the local university. The women discussed the possibility that the high school students may register for the class and receive university credits. St. Katherine's already had a

Bridge Program established. Dr. Lamb created the program and agreed to the proposition. The High School Honor students will register for the class, learn about dogs and their connection to humans and intern for three hours per week at The Plainledge Animal Shelter or Aaron's Dog Park.

Seth loved the idea. Ms. Blake immediately started on the internship plans. She spoke to the students in the Honor's program. Three students were eager to begin as soon as possible. The dog class would be taught during the last period. Irmgard asked her husband Helmuth if he could transport the students to the animal shelter or dog park once a week after class. He was so excited with the idea, he made sure to finish his workday early on Fridays and drive to St. Katharine's University to pick up the students and transport them to the two locations.

Sam and Shaggy were so interested in Ms. Blake's program, they decided to enroll in St. Katharine's University. Sam decided to major in Business to learn about management and leadership. Shaggy always loved psychology, so chose to major in the field. She discovered a clairvoyance course taught by a renowned Professor Jones.

Of course, they both registered for Irmgard's dog course. Although students were not usually allowed to opt for a course their parent taught, the university granted an exception since Shaggy worked at the animal shelter and wanted to learn how to apply her knowledge to the business and to the care of the dogs. They enrolled in the online program. This gave them the opportunity to study and complete their assignments at their convenience. Dr. Kara was their advisor. She advised every student in the online program. She enthusiastically answered their questions, registered them for their classes and guided them through the process. The semester proceeded nicely. The three interns loved working with the dogs; Shaggy and Sam earned fantastic grades on their exams. The dog park and animal shelter flourished.

One day in Clairvoyant Psychology, Samael shared his relationship with his grandfather and the horrible manner in which he died, the accident, the inheritance and the reason he named the dog park after Aaron. Unfortunately, the story spread and changed, as in telephone game we all played when they were young. Gossip and a dark interest escalated to dangerous proportions.

Nina was one of the High School honor students interning at Aaron's Dog Park. She had long brown wavy hair, deep brown skin and black eyes. She wore those cat style glasses, which accentuated her intelligent appearance. She was tall and lean at 5 feet, 7 inches tall and 120 pounds. She was also Yanna Lane's niece. She longed to try to reach her aunt ever since the family disappeared. She thought it would be interesting to try to communicate with the spirit world.

Nina and 4 of her teenage friends, three boys and another girl, decided to hold a séance at the dog park. They searched the internet for proper procedures and they watched a few horror movies to understand the correct methodology. They waited for the dog park to close. There didn't notice any security cameras or motion detectors. They easily squeezed into an open window in the basement storage area. They sat on the floor in a circle and surrounded themselves with candles. They drew a five-sided star with white chalk in the middle of their circle. They laughed nervously at each other, not knowing what to expect, but nervous at the possibilities.

Nina instructed everyone to be silent, hold hands and to focus on the candles and her voice. She started by summoning the spirits to join the circle.

"We would like to contact anyone who has departed and desires to send a message to their loved one. Any lingering soul may enter and connect with us at this time. We welcome you to communicate with us with a signal, a sound or a touch, whatever means you are able. I can act as the vessel for your soul. If Aunt Yanna, Uncle Walter, Kevin, Connor or Bella can hear me, I would like to specifically invite them to join us. I miss you. No one knows what happened to you all. You simply vanished. We couldn't even find the dogs. Loki, Jenna, Cody, can you hear me? Are you able to smell my presence?"

Nina felt a sadness course through her body. She figured the feeling was a sign of her aunt's presence, but she was wrong. Nina explained to the spirit that a woman named Lucy and her dog, Dakota, moved into their house. She had not met them, but heard nice stories about them. She described how Lucy rescued Dakota from the same shelter they rescued their three dogs.

Nina felt a rush of air blow through her hair and snuff out the candles. She was cognizant of her environment, but had no control of her body. Her own thoughts were cloudy, but she was aware of an alternate internal voice. She did not recognize the voice. It wasn't her Aunt Yanna. It was an evil entity. It attempted to use Nina's body to throw the toolbox off the shelf. Nina was helpless as she pointed to the toolbox, wriggled her hand, which started to smoke, and she watched the wrench hurtle toward Jonathan.

It bashed Jonathan in the head with such force he crashed to the ground. The wrench-head lodged deeply into his left eye while the handle stuck out at an irregular angle. He hopelessly attempted to remove the object with his left hand during the remaining seconds of his life.

The air morphed into a maelstrom, whipping around the room. The friends let go of each other's hands and screamed in panic. They covered their eyes with their hands as dust and debris whirled around them.

Nina spun around and the wind mimicked her movement. It picked up speed. The window shattered; the candles flew out the broken window. Some of the smaller objects on the shelves surged through the new hole in the wall. The force had no effect on Nina. She stood upright in the middle of the room, spinning without falling.

She shrieked, "I'm coming for you."

Lori, one of Nina's friends, witnessed the wrench slice through Jonathan's face. She saw Nina's eyes cloud over. She was confused and frightened as she observed Nina's strange behavior. Nina appeared possessed by a force powerful enough to allow her to telepathically push an object off the shelf. Lori bent to help Jonathan. She wasn't sure if he was dead. He no longer looked like himself, but another person's hazy reflection. He was old, decayed and withered. She was suddenly afraid of him, changed her mind to offer help, and turned away. His hand seized her arm. He glared at her without sight, his eyes glazed over with a thick white substance covering his pupils and irises.

He spoke in a deep, slow-spoken voice, no longer his own, "Thank you all for inviting me in."

The last two friends, Liam and Joseph, checked Jonathan's pulse and breathing. They seized the instant they touched his body. The fell backward, their eyes rolling in their heads, their tongues lolled from their mouths. They jiggled together like a couple dancing to their favorite disco song. They weren't able to complete the fictitious song when their bodies, along with Jonathan's body, were plunged beneath the floor, vanishing without a trace. None of the friends noted the simmering circle left behind.

Nina walked home robotically. She woke the next morning in her bed as if it were a normal day. She remembered nothing after she finished school the day before.

Lori didn't wait to watch the dance. She bolted from the building, tripped on the steps and face-planted, extracting her two front teeth. She felt no pain as the adrenalin rushed through her body. She continued to the top step when she slipped through a hole. Her body, engulfed by a gravitational force, descended rapidly. She hit bottom, cracking both of her legs. It took her a minute to register the pain. She touched her legs and noticed a bone protruding from each leg. She recalled the recent incident at the séance and couldn't process the pain and the trauma. She screamed until her throat was burning. She was exhausted and thirsty. She sat in the same position, scanning the area. It was difficult to see any distinguishing characteristics, as it was dim and gloomy. However, she did hear voices and what may have been a dog yowling quietly from beyond when she finally stopped screaming.

She emitted a soft, "Is anybody there."

A man's voice cried out, "I'm here, keep talking, I'll follow your voice." He pursued the sound of her voice coming from the tunnel to the right side of his family.

Lori continued to cry out, "I'm here." She was drained, terrified and in extraordinary pain to muster any additional words. She was utterly relieved to see the man approached. Two beautiful dogs led the rescue team. Walter Lane introduced himself, Loki and Jenna. Lori explained the séance and disturbing events landing here in the cave. Walter assessed her physical health and realized he could not transport her to his family. The dogs remained with Lori while Walter returned to his family. They were in adequate condition to trek the short journey.

Yanna was hesitant to move the children, but understood she had no options. They couldn't abandon a child in this horrid place and it was necessary to explore the area for means of escape.

Kevin and Connor agreed easily, as they wanted their dogs. Bella didn't react, slowly stood up, clutching Cody in one arm and grabbed her mother's hand with her free one.

The dogs protectively hovered beside Lori when their family arrived. Lori was grateful for their help and comforted with the presence of others, but her legs felt like the bones were kindling, emanating a fire inside her body. Bella sat close enough so Lori was able to pet Cody. The threesome bonded immediately. Walter, Kevin and Jasper chose to investigate a possible means to find a way back home. Yanna remained with the other children, Cody and Jenna.

Jasper and Jenna caught the whiff of another strange smell before Walter and Kevin. They zoomed ahead without concern.

Two repetitive words resounded along the cave, "Here doggies, here doggies."

The dogs were excited to locate another human, but this voice sounded anything *but* human. It was a sinister drawl. Although we had to strain to hear it, it vibrated in our heads. We held our hands up to our ears to muffle the internal noise. It did not affect the dogs in the same manner. They continued to run toward the voice, while we hesitated due to the increased pressure in our heads.

Walter took note of the vision unfolding before them. The antique mirror stepped out of the wall. Its legs were demon-like, growing from the bottom of the mirror. It pulled itself out of the wall with lengthy arms. The face was imbedded in the mirror, covering its entirety. It was ghastly. The black, vacant eyes occupied most of the upper portion. The mouth was open wide like a cobra ready to swallow a mouse. The mirror lost its physical attributes and morphed into a full-bodied monster once it entirely emerged from the thick mucky wall.

Jenna and I attacked. We first froze in fear as this abnormal figure loomed over us menacingly. It advanced on us; its heavy stomping shook the cave. We bared our teeth and growled threateningly. The beast advanced on us quickly, as its stretchable legs moved with huge strides. Before I had the chance to step in front of Jenna, she threw herself at the Stretchman, aiming for its throat. Its reflexes were too fast for her. He caught her by her throat and squeezed. I leaped over and bit down on its ankle, tearing on the vinous substance. The beast didn't flinch, nor did it release its hold on Jenna's wind pipe. It reached down, taking my collar in its other arm, hanging me. I hung suspended from its outstretched arm. I made eye contact with Jenna. We looked into each other's eyes lovingly during those last few seconds.

Walter heard the dogs struggle from a distance. Kevin darted past Walter to save the dogs, but Walter held him back. He knew there was no hope for the dogs. He didn't want to expose Kevin to the potentially gruesome scene.

Kevin doubled over in pain. He couldn't live without Loki. Loki was his best friend. He already sensed a part of him disappeared with Loki. It felt like a chunk of his body was ripped out of him. It hurt worse than physical pain. Walter hugged Kevin for a minute. He wanted to give Kevin time to grieve, but they had to find an escape route. He thought the mirror could be a portal to their house. Kevin was immobile. He would not stand up and follow his father. He heard his father tell him they must help their family escape, but Kevin only heard indistinct utterances. He was incoherent with grief tugging at his heart. Nothing else mattered except the overwhelming feeling of loss and the desperate longing for Loki.

Walter realized Kevin was unable to resume their journey. He carried Kevin back to Yanna and the children. Connor noted the dogs did not accompany his father and brother.

He asked, "Did Loki and Jenna find the boogeyman? Are they beating him up for us? You know, Jenna is like a super dog, she'll protect us."

Walter gazed at Yanna, shook his head and handed Kevin to her. She sat down and rocked Kevin back and forth like she used to do when he was a younger boy.

Connor sat next to them and patted Kevin's shoulder. He said, "It's OK Kev, Loki and Jenna will come back as soon as they win the fight with the boogeyman." Kevin gripped his mother's arms with his fists clenched and emitted a long, sad, yearning bellow. Cody responded in a similar howl and Bella started to weep in tandem.

The family huddled together, supporting each other in their grief and uncertainty when the earth began to quake again. Walter signaled to Yanna to scoot the children closer to the wall. He stood protectively in front of them. He realized his mistake when he detected a reflection in the cave wall. He should have moved his family away from the wall, not close to it.

The mirror forced its right stump leg out of the wall and grabbed Connor. He disappeared in an instant, unable to utter a word. Yanna couldn't move fast enough as she was sitting on the ground, embracing Kevin. Walter leaped toward the mirror-thing and Connor. Time seemed to stop. Walter felt as if he was vertically extended forever, desperately reaching for his son. The mirror's arms stretched out too far to seem logical, and took hold of Walter's neck. Walter caught sight of Connor, Loki and Jenna. They were stuck deep inside the glass. The last sound he ever heard was Yanna yelling, "No!" A sense of dread encompassed him and he existed no more.

Yanna watched the mirror-monster snatch her son and her husband. However, it wasn't finished with its task. She caught its reflection in the glass. The vision staring back at her was an angry creature. Its arms and legs stretched through the wall, morphing into an elongated monster. Yanna yelled in disbelief as it pushed itself from the barricade.

It clamped two fingers on Cody, pulling him from Bella's grasp. Bella looked at her mother pleadingly, but Yanna was more concerned for her children and could not address Cody's predicament in the moment. She hovered over them, offering her body for protection. The stretchy-thing leaned closer, its head tripling in size. It exhaled a powerful stream of smoke and shrapnel, forcing Yanna backwards. The shrapnel bulleted her. She covered her face with her arms and the flying glass shredded her arms. She hugged herself and ducked her head to her chest trying to dodge the sharp objects, but they found their way to her eyes, mouth and cheeks. She was blinded, large chunks of glass embedded in her eyeballs, her face cut and bleeding down her neck. She was confused, couldn't figure out which direction she left the children.

The Stretchman stole Bella first. Yanna heard her petrified screams. She called, "Mommy…. mommy" then there was silence. Yanna released Kevin in an attempt to grab Bella. She searched for her desperately, her hands floundering in the air.

The Stretchman snatched Kevin as soon as Yanna released him. The monster took delight in holding on to Kevin's ankle, raising him above its head and shaking him in Yanna's sight. Yanna barreled into the Stretchman without a concern. She would protect her son with her own life. The monster flung Kevin into the wall with a chuckle. Kevin vanished into the bowels of The Dark Place

Yanna tripped on a large sharp object spewed from Stretchman and landed on her hands and knees. She felt immense pain on the back of her neck and realized the monster was stepping on her head. Her face was smashing into the impenetrable earth. She hopelessly tried to inhale. There was no space, no air between the earth and her lips. The Stretchman pounded on her back and neck. The pressure building on her spine and the terror she felt was unbearable. She didn't hear the sound of her own neck snapping.

Her paralyzed, beaten body dissolved into the ground without a trace.

Lori crawled away and cowered behind a large rock jutting from the side of the cave wall. The monster picked her up with its left hand and held her to eye level. It studied her, moving its head from side to side. The Stretchman was fascinated. It planted its right hand on her head as if it was a golf ball. The evil giant twisted Lori's head and popped it off her neck. It hoisted her dead face up to its own and shoved it into the spot where its own once perched. The monster reveled in its new gorgeous appearance. Unfortunately, the new face deteriorated quickly. The Stretchman discarded the rotted face and returned to its usual gruesome appearance within minutes.

Chapter
THIRTY-ONE
Nina

Nina refused to tell her mother what transpired. Her mother, Dina, did not approve of paranormal experimentation. She was aware of Nina's interest in the supernatural, but did not support her curiosity.

Dina enjoyed palm reading. She was quite the entrepreneur at ten years old. She charged the neighborhood kids a small fee to read their palms. She predicted good grades, a cute boyfriend (or girlfriend) or winning the lottery for her friends. She envisioned negative fortunes, going blind, losing their hair or their parents dying to those she disliked.

One of the girls ran to the principal's office in terror, thinking her parents were dead. Mr. Crowley, The Plainledge School District principal, called Dina and her parents to his office. Dina was reprimanded, was required to apologize and was forbidden to read any more palms.

Dina and her sister, Yanna, delved in Tarot cards and palm-reading before they had children. They practiced their skills on each other. Dina set up a dimly lit room with candles. Yanna covered a small table with an incantation book and the cards. They helped each other hang a curtain through the ceiling fan and draped it around the table.

Yanna quit the game when Dina turned over a Ten of Swords and a Five of Pentacles. Dina told Yanna the Ten of Swords indicated suffering and grief, while The Five of Pentacles symbolized the number of people who would be involved in the misery, five. Dina said Yanna would have three children and a husband, completing her family with the five people the cards envisioned.

Dina was forced to deal her own hand since Yanna left the room. She turned over a Three of Swords, which indicates a separation, and The Child. The Child symbolizes a happy child who loves to learn and experiment. However, it warns how curiosity may expose dangerous situations. Her third and last card was Misfortune. This was self-explanatory, but could also signify caution.

Dina didn't place much value in the cards until Yanna and her family disappeared without a trace and her own life unfolding as the Tarot cards predicted. Her husband deserted her years ago and recently, Nina's change in behavior and secretive nature.

Her father was not involved in Nina's life. He abandoned her and her mother years ago. He called Nina a few times a year, mostly on her birthday and holidays. The calls dwindled and stopped completely about a year ago. She was an only child who substituted good friends for siblings. She was smart and popular until the séance.

She attended classes and continued her internship at Aaron's Dog Park, but she felt uneasy and anxious most of the time. She walked around in a daze after the séance. Rumors circulated about the disappearance of her four classmates, all her closest friends. She suffered from severe panic attacks whenever she thought about them, but couldn't understand why they surfaced only on these occasions.

She was lonely. She missed her best friends. Jonathan had recently asked her to be his girlfriend. They were both excited to move forward with their relationship. They were friends since Elementary School and flirted with each other ever since. She vague flashbacks; Jonathan laying in the floor, writhing in pain. It didn't make sense. They attended classes together yesterday. He was healthy and behaved normally. Her memory seemed foggy. She pictured eating lunch with her four friends. She questioned if that really happened, was she losing her mind?

The other students made jokes about it, asking her if she killed them off. They wanted to know if she was jealous of Lori's and Jonathan's friendship, maybe she caught them kissing, got angry and retaliated. Did she hide them in her basement, along with the two other students? Nina found no humor in their ribbing. She withdrew completely, ignored their questions and chose not to speak at all. She ate little and lost a lot of weight.

Nina dreamt of her Aunt Yanna. They were in a cave-like setting, dark and gloomy. However, Yanna appeared beautiful and healthy. She was tall and muscular just as Nina remembered her. As the dream progressed, Yanna' figure faded. She thinned out, losing her muscle tone and a few inches off her height.

Nina yelled out to her, "What's wrong Aunt Yanna, what's happening?"

Yanna was unable to respond. She moved her mouth and lips, but no sound emerged. She placed her hands on the sides of her face and opened her mouth and eyes wide. The figure reminded her of the picture she had seen in art class, *The Scream*, by Edvard Munch.

Aunt Yanna moved closer to Nina. Nina was too frightened to step toward her aunt. She stood her ground and waited for Yanna to reach her. Yanna extended her hand. Her finger was just about to touch Nina's face when the rumbling began. The structure rocked around her. She was caught off-balance and bumped into the wall. Pain shot through her elbow up to her shoulder. She let out a cry, but Yanna placed her index finger to her mouth, signaling Nina to be quiet. She understood and shook her head. She stifled her sobs and rubbed her bruised arm.

Nina gasped when she heard an unseen entity say, "You invited me in. Now, I welcome you to my home." The voice was scary, slow and deliberate. Nina never felt so afraid and alone. She looked to her aunt for comfort, but she vanished upon the sound of the voice.

Nina fell to the ground, curled in a ball and…woke up screaming and perspiring. Her nightgown was completely soaked.

Chapter
THIRTY-TWO
Aaron's Wake

Sam and Trista decided to wait until Seth was discharged from the hospital before organizing Aaron's wake. It was arranged in the Town Hall, which also substituted for the church. Seth was looking forward to contributing to the send-off with a beautifully-written eulogy. Sam was surprised at his father's offer. Seth was in such a good mood; he permitted Trista to attend the ceremony. Friends from the auto garage, now turned dog park; those from The Plainledge Animal Shelter and people from The Pleasantville school district arrived in droves. The dogs waited outside the town hall, as per Seth's request. He begrudgingly made an exception for Chestnut. He despised all animals, especially dogs.

Sam posted pictures of Aaron on an easel. Some displayed Aaron and Sam at the auto shop, the park and at Sam's school. Others depicted pictures of his grandfather and his grandmother, Joanie. Aaron's coworkers offered pictures of him fixing cars, cleaning the shop and enjoying a cup of coffee with his employees during break. He was well-liked, always smiling. Sam found a few various older pictures of Aaron holding a toddler giving him a bath and teaching him how to throw a baseball. Sam couldn't find any photos of Aaron and Seth after toddlerhood.

223

The attendees made their way to the casket and said a little prayer. Some were comfortable enough to bend down and kiss his forehead. Others touched his hand, his clothing or left a memento next to his body. Babs didn't want Daniel to view the body, but he managed to slip an object in her hand. He pointed to the stage where Mr. Ravana rested in eternal peace. Babs understood Daniel's wish and positioned the gift on Aaron's chest.

Chestnut approached Daniel before they proceeded to the wake. He picked up a stuffed animal from Daniel's room and carried it softly in his mouth. Chestnut told Daniel to leave the gift in the box with Mr. Ravana. Daniel was excited to acquire an important task. He considered himself a vital part of a powerful circumstance.

Seth healed faster than his doctors predicted. He assumed it was due to his perfect physical condition. His left arm hung in a cast and he required a walker to support him. His legs were swollen and bruised. Some open wounds were bathed in medicated ointment and bandaged. Scars formed due to some of the deeper lacerations. He didn't focus on these temporary setbacks. The audience eagerly awaited his speech. Sam introduced him to those who only remembered him as a child. His walker steered him to the podium.

He began by giving a lovely definition of a father and how lucky children are to be blessed with a supportive male figure. He talked about playing football, going on hikes, helping with homework and so many other great activities fathers preformed for their children. He peeked at the audience and noticed some of those idiots dabbed their eyes with tissues. He even detected a few sniffles.

His attitude changed, "But my father was nothing like this."

The guests gasped. They did not expect this contradiction. Seth lied, exclaiming how his father molested him, how he beat him, starved him and locked him in the closet.

Principal Blake, who had contact with The Ravana's for years, was not surprised at these accusations, as Seth was an angry young man, a bully in and out of school. In actuality, Seth was the one who abused his father.

Ms. Blake wouldn't allow the eulogy to continue. She would not permit Seth to ruin Aaron's pristine character with fabrication. She planned to take the microphone from Seth when she observed a furry tiny head emerge from the casket. It was quite cute, although it was out-of-place. It climbed onto the edge of the casket. It had a grey coat, small black eye and a bushy tail.

Sam heard some peculiar little sounds emanating from the same. Most of the parishioners seemed unaware of the commotion. More furry heads popped up, scurrying from their hiding place directly toward Seth.

Squirrels! Multitudes of them. They circled around Seth. He tried to stomp on them, but his damaged legs were no match for their speed and agility. He twisted from one squirrel to the next, madly kicking at the rodents. He tripped over his walker and thumped to the ground. The grotesque creatures crawled up his legs. He felt their scuzzy bodies burrow up his pants, clawing their way to his groin area. He tried to fight them off, but six of them attacked his hands, three on each, disabling them. His hands were on fire, hundreds of little bites munching on his fingers and palms. They were eating him alive. He shrieked in agony. He flailed his arms like a human windmill. He spied one mini-demon who stopped chomping to look at him. The beady red eyes locked onto Seth's. Seth was convinced he observed a grimace on its repulsive face. Blood dripped from its mouth, Seth's blood.

He yelled, "I'll kill you."

The squirrels stopped feasting. Seth was sure he scared them. The five accomplices watched mini-demon, who scampered into Seth's sleeve. They squeezed into his cast and gnawed on the skin inside. His cast marinating in his blood, the smell further excited the animals. They sucked on the blood, wearing out the blood-soaked plaster.

The pants-attackers bit off the bandages and chewed on the open wounds. The pain was excruciating. He begged them to stop, even screeched out an apology to his past misconduct. Yet, they persisted. The fuzzy-tailed creatures nestled in his hair, digging furiously at his scalp.

He yelled, "I'll set the whole useless park on fire!" and he passed out.

Before the critters could accomplish further damage, Sam stepped onto the platform. He knelt down and lovingly placed his hand, palm up on the floor. He didn't utter a word. The first squirrel noticed him and paused. He scampered over to Aaron's body and jumped back into the casket. One by one, the others followed the leader until the last of them resided with Aaron.

Ms. Blake and Sam rushed to help Seth. Ms. Blake called the police and an ambulance. Sam felt for a pulse and breath. His father was unconscious, but alive. Sam turned to the guests. Some were speaking softly to each other; others were scanning the psalm booklet awaiting the next song. Sam cleared his throat and began to speak when the audience glanced at the podium. They had just noticed Seth lying on the floor covered in blood. They had not any recollection of the attack. They started screaming and ran from the building. Helmuth and Irmgard tried to control the panic, ushering the adults outside and carrying some of the younger children. Shaggy, Babs, Paul-Anthony, Lucy and Ms. Blake remained in the church with Sam. Kyle and Maddie ushered Daniel and Chestnut from the building.

Sam and Ms. Blake reluctantly described the incident to their friends. They weren't sure they would believe them. They were exhausted after they relived the story in great detail. They wondered if their friends found them credible. Shaggy slid her hand in Sam's and smiled at him. Babs let them know she believed them and revealed her night terrors for the first time in her life. She was somehow aware that her nightmares were connected to this freakish disturbance. They were grateful the group trusted them although they did not witness the events.

Paul-Anthony said he remembered walking into the building, chatting with the neighbors, saying a prayer for Aaron and returning to his seat. Then he sat and waited for the eulogy. He was confused and concerned when he suddenly noticed Seth crumbled and bleeding near the podium. He looked around; everyone had the same confused expression. The rest of the group agreed. They wondered what they missed; how did it happen? They all watched the others panic and stream for the building, knocking over chairs and tumbling over each other. They hung on to each other, helping those up who fell, grasping the children and leading them to safety. Helmuth and Irmgard Weber strained to control the panic.

Babs recalled Seth's wife. She didn't panic like the rest. She was unphased. She calmly rose from her chair, clutched her pocketbook, smoothed her hair and glided across the cluttered aisles. She held her head high without any expression, like a runway model.

The police and ambulance arrived. The paramedics lifted Seth's bloody body onto the gurney. He was in enormous pain, but none of the bites were fatal. They said he was fortunate no major arteries were broken. They rushed him to the Plainledge Hospital Emergency Room. The police officers questioned the guests. They were suspicious as to how a man was badly mauled, in front of a crowd of people without any eye witnesses. Samael chose to repeat the same story to his confidants. He doubted they would believe that a scurry of squirrels rose from a casket to attack his father.

The officers insisted they all leave the building, as it was considered a crime scene. The cop allowed Samael to say a final good-bye to his grandfather. He ambled over to Aaron, bent down to kiss his forehead and saw a stuffed toy squirrel resting on Aaron's chest. The squirrel had a beautiful smile forever stitched upon its face.

Chapter
THIRTY-THREE
The Apartment

Helmuth and Irmgard were impressed with Shaggy and Samael. They were dealing with Aaron's death, his father's hospitalization, the opening of the dog park and the upkeep of the animal shelter. They wanted to reward their accomplishments. Since Shaggy and Sam recently decided to rent an apartment together, Helmuth and Irmgard figured they would construct a top level to the dog park where the two could live. It would include two bedrooms, a kitchen, a living area and a separate room for two dogs. They would also gift them each a dog from the shelter. They hired Paul-Anthony Waldron's construction company to build the apartment.

Shaggy and Samael were elated with her parents' surprise. The timing was perfect. Their relationship flourished in the short time they had known each other. They spent time together in the shelter, at the dog park and at St. Katharine's University. Neither wanted Sam to remain in his house with Seth and they felt a strong bond, a developing relationship. They decided to rent a local apartment and pursue their budding connection.

The five met to discuss the plans. Paul-Anthony and five employees began immediately. They closed the dog park for a few days. They didn't want to risk any injuries in the building process. Helmuth and Irmgard worked on improving the grounds. They purchased tress, seeds and flowers from the nursery. They planted, mowed and pruned.

Shaggy and Sam learned a lot while watching the construction crew. They supervised, took notes and checked on them frequently. They assured the workers utilized their breaks, remained hydrated and offered them snacks throughout the day.

The first hour was uneventful. It was the usual setting up the equipment, reviewing the master plans and delegating tasks. Afterwards, multiple tragedies occurred.

Helmuth was clipping the hedges with garden shears. Irmgard was engrossed in planting the beautiful flowers nearby. She inadvertently grabbed a bee while she reached for a daisy. She stood up and yelped. Helmuth walked over to check on her. He tripped on a piece of hedge trimming. He fell, holding the garden shears face-down. They impaled Irmgard's left foot. Helmuth scooped her in his arms, ran for his car and transported her to the hospital without waiting to call an ambulance. None of the others learned of the accident until later. They didn't hear the noise. The construction muted the commotion.

The electrician, Bryce, was installing the electrical wiring. His vison blurred and he could not perceive any difference between red and blue wires. He hesitated, unable to make a decision. He reached toward the wires unwillingly. He felt his hand move without his permission. Something controlled his movements. He fought with the urge to touch the wrong wire. He used his left hand to hold down his right hand. He slammed his right hand on the table once, twice, three times. The pain radiated up his arm, but the hand continued its quest.

He wielded a hammer and struck his hand, breaking his metacarpal bones. He heard the crunch, turned, and vomited from the pain. The hand kept moving toward its target. He selected an axe from his toolbox. He didn't want to harm himself, but he had no options. He lifted the axe with his left hand, hitting his target. He sliced off four of his fingers, leaving only his thumb intact. He held himself up with his left hand. He leaned on the table for support. Blood gushed from his fingers. He sensed the room spinning. He was dizzy with pain. He fell, landing on his right elbow. He heard another crack as the bone broke.

He looked up to see the live wire drop from the fuse box and dangle in front of him. He rolled to the side to dodge the wire, but it followed him. It flicked closer and retreated, as if it was teasing him. He screamed and cried out, but no one came to his aid. The live red wire zapped him in his eye. The electric shock coursed through his system. It knocked him unconscious. He seized. His head banged against the floor; foam drooled down his cheek. Paul-Anthony heard the banging and sprinted to Bryce. The seizing ended, but Bryce couldn't speak or move. Paul-Anthony wasn't sure if he was dead, but was afraid to touch him. He called for an ambulance.

The doctors revived Bryce. He was unable to speak or move from the neck down. He rolled his head from side-to-side, trying to communicate in some fashion. He moved his lips, but no sound emerged. He laid there for hours before his body succumbed to the injuries.

Jackson was hanging the drywall. He worked with Paul-Anthony for ten years. When they found him, his co-workers never understood why he wasn't wearing his safety goggles. His screw gun jammed. He thwacked it a few times and changed the batteries, to no avail. He felt a presence forcing his hand to point the gun turn toward his face. He was frightened; he was unable to control the pressure. He reluctantly unfastened his goggles.

He said to himself, "What the heck is going on here?"

He placed both hand on the gun. He struggled to push against the opposing force, tugging with all his effort, yet the gun inched closer to his face. He couldn't wrench it away. He yelled out for help, but again, no one answered his calls. The gun vibrated. He attempted to run, but slipped on a sheet of drywall. The gun discharged, blasting screws from its nose, blanketing Jackson's eyes, checks and nose. His skin shredded from his face. His eyes imploded; his teeth were extracted, his nose disintegrated. Blood covered the remnants of his face.

Chaos erupted. Paul-Anthony called the police and another ambulance. The other employees, three brothers, heard the news and exited the building instantly. They considered the first incident an accident. However, after Jackson's unexplained tragedy, they perceived an evilness lurking around. The hellish presence was palpable.

They bounded to their four-door, blue Chevrolet Silverado. The three brothers purchased the truck for various construction jobs. It seated five and had ample room in the cab for their tools and equipment. They had no time to think. They were frightened and wanted to take off as quickly as possible.

232

Jeb sat in the driver's seat, already revving the engine.

Joe took the passenger seat, yelling, "Go, go!"

Javier was behind the truck, hurling the toolbox into the cargo bed. The toolbox opened on impact. A wrench propelled upward, ricocheted off the cargo wall and smacked Javier on his forehead. He was disoriented and grabbed the rim of the truck to regain his balance. Jeb floored the gas pedal without realizing what was happening behind him.

Javier couldn't release his grip. His fingers would not move. He saw malignant shadow enter his nose. It squirmed up to his eyes, clouding his vision. It reached his brain, dominating his mind. He heard it command him to "Hold on." He was aware of the implications, but was unable to let go. He heard the roar of the engine. The truck jolted and moved at an abnormally rapid speed. His feet scraped the ground. His phalanges and metatarsals pulverized. The fibula and tibia crushed and grinded. He was dead before his patella turned into dust. His piercing screams were smothered by the truck's clamoring. His brothers were unaware of his torturous demise.

Jeb couldn't drive fast enough. He tried to get as much space between his brothers and the shelter as possible. He executed the curves recklessly. He believed he perceived a tree in the middle of the road, up ahead. It possessed extensive branches.

Jeb, in his surreal state, perceived them as arms stretching out to grab him. The tree trunk contained an enormous cavity, which Jeb thought was a mouth attempting to swallow him. The roots didn't touch the ground, but hovered slightly above. They looked like footless strands of bleeding filament dangling from a gigantic beast. Jeb slammed the brakes to avoid contact. Joe, who had no time to fasten his seatbelt, catapulted through the windshield. He sensed his body fly through the air. It was exhilarating and terrifying. He experienced no pain as his head smashed into the tree-like monster. His teeth shattered. His bones crunched. Before he completely disintegrated, he was swept into the tree hollow. His dead body tumbled down a dark shaft. The Stretchman absorbed his energy and cast his corpse into an underground cemetery where no living soul visits.

Jeb was distracted with his own predicament. The truck rolled over. Jeb was tossed around inside. He reached out his arms to protect himself. His chest slammed into the steering wheel; his neck whiplashed backward. The car flipped over. Jeb hit his head on the top of the truck. It bent forward at an unusual angle. He heard his neck crack. He couldn't feel any sensation from his neck down to his toes.

He cried out for help and caught site of the tree-thing drifting his way. It extended a branch to Jeb. He mistakenly thought this was as a peace offering. Another branch was stretched horizontally, crisscrossing the first one. The Stretchman tree-monster rubbed its limbs together creating heat and smoke. A spark produced a flame, which generated a full-fledged fire. The monster dipped his boughs under the gas tank and dispensed them as if it amputated its own arms. Jeb watched it coast away as the truck was engulfed in flames. His flesh began to burn, tearing from his body. The pain was excruciating. He emitted a brief savage scream. He wasn't able to shout for help any longer as his lungs were full of smoke.

The Stretchman returned, collected Jeb's smoldering carcass, dumped him into the awaiting cavity, and launched Jeb into his ultimate tomb.

Sam and Paul-Anthony terminated the project until further notice. Sam realized he had not seen Shaggy in a while. He panicked, started running around calling her name. She didn't answer.

He raced from the vacated apartment, glancing out the windows, to the lobby and the main office, when he noticed her standing still near the restroom. It seemed as if she was about to enter when something prevented her. The door was ajar. He walked over to her and placed his hand on her shoulder, repeating her name. She was unresponsive. He shook her gently, but she remained unaware.

He noticed something in the mirror within the bathroom behind her. The image shocked him. It was monstrous, vacant eyes, a large open mouth. He forced himself to look away. He patted Shaggy's face more sharply, yelling her name loudly.

She stared at him with dark swirling eyes and vigorously said, "Get out. Heed my warning." Then she collapsed.

Sam carried Shaggy outside and rested her on the grass under a shady tree. Shaggy was incoherent, her head flopping side to side. Every few seconds, she would blurt out unrelated words, "cursed," "tree," Nick," "truck."

Sam yelled loudly for someone to fetch some water, but he received no response. He scanned the area and noted it was deserted. He phoned Shaggy's father. The line rang ten times. He almost disconnected when Helmuth answered. Sam briefly explained Shaggy's condition. He was worried about her. He wondered why Helmuth was not at the dog park. Helmuth described Irmgard's accident and told Sam they were waiting in the Emergency Room for the doctor to stitch her wound. Sam rambled about the devastating events at the construction site. Helmuth advised Sam to either call an ambulance or drive Shaggy to the hospital himself.

Sam chose to drive Shaggy to the Emergency Room. He didn't want to wait for an ambulance. He gently placed her in the passenger seat and fastened her seatbelt. She starred ahead blindly, repeating the words, "Don't go back, don't go back."

The psychiatrist assessed Shaggy and admitted her to the Psychiatric unit for further observation. They administered an anti-anxiety medication and settled her in the facility on a comfortable bed.

Roma, a veteran patient, approached Shaggy. Roma was cuddling a stuffed dog. Roma spoke rapidly and loudly. She claimed she used to own a real dog named Cameron. A giant monster stole Cameron inside her own house. She said the monster scared her when it snatched her dog. She couldn't stop shaking and crying. She ran from her apartment and raced around the courtyard hollering for help. One of her neighbors exited her flat and caught Roma in a fierce hug. Roma's friend attempted to calm her, look for her dog and listen to her story.

Roma said she had an appointment to take Cameron to The Plainledge Animal Shelter for a bath and grooming session. She paid Cathy, the regular groomer, and offered a generous monetary donation for dog care and supplies. They returned home, she assembled a turkey sandwich for herself and a fresh bowl of water with a homemade dog biscuit for Cameron. They sat together on the couch to watch the news.

Roma stated she heard a rumbling and felt the room wobble. She claims she observed a dark shape arise from the back of the couch. It resembled a hand, but the fingers were inordinately long. The arm stretched unrealistically over the sofa and wrapped itself firmly around Cameron's body. It lifted her like the crane toy Roma used to play at the amusement park. She attempted to free her dog from the stretched arm, but her hands were unable to maintain the grip. It seemed as though the dog's fur was coated with oil. Her fingers slipped from Cameron with every effort.

Roma was aghast. She remained, unmoved, in her spot for hours. She admits she may have heard the phone ring, but she had no desire to rise and answer it. She patiently waited for Cameron to reappear.

Days passed. Her neighbor knocked on her door numerous times, and then decided to call the police. Roma was dehydrated and unresponsive. The ambulance drove her to the Emergency Room. They administered an oral rehydration solution and offered her some broth. When she continued to jabber about her delusional experience, they admitted her to the Psychiatric Unit.

Shaggy did not explain her experience to the doctors. She recognized the unbelievable quality of her story. The psychiatrist would no doubt admit her if she told the truth. However, when Sam picked her up, she told him about her encounter in the car. A strange feeling coursed through her body. It felt like an intravenous drip of cold gel traveling through her veins.

At first, she was petrified. She fought, struggling to gain control. She couldn't move. She strained to flap her arms or command her legs to step forward.

She tried yelling for Sam, but no sound escaped her lips. As her veins filled, her body relaxed. A malevolent entity gained full control. She reluctantly submitted to the intrusive residence. Her eyes turned dark, churning; her movements, robotic; her voice, slow and expressionless. However, she was aware of the thoughts bewitching her mind.

The being informed her of a horrific truck accident, involving three brothers from Paul-Anthony Waldron's construction company. It described a stretching malevolent tree siphoning dead men. It detailed the manner in which it cursed The Plainledge Animal Shelter. She heard dogs whimpering and people crying in a far-off site. The most frightening component was the anger. It was all-consuming. A hateful sentiment full of revenge, capture and torture.

Chapter
THIRTY-FOUR
Babs and Nina

Shaggy and Sam met her parents and Paul-Anthony at Aaron's Dog Park to discuss the plans for the apartment. Babs covered The Plainledge Animal Shelter with Nina, one of the dog park interns. Her dog, Siggy, wasn't feeling well and she wanted to examine him.

Nina behaved peculiarly lately. She hardly spoke, she jumped at every small sound, she lacked facial expression and she seemed frightened of something unknown, like she was living in a nightmare.

She relaxed a bit when she was with the dogs. She gained comfort in holding the dogs and stroking them, like Daniel did with Chestnut.

Babs thought the shelter would be a more appropriate place for Nina since the noise from the construction on the dog park would agitate her.

Nina loved the shelter. She took a liking to a Newfoundland, although she usually chose the smaller dogs. This dog was a beautiful giant, weighing 160 pounds. When he laid on the floor next to Nina and gently rested his head on her feet, she fell in love. She sat down and hugged him, snuggling her head in his fur. Her arms couldn't even wrap around his whole body, as he was tremendous. She felt protected and secure. Babs told her the dog's name was Tonka. Nina gazed at Babs with a twinkle in her eyes and said, "Hi, my name is Tucker."

Babs almost fell over. She trembled all over. *Tucker is the dog's name in my nightmares.* When Nina mentioned the name, Babs clearly remembered her dream. Tucker died in the Dark Place in her dream when he tried to protect her. Babs sensed an evil premonition. Nina insisted on the name. She said it popped into her head the moment she laid eyes on the dog.

Babs panicked. She paced. Siggy followed her. She picked her up and held her close, denying the coincidence. Dogs are always a comfort to their humans. They don't need training for this. Their presence is enough to cause a calming reaction. Nina cowered; she lowered head looked up at Babs with her eyes. She asked if she upset Babs when she called the dog "Tucker." It seemed appropriate to confide in Nina about her night terrors. Perhaps they would find a connection between Babs's dream and Nina choosing the same name. Maybe it would spark her memory and she could recall what happened the day her friends disappeared.

She listened meticulously to Babs's nightmare. She became agitated when Babs explained how Tucker tried to protect her and he lunged at the beast. She told Nina she heard her dog yelp, but he didn't necessarily die. Babs woke up before the dream concluded. Tears flowed down Nina's cheeks when she asked Babs if her nightmare could come true.

She suddenly sobbed. Her body shuddered. She buried her head in Tucker's body and repeatedly screamed, "No, no, no."

Babs caressed her back and allowed her to cry until she exhausted herself.

Nina looked at Babs and whispered, "I remember."

Babs asked Nina if she would like to talk to her about her experience and her feelings. She was afraid Babs wouldn't believe her or she may get angry with her for the part she played. Babs assured her she would listen without judging.

She explained the séance. When she found out Aaron died in the Dog Park, she wanted to contact his spirit. She revealed her relationship with the Lanes and that they and their dogs mysteriously disappeared. She watched movies focusing on holy grounds, spirit energies and processes for contacting the dead. She thought she understood the procedures. Her friends were excited to participate. They purchased candles, pentagons and sage.

She told Babs about her the details, her friend's death and disappearances. She blamed herself as she coordinated the event. She was specifically afraid of the voice that thanked her for inviting it in. As the story unfolded, Babs sensed that the séance, Tucker and her night terrors were connected in a sinister manner, but she didn't know how. Babs planned to discuss this with her family and co-workers. The accumulated knowledge may shed some light on the disturbing events.

Babs started to reassure her when the building swayed. They held onto the dogs. Siggy jumped from her arms. The trembling continued, mounting to a frightening upheaval. The shelves reeled; packages of dog biscuits bowled over. Babs placed a few of the Limited Ingredient Dog Biscuits in her pocket. Siggy loved them. They calmed her. She stopped whatever she was doing to receive a biscuit, but Babs couldn't

241

procure her from where she stood. Dog cages flipped to their sides and the lights flickered.

Nina and Babs grabbed each other and hugged tightly. Siggy darted around the room frantically searching for the source of the commotion. The wind tossed her back and forth. She finally dropped near the rear door when the ground collapsed. She wrestled to maintain her balance. He little paws scratched violently to secure her stance, but she plummeted into the abyss. Tucker watched her and lagged closely behind. He swiftly dug his head in the hole and snatched Siggy gently by the nape of her neck. He struggled to free her. The opposing force fought with him, threatening to pull them both in. Nina and Babs released their hug and unsteadily moved toward Tucker. Babs reached her hand into the emptiness and located Tucker's collar with her fingertips. She gripped it securely. Nina held onto her waist to support her. The gravitational pressure was too much for them to combat. The four of them descended into the unknown.

The Dark Place was not unfamiliar to Babs. She visited it in her nightmares. This was slightly more disturbing because she understood it was genuine. She was never so completely afraid. She could feel her heart beating rapidly, her mouth dry as cotton. She had difficulty swallowing. Nina was pale and her lips were blue. Babs had to convince herself to act calmly for Nina's sake. Siggy sat by Babs's side panting. Her head crouched, her tail between her legs and she displayed the moon eye.

The moon eye signifies a dog's distress. The white part (the sclera) appears as a crescent moon shape. It is similar to when humans are anxious and open their eyes wide. Tucker stood tall and upright next to Nina.

The hair on his back stood on its end, he bared his teeth and he waited to attack the enemy. They didn't wait long. The monster clawed its way out of the wall, stretching its head and arms first; it flopped out like a fish caught on a hook. It stood up and slowly clambered to eight or nine feet tall. It pointed its thin, long finger at Nina and hollered, "You."

Nina emitted a guttural sound that panged Babs. Tucker sounded like a bear as he produced the nastiest, most threatening bark he could muster. The Stretchman grimaced with its empty mouth, stepped one long stride toward Tucker and took hold of his collar like he was a rag doll. Tucker dangled in midair, desperately fighting to breathe and free himself.

Siggy ignored her own discomfort and prepared to strike. Babs didn't give her the chance. She snatched her before she could advance. Siggy acted on instinct and turned to bite Babs in her frenzied state. Babs gently wrapped her hand around Siggy's mouth like a muzzle. Before Babs managed to make a move, Nina returned from her stupor. She scooped up two fistfuls of soot from the ground and charged at the Stretchman, full speed ahead. It caught her in mid-plight with its free hand, hugged her and Tucker firmly to its chest.

Nina pleaded for Bab's help. Tucker was slowly losing consciousness. Babs felt useless, defenseless. She reached into her pocket and lamely flung one of Karen's homemade dog biscuits at the beast. It touched its knee cap and thrust deep into the sinewy bone. The biscuit glowed brightly, turned a deep crimson and ignited. Stretchman's legs acted as if they were kindling. The fire moved up the beast's body. It shrieked loud enough to throw Babs backward. She felt a hot, fetid rush of air pulse through her hair,

243

drops of spittle gathered on her face. The light of the fire briefly blinded her.

The Stretchman pointed its finger at her and swirled it around and around. Babs crouched down, securing Siggy in a tight hold. She was terrified to the point of nausea. She closed her eyes, hoping this was another night terror, but she knew otherwise. She felt a dizzy sensation consume her. Siggy wiggled and whined. They were moving, circling in the direction of the Stretchman's finger. She glimpsed a vison of the monster as he pushed himself backward, disappearing into the cave wall with Tucker and Nina.

Siggy and Babs struck the floor with an unyielding bump. He yelped as she inadvertently squeezed him when she hit the ground. She was sick to her stomach, frightened and worried. A multitude of horrible thoughts raced through her mind. Where are Nina and Tucker? How can she help them? Are they alive? She didn't even have a plan. How could she return to The Dark Place and how could she crush the Stretchman?

Babs needed collaboration from a team of dog-loving, supportive, trustworthy friends. She called her husband at Aaron's Dog Shelter. He was busy with the construction, but ceased working instantly when she told him she had an emergency. She requested assistance from Shaggy, Samael and the rest of the group, and their dogs, to head over immediately. She phoned

Ms. Blake and informed her about the emergency. She asked if she could take Maddie, Daniel and Kyle with her to The Plainledge Animal Shelter. She would have to stop at their house first and pick up Max and Nick. Daniel would already have Chestnut with him.

They would require as much help as they could find.
They had to figure out a course of action.

Chapter
THIRTY-FIVE
Trista

I learned to hate dogs after they attacked Seth. My life would have been completely different. I envisioned Seth playing professional football, earning a significant salary. His attitude toward me would have changed dramatically. Between his career and a newborn son, he would have been happy, less angry. I would live in a beautiful mansion, wear expensive clothes and entertain the celebrities. The three of us would vacation together and travel the world.

It didn't work out that way. Those three wretched animals destroyed my chances for a prestigious life. Instead, I was trapped in an abusive marriage without any friends, any freedoms and a stupid fragile son. I reminded Seth that our tenth anniversary was approaching. I hinted that the ten- year gifts are usually composed of tin or aluminum. I never received a gift from Seth, but I mentioned an aluminum wind chime that I wanted. It resonated a beautiful sound, a sad calling, haunting but enchanting. Eleven chimes dangled from an oblong block of wood. Five chimes in increasing lengths hung to each side of the longest chime. The eleventh chime, situated in the middle, was the lucky chime predicting another year of marital bliss.

Seth arrived home after work that day with an aluminum baseball bat. He struck me ten times. I cowered, dropped to the floor and protected my head with my arms. The bat pummeled my body, hitting my back first. The pain was excruciating. I think the fifth blow broke my arm, but the penetrating pain was my concern and focus. After ten strikes, he reminded me that eleven is for good luck and another year of marital bliss. The weapon smashed into the back of my head and I lost consciousness.

When I regained consciousness, I was lying in my bed. Seth would always treat me nicely after a beating. The typical, "I'm sorry babe, it won't happen again." This time, I received an unexpected anniversary gift after the assault. It was a stunning antique mirror. It was soiled and smelled foul, but I immediately saw its beauty.

I glimpsed my reflection. It resembled my own, but looked faded, unsubstantial. It appeared as if it was disappearing. I was curious, as I felt those qualities mimicked my own perceptions of myself.

I positioned the mirror in the middle of my bedroom. I sanded and stained the wood frame. I cleaned the glass and draped it with pleasant-smelling lavender. I stepped back to view the restoration. This project raised my self-esteem. I felt worthy that I accomplishing a memorable task. I again observed my reflection. It changed. It was no longer dreary. It was livelier, more enthusiastic. The image portrayed my feelings in a physical state.

I contemplated what I wanted to undertake next. A shower would be appropriate, as I was full of stain and grime. I took a long relaxing shower and washed my hair. I donned clean clothes, selected my favorite music and returned to the mirror. I was stunned. My reflection was more beautiful than my own physical appearance. I detected a strong, powerful woman in that glass. She obtained qualities that I may have acquired before the rape, assertiveness, esteem and authority. I imagined my real self as my mirror image. I desired to transform into that potential self.

The mirror became my best friend. I stopped thinking of myself as a powerless victim. My negative self-talk convinced my brain to believe my own doubts. The mirror reflected my pessimistic thoughts. I lost sight of my potential, my true qualities. Each time I took care of my own needs, set a goal or ignored others over myself, the mirror reflected a more powerful figure.

The greatest change occurred when I left Samael alone crying in his crib. The sound reverberated in my brain. I wanted to choke the life out of him, just so I wouldn't hear his pathetic calls. I filled the bathtub with warm and relaxed in a bubble bath for two hours. I blocked out his screams with my headphones and my favorite music. When I was finished, I dressed in my only comfortable cotton dress. The brat was no longer crying. He laid still in his crib, staring at the ceiling. He kicked off his blankets during his tantrum. I touched his cold skin. He looked at me and smiled. He probably wanted me to pick him up and comfort him, but I wasn't in the mood. I skipped back to my mirror-friend and was pleasantly surprised. Yet, another delightful and mysterious image looked back at me.

My new likeness had less hair, enlarged hollow eyes and a menacing grin. She was intimidating; taller, with long arms and legs. I was awestruck. Physical beauty may sometimes deteriorate with inner hatred, revenge and a need for power. However, I was grateful for the trade-off. I desired to transform into a superior self.

I reached for the glass. My finger and my mirror-finger connected with an electrifying jolt. Instead of throwing me backward, the force pulled me into the mirror. I felt my physical body dissolve into the image. We merged as one substance. My body magnified with my self-esteem. I mutated into a superhero, albeit, not necessarily benign.

I sensed a diabolical presence attached to the energy. I was terrified at first, the evilness chilling. Did I want to take part in a fiendish lifestyle? The monster displayed pictures of my life before my eyes, the abuse, the isolation, the suffering. My ambivalence turned to craving. Yes! I accept the wickedness with the capability. I am in control now. I will seek revenge on those who hurt me. I will curse their ridiculous animal shelter, the unwarranted dog parks, even the places the dogs and their rescuers lived. I will capture and kill the treacherous dogs and torture those who help and rescue them. I will stick them in The Dark Place like tacks in a corkboard. They will all pay homage to me.

I launched into my new life one year later. I watched the neighborhood, observing the stupid people who rescue, care for and walk their dogs. I wasn't sure who I despised more, the humans or the dogs, probably the dogs. I focused on a specific ugly black family with three grotesque children and three old, loathsome dogs. I suspected these dogs were the ones who attacked Seth. Their description and age matched perfectly. I felt my face flush and my rage escalate every time I observed this revolting group of eight.

They chatted and smiled at each other when they walked their dogs. They displayed a friendly façade as they strolled the neighborhood. I noticed they were friendly with the freaky lesbo neighbors who owned the dumb big animal, who looked more like a Jackass than a dog.

I planned my attack with my newfound strength. I approached the mirror. I rested both palms on the glass. I summoned it, called it to join me, to join forces. I was ready and willing to accept the gift. My feet lifted, my body rose horizontally and my hands remained glued to the surface. It pulled me in. I felt a jolt of power rush through my body. It pushed and pulled me in all directions. I grew, six, seven, maybe eight feet tall. I seemed to lose my feet in the process, but I wasn't concerned. I evolved into a superior being and had no use for them. I hovered above the ground, floating freely.

I looked around and enjoyed the view. I touched down in a safe place. I welcomed the darkness. I was no longer doomed to watch the repulsive people invade my neighborhood with their dirty mongrels.

I spun around in delight. I wanted to absorb every piece of this amazing place. It was cold and damp, much better than the hot, humid climate I previously endured. I touched the ceiling and it shifted. I curiously continued to rub my hand in a circular motion. The falling rocks and debris tickled me as it landed on my head and shoulders. It was like a rain massage, caressing me, loving me, becoming a part of me. This enchanting, lovely cave was now my home.

My hand created an opening, a window into reality. I could see the black family inside their house, their dogs chasing the children around, the mother and father preparing dinner. This was my golden moment. I reached my arm into the portal as the little girl ran into her parents' bedroom. My arm stretched further than I thought possible and I snatched the toddler. Her dog immediately came to her aid, barking a warning as if she possessed any power over me. I seized her also, laying them both on the ground in my cave.

The dog's barks alerted her brothers. I allowed them to hear her cries so they would follow her path. They flowing her voice from the portal under the bed. Their dogs barked behind them. I reached over the boys and grabbed their dogs first, flinging them into their new home without concern. The boys screamed for their dogs. I captured one brat in each hand. Their arms flapped above their heads as they shrieked in terror. I discarded them as I did the others.

The two big ones appeared not five seconds later. They heard the clamor and reacted faster than a speeding bullet. I despise parents who defend their children if their own lives are at stake. The act as if they are Superman or Superwoman. Their vigilance fueled my rage. I took hold of them, squeezing so they had to struggled to inhale. I let them linger in midair before I released them. They landed next to their pathetic family in their forever home.

We were so happy living with the Lanes. They rescued us from The Plainledge Animal Shelter after we fled from the puppy mill. Jenna, Cody and I celebrated each time they had a baby. I felt an attachment to Kevin, where Jenna formed an attached to Connor, and Cody loved Bella more than she loved anyone else. We were getting old, but the children kept us feeling young. They played with us, walked us and allowed us to sleep with them in bed. The parents treated us like their own children. They are the best family a dog could ask for.

The start of the day was great, as always. School was closed for the summer. The children got up late. Walter and Yanna prepared chocolate chip pancakes and bacon for breakfast. Mom cooked extra bacon for us. She knew bacon was our favorite food. She cooled it in ice before she put it in our bowls. We wanted to lick her face to thank her, but she laughed and said we had bacon breath. She moved away from us and the children erupted in laughter. The family brushed their teeth, got dressed and clipped on our leashes. We all went for a long walk through the neighborhood and to the dog park.

We met Morgan there and made friends with many other dogs. Dogs don't care what you look like, how smart you are or what you're wearing. We just want to play and have fun. The trouble began when we returned home. Jenna and I heard Cody bark and Bella scream. We galloped toward the bedroom only to find a smoke emanating from under the bed. Kevin and Connor arrived in seconds, struggling to turn over the mattress.

Smoke smoldered forming a circular pattern in the wooden floor. We could hear faint crying and far-off barking. Jenna and I leaned into the circle, scratching and digging. We had no luck. The floor was solid inside the simmering enclosure. I heard Kevin yell my name. Before I was able to respond, an arm inconceivably stretched up from the area we just searched and hooked our collars with its nail-like claws. It threw us into a cavernous dungeon. Jenna hurt her leg, but she was usually quite dramatic. I licked the pain away easily.

Cody was sitting close by on Bella's lap trying to sooth Bella. She was scared to death. A powerful rush of air knocked us over and Kevin and Connor crashed into this hellhole. It was cold and dark. We huddled next to our humans to keep them warm.

A few minutes later, another windstorm occurred. We planted ourselves on top of our humans to prevent the turbulence from carrying them away. We gripped our nails into the moist ground and held on tightly. Our humans hugged us closely. Our *combined weight secured us to the ground. The wind subsided at the same time Yanna and Walter bounded down with a thunderous thwack. They rushed over to us. They embraced the children, patted us on our heads and told us we were safe. Dad spoke calmly and required us to sit quietly so he and Mom could devise a plan to return home.*

Chapter
THIRTY-SIX
Seth

Seth lay in the hospital after his surgery. His face, torso, arms and legs were stitched fully. He remained on an antibiotic drip, as the unknown bites could have caused an infection. The doctor was not aware of what exactly caused the lacerations. Sam and the other witnesses never revealed the culprits. The surgeon operated on him for two hours to repair the shredded skin and muscles in his cheek. His leg was re-casted.

Seth didn't mind lingering in the hospital. The painkillers were phenomenal. Another favorable outcome was his ability to abuse the female employees without consequence. He especially fancied Ola. She was an eighteen-year-old high school senior. She planned to attend St. Katharine's University to major in Nursing. Her guidance counselor suggested she volunteer at The Plainledge Hospital for experience and for community service. Ola started a non-paid position a year ago and did not encounter a problem until she met the man in room 113. His name was Seth Ravana.

Ola felt sorry for Seth. Rumor was he was savagely attacked by an unknown entity. He was swaddled in gauge, bandages and topical ointments. She spent extra time in his room, chatted with him daily, even laughed at his ill-humored jokes. She hoped her company would help him feel better, since no one visited him. She felt uncomfortable when he called her, "Baby-Cakes," but choose to ignore him.

She walked over to his bed to fluff his pillows, at his request. He picked up his head when she bent down to reach for the pillows. Seth stuck out his tongue and licked her cleavage. He wrapped the call monitor around her neck and drew her closer. He resumed nibbling on the top of her breasts. He maneuvered his free hand under her skirt and squeezed her buttocks. She struggled to twist from him, but the cord choked her when she moved. Seth had no intention of hurting her, he just wanted to play with her. He only took advantage for a few minutes, then he untangled the wire around her neck.

Ola jumped back, red-faced and mortified. She was dumbfounded, her eyes filled with tears. Seth harbored a wide smile across his partially bandaged face. He held her hand gently. He tried to apply increased pressure, but it caused him pain.

He stared at her with his eerie half concealed face and said, "If you say anything, Baby-Cakes, they will fire you. I am a paying customer functioning on pain medications. I have no control over my actions. The administrators will consider you unduly sensitive and incompetent to succeed in the helping profession. This will be the end of something you hardly had a chance to start." His smile never wavered.

Ola walked inconspicuously to the rest rooms and splashed her face with cold water. She bumped into a senior nurse on the way out of the bathroom. Nurse Jamie noticed Ola's flushed face and nervous appearance. She confronted her and inquired about her agitated state. She advised Ola leave until she felt better. Ola assured Nurse Jamie that she just encountered an allergic reaction to something, sneezed a few times and went to blow her nose and freshen up in the ladies' room. She was prepared to finish her day.

Ola finished her day at Plainledge Hospital, but did not return. She never mentioned the incident her supervisor or Nurse Jamie. However, she spoke to Ms. Andrea, an admission's counselor at St. Katharine's University. She explained her desire to major in a helping profession, but was no longer interested in Nursing. Ms. Andrea advised Ola to major in Biology and seek a career in Veterinarian medicine. The two discussed The Dog and Human Bonding course and St. Katharine's affiliation with Aaron's Dog Park and The Plainledge Animal Shelter. Ola left voicemails at both locations. She was excited to try a new venue in the helping profession.

Seth whooped when he heard that stupid, feeble girl quit. She reminded him of the good-for-nothing Samael. The world was full of ignorant, fragile idiots. Thankfully, Seth was kind enough to assist them in acknowledging their limitations and offer them a strong motivation to run from their unreachable goals.

Seth couldn't believe his luck continued. First, he tasted the delicious Ola. Now, to his great surprise, another visitor appeared. His own loving wife Trista arrived to nurture him. He expected her to rush in and fling herself desperately on his ailing body; to sob, simultaneously with grief and relief. She was probably distressed over his attack. But this was not the case.

She ambled in with her head held high, a confidence he never imagined. He didn't appreciate her new-found self-assurance. He would beat her down to her deserved demoralized statue as soon as he was discharged. For further enjoyment, he hoped an opportunity would arise for a hospital thrashing.

Trista decided to play her own game. She lifted a piece of broken glass from her satchel. She broke it from her antique mirror. She was well aware that Seth derived his confidence from his physical appearance and prowess. Trista planned to use his narcissistic predisposition against him. She admired her own powerful reflection before she turned the mirror toward Seth.

Seth gasped. If looks really could kill, Trista would have spontaneously combusted. He realized Trista discovered his vulnerability. He was furious she gained delight in his hideous appearance and impotency. He glared at her with pursed lips, squinted eyes and furrowed brows. His face flushed a blood red color. Anger surged from his gut, bubbling like a witch's caldron. Yet, he couldn't look away. The mirror gained his full attention.

Seth glimpsed images in the mirror aside from his own. Dark, hazy shapes floated behind him. Tortured faces, frozen in silent screams searched for salvation. They reached for each other, but their lack of substance did not permit a solid grasp. They slipped through each other like ghosts.

The mirror's concavity caused the figures to bulge in awkward positions. Faces were out of proportion to the bodies. A five-foot head sat upon a twelve-inch body; the neck stretched to accommodate the significant head. Fingers grew bigger than arms, appearing like a deformed trese stump with five four-foot branched jutting from its core. The nose covered the place of the entire face. Tiny little eyes, like black raisins, peeked out from each nostril. Then the shapes reversed. The bodies enlarged as the faces diminished. They reminded Seth as giant freaks with golf balls for heads. The eyes, mouths and noses were just dimples in tiny white balls. The fingers retreated as the arms expanded similar to a sloth. The nose disappeared as the eyes expanded, mimicking the Bratz dolls.

Seth was horrified and fascinated. He would love the opportunity to torment stupid, weak, useless people in this fashion. He met so many in his day, they were an abundant supply. He focused on his hideous reflection while the warped figures danced around his head. He desired, he wanted to be a part of the macabre activities. He spoke to whatever being offered him this great opportunity and agreed to its invitation.

Trista remained still, clutching the mirror with both hands, a crooked, menacing grin plastered on her face. She was the one who held the power, the control.

Chapter
THIRTY-SEVEN
The Fundraiser

Helmuth discussed the possibility of a fundraiser event for The Plainledge Animal Shelter with Ms. Blake a The Plainledge High School. He was hoping he could use the aid of the students to raise money for the shelter. It was in dire need of food, medications and supplies. He thought it would be a great learning experience for the students, a means for them to apply their courses to the real world. Most of the Plainledge residences owned dogs, so it would most likely be a welcoming and profitable fundraiser.

Ms. Blake was friendly with Babs Waldron, who was an expert in dogs and their relationship with humans. Babs had three children, her oldest was Kyle. Kyle was in the Plainledge High School honor's program, was very popular with his peers and played the trombone in the band. He may have some ideas. Ms. Blake called him to her office. She phoned his mother, Babs, but she didn't answer.

Ms. Blake explained the project to Kyle. Kyle said he would love the chance to help the dogs and raise money for the shelter. He suggested the Plainledge Junior High and High School band and orchestra perform at the event. Many of his friends played instruments. He was certain they would volunteer.

Helmuth would ask Sam if they could hold the event at Aaron's Dog Park.

Helmuth volunteered his services, as always. He would conduct free dog training sessions. Kyle figured his mother would offer free dog examinations. Ms. Blake would follow up with her. Ms. Blake would also ask the music teacher if any of the chorus students would be interested in singing a few songs. She would talk to the theater teacher regarding a potential performance.

They all made their inquiries. They were delighted with the students' motivation and commitment to the cause. The fundraiser would be held at the dog park. The entertainment and programs would be free. The attendees would pay an admission fee. Additional monetary donations, food or supplies would be gladly accepted.

Paul-Anthony and his crew constructed a stage for the performances and tables for the merchandise. Many students solicited items from the local merchants. They packed them in beautiful baskets and sold tickets for a raffle. The elementary and middle school parents baked cookies and cakes to sell at the concession stands. Karen baked her limited ingredient dog biscuits using her secret recipe.

Daniel and the students on the spectrum were excited to join the adventure. Ms. Blake purchased materials for them to color and paint bandanas for the dogs. They met with their parents in the school cafeteria on the opening day. They were quietly concentrating, in their zone, created masterpieces. The smiles on their faces communicated more than the words they were not able to speak.

The Plainledge Hospital was instrumental in advertising for the fundraiser. They hung flyers in the lobby, the cafeteria and in each wing. They strategically positioned donation boxes at all the nurses' stations. Babs asked them to sell Daniel's and his friend's bandanas. The hospital gift shop agreed to sell them without taking a cut in their profits.

Aaron's Dog Park filled up quickly. Generous donations streamed in. The chorus sang *The National Anthem* and *America the Beautiful.* The band and orchestra accompanied them. Kyle had a solo at the end, which was unusual, but the band teacher wanted to reward him for coordinating the band performance. During the words, "*from sea to shining sea,*" the chorus and the band went silent. Kyle stood up with his trombone and played those five words slowly and hypnotically. The crowd roared.

The theatre group performed, *"The Three Dogs,"* instead of, *"The Three Bears."* Ola played the part of Goldilocks. She regained some of her confidence after the hospital incident. The students changed the theme and plot themselves, wrote their own prompt booklets and used their own dogs as the star characters. They thought it would be an adorable change in the story if the dogs arrived back at their house, after taking a walk in the park, and allowed Goldilocks to stay and live with them, rather than chase her away. The Mama dog cooked extra porridge for her, the Papa dog built her a chair, perfect for her own size and the Baby dog shared his bed with her. He always wanted a litter pup, his dream came true.

Of course, they all sported the bandanas. They received a standing ovation. The feedback was so wonderful, the students decided to present a second show later that day. The audience enthusiastically transferred money over to The Plainledge Animal Shelter.

261

The children on the spectrum were full of glee. It was such a pleasure watching them engrossed in their activity. They smiled and laughed and loved petting all the dogs. The visitors liked the bandanas so much and appreciated the effort, they not only purchased them for their dogs, but for themselves as well. There was such a demand for the silk cloths, the children were asked to create more. Babs set up a picnic bench with supplies and gathered the children. They were excited to resume the activity. They cranked out dozens of additional creations.

Daniel sat with Chestnut. Chestnut donned all of the bandanas Daniel produced. He spoke to Chestnut as he worked. Maddie convinced Daniel to walk around with her and Nick. Chestnut would be the advertisement. The good-natured dog wore three bandanas on each leg, two tied loosely around his neck and four surrounding his tail. Those passing the humorous spectacle inquired about the product. Maddie directed them to the picnic area where they could make their purchases.

Suddenly Daniel's mood and behavior changed. He stopped moving, stood perfectly still. His eyes glazed over and his lips quivered.

Maddie bent on her knees, hugged him gently and asked him what was happening.

He said, "Chestnut said something is wrong. A monster is coming. Get the dogs and people together." Then he sat on ground quivering and refused to move.

Maddie called her father, Paul-Anthony, and notified him of Daniel's condition and advised him to meet her at the theater area as soon as possible. Babs was covering The Plainledge Animal Shelter

Paul-Anthony arrived within minutes. He picked up Daniel, sat on a chair and placed him on his lap. Chestnut, practically hidden by the bandanas, was cradles in Daniel's arms. Paul-Anthony rocked Daniel rhythmically, which slowly calmed him down.

He asked his son, "What happened, baby? Can you tell me what Chestnut is thinking?" Paul-Anthony knew the best way to communicate with Daniel was through his dog.

Daniel shook his head from side to side, stroked Chestnut and said, "Chestnut said we need to gather the people and the dogs. We'll be safer together."

Then, the ground rumbled. Maddie reminder her father of Daniel's unique relationship with his dog. He had the ability to sense oncoming danger, via a telepathic connection with Chestnut and sometimes, other dogs as well. Either Daniel was able to transmit messages on a supernatural level or he experienced hallucinations and delusions. The end result was the same. The foreboding Daniel described always presented itself. They should heed the warning and take some preventative measures.

Paul-Anthony proceeded to the band and orchestra members, who just finished playing *America the Beautiful*. He motioned to Kyle to join him, but he never reached his father. On the last note of his solo, as the audience applauded, he experienced a choking sensation. His trombone's mouthpiece softened and slid into his mouth. It continued down his throat and expanded. His bandana was torn off his head and fell to the ground. He felt a fullness in his body, both uncomfortable and unequalled.

He was not only a musician; he *was* the music.

He body bent and twisted. His head spread like the trombone's bell. His arms elongated into the slide.

He yelled out for help, but only a blaring toot escaped from his lips. His neck contorted into the turning slide. His legs shortened until he was three feet tall. He looked around and took notice of other transformations.

His friend, Marisa, currently looked like her violin. Her neck extended, her upper and lower body positioned exactly like the upper and lower bouts of the instrument. She screamed, but all that was heard was a squeaky untuned timbre. Her bandana flew from her neck. The four strings snapped off. Her arms converted into two of the strands squirming wildly. The other two strings dropped to the floor, creating insecure legs. She tottered fanatically, trying to control her balance.

Neil morphed into a circular drum. His face flattened against the batter head. The air holes expanded, affording room for his arms and legs. They looked like four drum mallets. The crash cymbal jutted from the shell, above the batter head. It appeared as if he wore a gold beret.

The beautiful lush grass turned brown, the colorful flowers wilted, the leaves fell from the tress. The dog park was dying.

The students circled the stage and ran between the chairs like a moving concert of real live music. The noises emanating from their newly formed bodies no longer resembled word, but music notes. The atrocious blares and clamors prompted the dogs to yap incessantly. The parents chased their children, not knowing what to do if they caught them.

The theater students were busy washing their dogs for the next performance when they heard the commotion. They quickly rinsed and towel dried their dogs and hurried over to the stage. They were horrified at the sight, froze in fear, grabbed their dogs and combed the area for help.

They spotted Paul-Anthony. He signaled to them to accompany him. They followed him to the picnic bench where he left Maddie and Daniel. They all spoke at the same time, trying to find the right words to describe the horrors. None were sufficient. They couldn't listen to each other as they all needed to vent. Paul-Anthony placed his hands on their shoulders, one at a time, and firmly sat them on the bench. He was unnerved himself, but had to calm the students.

Daniel stood stoically, caressing Chestnut, watching the students and his father gather on the bench with their dogs. He smiled, aware that they had power in numbers. Maddie was terrified at the look on her father's face, but found her own courage and took charge of the situation. She knelt near each student, Nick following her every move. Nick whined and nudged each dog individually as they cuddled closer to their human.

When the theater students calmed down a bit, Paul-Anthony asked them to follow him. They headed toward the arena where the living instruments wandered. Daniel placed Chestnut on the ground. Chestnut communicated to the dogs. The Border Collies circled the students in the arena, condensing their space. The Greyhounds ran in circles, barking wildly. Nick followed, pulling a cart of Karen's homemade dog biscuits to reinforce the dogs' good behavior. They needed to combine their strengths.

The theater students' dogs followed behind Nick. The band and orchestra students' dogs acted in accordance. At least thirty loving, caring dogs surrounded the deformed students. Then they stopped, following Chestnut's lead. They moved forward, one step at a time. The Australian Shepherds directed the dogs, herding the metallic children inward, forming a shortened area.

When they were close enough, each dog took their position beside their human and laid the heads on their feet or whatever part was exposed. Daniel and Chestnut, and Maddie and Nick collected the numerous bandanas tenderly created by Daniel and his classmates. They deposited them next to the dogs. Daniel was aware that the combined efforts of the humans and the dogs and their love and loyalty for each other would be powerful enough to break the spell. The bandanas afforded an additional symbol of human goodness, tolerance and acceptance.

The ground shook. The people heard an angry hiss throughout the park. The monster was unable to retain its hold on the students. It was furious. In one last effort, it emitted an angry howl and an ominous stream of fog. However, the fog dissipated quickly.

The howl backfired. It compelled the dogs to move closer to their humans. The monster was losing its powered. It rose up from the ground, stretched at least twenty feet tall. It spread its arms out, over its head, then horizontally, down to its legs, completing a circular shape. It mustered as much strength as possible, but it wasn't enough. It spiraled downward in a reverse tornado, drilling itself back into the earth from where it emerged.

The flowers bloomed; the grass was restored to its natural green field, the leaves whirled back to their branches. The park returned to its original state. Unusual combinations of clangs, clicks and bangs erupted, like the sounds of novice musicians. The students began to reform into their human structures.

266

They morphed more easily, no pain or fear, just a patient waiting to return to their normal selves.

When the transformation was complete, the students were exhausted. They laid down next to their dogs and fell asleep. The parents who'd been chasing them sat near them while they slept, afraid to leave their sides. They stoked their children, their dogs, and chatted quietly amongst themselves.

I knew we had to help our humans. I especially wanted to support my Maddie. Daniel gave the warning and I immediately dove into action. The evil force invading our space and distorting our humans can only be stopped by overpowering its anger and hate with our love and loyalty. I communicated this sentiment with each dog. I jabbed them, assuring their bodies made contact with their humans' hearts. I told them we needed to band together to fight the invisible beast within the complex.

The humans heard this as a whine. However, I know Maddie and Daniel were aware of my antics. Our goal was to get the deformed students in a compact area, surround them and protect them. We used our best qualities, herding, running and patience. We took advantage of the bandanas the kind little children fashioned for the fundraiser. All these symbols of limitless love were damaging to the lurking diabolical forces that attempted to destroy our delightful event.

As the saying goes, we won the battle but not the war. I glanced over at Chestnut and Daniel. Daniel held Chestnut to his ear. I heard Chestnut mewl softy and I heard Daniel say, "It's OK Chestnut, we can do it again."

Chapter
THIRTY-EIGHT
Shaggy

I regained full consciousness and mobility from the dog park incident, but I experienced occasional weird occurrences. It was debatable if they were delusions, hallucinations or paranormal activity. Either way, I never felt quite the same. I questioned my surroundings, my senses; I was often anxious for no apparent reason. The first night was the beginning of a harrowing, haunting situation.

My parents agreed to allow Sam to live with us until the apartment was completed. I was afraid to be alone or drift off to sleep. I sat with Sam until the early hours, chatting watching television and reading until I was exhausted. I drank a few glasses of wine for an extra sedative effect. I laid on my soft, warm queen-sized bed with my eyes wide open. I couldn't fathom how I could be so tired and not fall asleep. I played meditative music on the television and I took some deep breaths. I felt my body start to relax.

The music faded in the background and the hall light went on. I thought Sam was approaching the bedroom, but I didn't hear any footsteps, or breathing. The toilet didn't even flush. I froze. I was afraid to move or speak. I didn't want the possible boogeyman to detect my presence. Sweat dripped from my forehead. I wouldn't dare whip off the

268

blankets to flee from the room. I was overheating under the covers. I needed to pee, but anxiety prevented me from leaving the bed. I was worried if I placed my feet on the floor, a hand may emerge from under the bed and drag me under.

I waited until my eyelids were heavy with sleep. I closed them for a brief minute. I detected an eerie yellow glow and flicked them open. My bedroom door, which was previously open, was securely closed. The hall light radiated a sinister glimmer. The misty gleam seeped through the slits in the sides and bottom or the door. I heard a scratching sound like a single fingernail on a blackboard. It tap, tap, tapped methodically.

The fog swooped around my head. I think I heard my name. I was uncertain if I was dreaming, experiencing auditory hallucinations or if the entity that possessed me earlier returned to finish its goal. I wondered if it could have gained strength from me, stole some of my body and initialized a morphing process.

It whispered a quick, quiet, "Shaggy" that reverberated in my ear. It jolted me from my nightmare. I figured the voice was Sam's, he finally decided to join me. But Sam didn't appear. The voice resounded, repeating my name. I held the sheets to my neck and quivered. It was imperative I leave this room.

I counted to three, inhaled deeply, flipped the sheets over and darted madly toward the hallway. I took one step, two steps; on the third step a spindly arm stretched inconceivably from under the bed. It snatched my ankle like a bear trap snags an unsuspecting animal. Strong talons dug into my lower leg. I fell forward with a thump, my chin and arms taking the brunt of the impact. The gangly arm retreated underneath the bed, carrying me off with it. Brick walls emanated from the floor to the top of the mattress frame, circling me. A slate ceiling slid over the bottom of the bed frame, covering the space above my head. I was trapped, encased below my bed, a living body in a chamber-coffin.

Sam undoubtedly heard the pandemonium; I heard him enter the room and call for me. I answered him, yelling and pounding on my tomb, to no avail. Candy and Curly charged in with my parents. The dogs immediately sniffed at my location, lying on the floor with their noses to the bricks. Their continuous barking alerted them to my whereabouts. My father ran to the basement for a hammer and pounded the bricks unmercifully. My mother instructed me to remain calm. I think she was trying to convince herself as much as me. Sam flipped the mattress over. I detected more banging above me. Their efforts were in vain. They were unable to make a dent in the structure.

I was thirsty and alone in my crypt. I felt claustrophobic. I was limited in movement. I was able to shake my head from side to side and lift it about two inches. The tight enclosure prevented me from controlling my anxiety. I closed my eyes and inhaled deeply. I felt the cold, rough bricks tingle the hairs on my arms. I looked up and noted fog from my own breath accumulate on the slate planks above me.

I panicked. I propelled my feet and stubbed my toe on the ceiling. I pummeled my arms; I lashed out with my fists. They raked against the brick edges and bled from multiple scrapes. I screamed at the top of my lungs until I was hoarse. Curly and Candy were aware of my location. They were able to follow my scent. My family were aware of my presence but were unable to set me free. I laid prone, trembling and distressed while I remained captive.

Five claws crept up my legs, my belly and up to my chest. I watched them climb like carnivorous black spiked caterpillars ascending to the higher branches on the tree to the more plentiful leaves. I was certain they would choke and kill me.

They suddenly halted. They scratched a rectangular shape on the slate above my eyes and checks, down toward my mouth. They sliced through the material like paper across skin. The index and thumb snatched the cut-out, crushed it like an aluminum can and absorbed the material into its scrawny fingers. It created an opening where I was able to see my parents, Sam and the dogs, but I couldn't fit through. Creepy laughter echoed around me. I think the monster was playing a malicious game and it enjoyed my unwilling participation.

The dogs scampered to me, wagged their tails and delightfully licked my face. The monster's giggles changed to gasps and deteriorated to threatening, angry moans. It depside the dogs' happiness, hated their love for me and their display of affection.

Two decrepit arms shot out from within my crypt. They circled my waist and squeezed me tightly. The pulled me downward. I stared at my family, my mouth shaped in an "O," and my pupils dilated, I yelled, "No, no." I didn't have enough room to reach my hands out of the opening. I thrashed around, pressing firmly on the bricks in an effort to prevent the stretchy-thing from sucking me with it. The dogs barked furiously. Sam and my father were offering their last-ditch efforts to break the barrier. My mother paced, wrung her hands, prayed quietly.

I was fading from their world. I felt myself sink into the damp earth. My captor created a tunnel. The packed dirt separated, leaving a path for us to funnel through. Its vile arms constricted, inhibiting my ability to inhale. It dropped me into a dark cave with outlets on each side. As soon as I landed, the monster vanished. A minute later, Curley landed with a sickening thump.

Candy and I detected Shaggy's scent before we arrived in the bedroom. We were unable to get a visual, but we did alert the humans to her whereabouts. Shaggy hadn't paid us much attention since Tanya died. We understood. She was grief-stricken. She withdrew from giving and receiving love so she wouldn't risk experience a repeat of the depressing, overwhelming feelings. She wasn't thinking about how happy Tanya was when they were together and how she rescued Tanya from a miserable existence and a offered her a second chance.

Tanya enjoyed the love, loyalty and companionship only a human-dog bond offered. Shaggy would benefit greatly if she rescued another furry friend, after a reasonable period of mourning. Candy and I never stopped loving her. We would wait forever for her to open her heart to us again.

We were excited and relieved when her face was exposed. We smothered her with kisses. In that moment, we witnessed the former Shaggy, the one who accepted love rather than build barriers to protect herself. She smiled, we wiggled. Then she started to panic, but we couldn't figure out why. She was shrinking, disappearing from our view.

Candy moved toward Helmuth. She felt like a failure. We dogs are supposed to protect our humans at all costs. We honor and uphold this task. I glimpsed Candy's demeanor and understood. I was obligated to act quickly. I stuck my nose into the rectangular hole. It may have been a mistake, but I would have repeated the same behavior again if I was presented with a similar case. Three sharp, slinky fingers latched into my snout. I was frightening for a couple of seconds, and then accepted my fate willingly, if it meant I would receive an opportunity to help Shaggy. I wish I could hold my nose to block out the putrid odor in the same manner as humans are able. Instead, I was forced to deal with the nausea and the hideous claws clutching my snout. I hurt my front paw when I landed with a solid thwack. I forgot about the pain when I laid my eyes on Shaggy. She was genuinely glad to see me.

Relief flooded me at Curley's arrival. I checked her leg. It wasn't broken, just bruised. I sat up on my knees and hugged Curly for the first times since Tanya died. I thanked her for following me and I apologized for my rude and standoffish behavior. She didn't have to forgive me; she was never mad at me. She simply waited for me to open my heart and allow her back in. She tucked her neck in the crux of my neck and wiggled her entire body.

Suddenly, she backed up, perked her ears and waft her nose in the air. She emitted a shallow cry and retreated from my embrace. She ventured a few steps, stopped, looked back for approval and continued onward. She wanted me to follow her, I obliged.

We advanced about twenty yards when I heard a girl's voice. She said, "Is anyone there? Please help me."

Curley contacted her first, signaled a quick bark, and I found my way to them. The poor girl was crouched alongside the wall, weeping. A dog lay silently at her feet. His breath was raspy. He was either sick or injured. I assessed the dog while Curley comforted the girl.

She said her name was Nina and her dog was Tucker. She stammered as she explained the bizarre happenings at The Plainledge Animal Shelter. I hadn't previously met Nina, but I was aware of the séance and how Babs devised a plan to aid in Nina's recovery.

Babs would allow Nina to select a dog from the shelter for her very own. The unconditional acceptance the dog would offer her would facilitate her healing. I noticed a major coincidence in our situations. When Curley and Candy eagerly licked my face, the stretch-thing became enraged and used that fuel to capture us. When Nina chose to recuse Tucker to love and care for, chaos erupted at the shelter.

When I get the heck out of this place, I will have to further investigate this idea with Samael and my parents. Perhaps there are additional connections.

Chapter
THIRTY-NINE
The Meeting

Paul-Anthony and I called our friends and co-workers from The Plainledge Animal Shelter and Aaron's Dog Park to discuss and coordinate a plan to release The Dark Place captors and kill the Stretchman.

Helmuth and Irmgard agreed to close the shelter for the day. I included my children, as I had observed the paranormal activity surrounding them. I was certain Daniel would be an asset to the team. We met at the shelter with our dogs on a sunny Monday morning. Ms. Blake joined us with her two dogs and agreed to allow the children to miss a day at school without penalty.

Lucy, the Administrative Assistant, invited her friend, Cathy. Cathy experienced a similar disturbing phenomenon. She baked enough banana-nut muffins for the entire crew, Samael picked up a Carton-O-Caffeine at the local coffee shop. Karen, who could not attend the meeting, fired up a batch of her homemade dog biscuits as a special treat for our canine teammates. Kyle, Maddie and Daniel fed and played with the kennel dogs before the meeting began.

Our dogs romped around with them and took advantage of the extra food and playtime. Paul-Anthony used his PAWs construction van to haul over a sufficient number of chairs and a table. I called the children and we all sat down to discuss our concerns. I kept my medical bag handy in case of any emergencies. We attached leashes to the dogs' collars to keep them close.

I began with my recent experience in The Dark Place and explained that Nina was stuck there with her dog, Tucker. Daniel became agitated. He grabbed Chestnut, closed his eyes and rocked back and forth while he stroked the dog. I admitted my encounters with the Stretchman in my recurring nightmares. I told them that Nina named her new dog Tucker, which was the dog's name in my dreams.

Kyle gasped and discussed his night terrors. His dreams included a horrifying monster who had the ability to stretch his extremities and grow to unusual heights.

Daniel shared his own nightmares, speaking as if Chestnut told him what to say, "Chestnut said I saw a big monster. He tried to steal us. I had my slingshot, I put something in my toy, aimed and hit the monster. It hit him and made him disappear in the wall. I don't know what I put in the slingshot but it hurt the monster. The monster cried and screamed when I hit him. Chestnut said I was a hero and he reminded me that I used Karen's dog biscuit to injure the monster."

Lucy chimed in, pointing out the similarities in her confrontation with the Stretchman. He exhibited the same stretchable qualities. Its goals were to capture and torment those who loved and rescued dogs. She remembered dropping a homemade dog biscuit in The Dark Place floor. Not only did the room transform to a more positive atmosphere, but the beast cried out in a rage and lost some of its power.

Paul-Anthony agreed with the symbolic expressions of hope and love. He offered a summary of how they laid out the bandanas to aid in the band and orchestra students' recovery. They infuriated the entity at Aaron's Dog Park during the fundraiser. The nurturing symbols decreased the Stretchman's power. We will need to use these to fight the beast.

Samael finally felt comfortable to disclose Shaggy's and Candy's disappearance and the traumatizing events that led to their departure. He spoke rapidly about the numerous outrageous happenings at the dog park, the construction men, Irmgard's accident and Shaggy's possession. He was visibly shaken.

Daniel stood up, walked slowly over to Samael and gently placed Chestnut in his lap. He took Sam's hand and showed him how to caress the dog. Daniel returned to his chair. He felt comfortable leaving Chestnut with Samael. As distraught as Sam was, he couldn't help but smile at Daniel.

Cathy replayed the devastating circumstances that resulted in Janet's demise. She included Yukon's intuition, his ability to locate the portal via the foul odor and his willingness to defend them at all costs. It was beyond all doubt that the dogs were our finest weapon against the evil forces.

Lastly, we heard from Maddie. She confessed that she had neglected Nick. Her eyes filled with tears as she spoke. She explained her relationship with Ms. Ravana, how they met and how she became her protégé. She described the antique, evil mirror and The Dark Place; how her reflection changed after each infraction, each time she hurt or humiliated a fellow student. As her self-esteem and vitality increased, her physical appearance deteriorated. She landed in The Dark Place with Trista when she set her priorities on her need for revenge and power, instead of on her family and her dog   When she caught sight of Trista's reflection, she resembled the Stretchman they all described. It wasn't a Stretchman at all, rather a Stretchwoman.

The realization battered Sam worse than any abuse he suffered at his father's hand. Of course it was his mother. He should have known. She was abused, mocked and paralyzed with fear since she met Seth. Her rage increased after each maltreatment. She had no friends, no money, no love. He was angry with himself for not noticing this sooner. All the accidents, the deaths, the perversions; they were all his fault. He began to sob violently. He stood up and handed Chestnut back to Daniel. He sat on the floor and rocked himself, trying to process the information and calm down. He voiced his unease and stupidity the rest of the team. Chestnut squirmed from Daniel's arms and sat on Sam's lap. The others assured Sam that this was not his wrongdoings, but his mother's. We needed to focus on our goals, assist those caught in The Dark Place and find a means to kill the Stretchwoman.

Nina and her friends were able to summon the Stretchwoman during a séance. I thought that would be the manner in which to initiate the plan. The shelter was equipped with a great supply of homemade dog biscuits. We would use those and the bandanas for weapons. Paul-Anthony agreed to pick up the remaining bandanas we stored in our house after the fundraiser. Our dogs and the shelter dogs were already present and ready to assist us. Sam volunteered to drive to Target to purchase a Ouija Board. Daniel followed him as he walked out the door. We allowed him and Chestnut to go with him. Chestnut may benefit both of them.

Target wasn't crowded on this Monday morning. Sam and Daniel found a stack of Ouija Boards in the toy aisle. Sam selected the first board on the shelf, wanting to return to the shelter as soon as possible. His guilt was festering inside. He needed to succeed in accomplish this small task to keep his guilt and negative feelings at a minimum.

The Ouija board box scorched his hand and he dropped it. The cover flipped open and the board toppled out. The planchette jumped out onto the board. The heart-shaped plastic piece sprouted two short thick legs and tiny feet. An eye resided in the center, a sun on the upper-left bulge and a moon covered with fog sat in the upper right side. The open circular shape below the eye allowed the players to view the letters on the Ouija board.

Daniel closed his eyes and held Chestnut securely. Sam kicked the planchette in frustration and anger. The sharp bottom portion of the heart sliced into his foot. He struggled to pull it free and threw it over his head. It stopped directly in front of his face, dangling. Its eye hovered, stared at Sam and blinked.

The planchette dropped to the board, running over the letters. It hesitated, forming words and a message; "Warning, abort...warning, abort." The tiny little legs cruised around the board, continuously pausing on the same letters. Samael removed a second Ouija Board from the shelf, linked arms with Daniel, tossed a fifty-dollar bill on the register and fled the store.

Samael explained the new occurrence when they arrived back at the shelter. They understood the danger and the risk involved with their project. They remained committed.

I set up towels on the floor in a circle. Each of us sitting on a towel with our dogs, close enough to touch each other. The kennel dogs laid down beside us. I distributed bandanas and Karen's homemade dog biscuits to the humans and tied bandanas loosely, but securely around the dogs' necks. We filled our backpacks with these items and added bottled water, my medical bag and flashlights.

I used the information I obtained from Nina, lit some candles and placed the Ouija Board in the center of our circle. I dimmed the lights and asked everyone to join hands. Daniel motioned for Chestnut to sit by his side and he completed the circle.

We touched the planchette with the tips of our fingers. Since there were too many of us to fit close enough to the Ouija board, Paul-Anthony volunteered to sit back, as did Helmuth, Cathy and Ms. Blake. Daniel's hands were full with Chestnut. Maddie and I sat on the side of the board where we were able to read and decipher any messages from the spirits. Kyle sat to our right. Lucy positioned herself to our left. Irmgard and Sam took place opposite Maddie and me. They viewed an inverted visual of the alphabet.

I acted cautiously and requested Nina's presence first. "Nina, we invite you to our world. We want to help you. Can you hear me?"

Maddie started to giggle. I opened my eyes and met hers. I realized she was frightened because she recognized the danger and was aware of the Stretchwoman's power and ability. I reminded everyone to focus and absorb the strength and courage from our joined forces. Nick propped his head on Maddie's leg. She glanced at him, smiled and resumed her concentration.

I called for Nina a few times. We did not receive any signal. I refused to give up. I asked Sam if he was ready to call for Shaggy. Irmgard uttered a desperate moan; Helmuth squeezed her hand for support. Curley whined hopefully. Samael nodded with both apprehension and desire.

Chapter
FORTY
The Voyage

Sam invited Shaggy to join us if she was able. Once again, we failed to receive any indication that another being presided with us. Sam became impatient and frustrated and yelled, "Is anyone here? Can you hear me? I invite you to show yourself."

It was a mistake to invite anyone to reveal himself or herself. Nina voiced the same error during her séance when the Stretchwoman murdered her friends. However, one of our goals was to kill the monster, so perhaps this was a blessing in disguise.

The planchette moved quickly. We should have expected it, that's why we purchased the board, but we jumped back reflexively. Our fingertips were not required. The planchette, sprouted legs and glided over the alphabet, repeating the same message Sam received at Target, "Warning, abort…warning, abort."

A hostile voice shrieked, "You did not heed my warning."

The candles flickered and the ground began to shake. Most of us experienced these sensations previously but it unnerved us just the same. The dogs leaned closer to us and Chestnut jumped into Daniel's arms.

The rumbling increased; our bodies bumped on the floor. The dogs gripped their nails into the wooden floor to maintain their balance. The candles blew out, leaving us in shadows. We heard a menacing giggle echoing from the walls and ceiling. The shelter walls crumbed slowly creating a booming racket, leaving dust and soot in its wake. The roof whirled away like a child's kite in a tumultuous storm. The wind whipped around us knocking supplies off the shelves. It lifted our cups and muffins, spinning and weaving the debris between the dogs and us like a tornado of our necessities. The beast offered us a display of her power, warning us of our fate if we dare to confront her.

Samael yelled, "Where's Shaggy?"

Cathy cried out, "I'm coming for Janet."

Paul-Anthony shouted, "I will find my construction crew."

Maddie, who felt guilty about succumbing to Trista's antics and neglected Nick, screamed, "We will kill you."

A spark appeared near Maddie. It lengthened and spread behind us, surrounding us from the back of our circle. The twelve-inch flames burned through the ground like a buzz saw. We hovered precariously on the wooden disc that was now our base. The opening below us formed a ghastly abyss. Cold, clammy steam rose from the hole above our heads and down through the front of us like we were situated in the middle of a heinous water fountain. The pressure of the stream pushed us downward. We grabbed or dogs' collars for security and started to spin. It felt like we were riding the tilt-a-wheel at an unholy carnival.

The Ouija board took flight, headed straight for Ms. Blake, rotating at an extraordinary speed. Eddie sprang for it, thinking it was a Frisbee toy. It slashed through Eddie's mouth, tearing both sides of his lips.

He flopped on his side, groaning in pain. The spinning slowed. I reached for Eddie, slid him next to me and opened my medical bag. I cleaned his wound and swathed his cuts with antibiotic ointment. I bandaged the area with a bandana hoping he wouldn't pry it off. The pressure would help stop the bleeding.

Ethan ambled over and rested his paw on the bandana, protecting it from Eddie's desire to rip it from his mouth. The two litter pups were so engrossed in Eddie's injuries, they failed to notice the projection of the planchette. It bee-lined toward Ms. Blake's neck, striking her between her collarbone and her chin.

Her head fell to her chest and tumbled off her shoulders. It bumped loudly on our descending disk. Her face staring upward, her eyes and mouth open wide in shock and fright. Blood gushed from her neck, flowed from her nose and dripped from her ears. Her hair absorbed the blood, dying it a deep crimson red. Her body slipped backward into the void below. Kyle and Maddie screamed. Max and Nick sprang up and stuck their wet noses in their faces. Daniel closed his eyes and found comfort in Chestnut.

We stopped spinning but continued to drop. No one uttered a word. We were rattled, frightened and horrified. I was about to break the silence when the planchette shuffled over to Ms. Blake's lifeless head and kicked it into the void. I felt powerless and doubted the plan. I felt guilty and angry with myself for involving my children.

We landed with a soft thud and I started to sob. The group seemed to understand my feelings, as they probably felt similar. The dogs stood up first. They waited until their humans mimicked them. Then, we all gathered toward each other and huddled together, gaining strength in our companionship and compassion. The dogs stood around us. We created a human circle, surrounded by our dogs' strength and loyalty. Their actions caused a brief reprise from the devastating incidences.

Chapter
FORTY-ONE
The Dark Place

One by one, we stepped from our spot into The Dark Place. It was sparsely illuminated. Paul-Anthony and I took hold of each other's hand. We told our children and the others to huddle together with their dogs while we check out our surroundings.

Before we even took a step forward, we all heard a female's voice and a dog's bark. Sam recognized the voice immediately ran toward it before we uttered another word. Curley sprinted after him, sensing Candy's bark and smell. I yelled for him to slow down so we can assess the situation and act accordingly, but he either didn't hear me or he chose not to heed my advice.

Paul-Anthony and I gathered the rest of our group and tentatively walked toward Sam. We formed a line, holding on to the shirt of the person in front of us. Paul-Anthony was the trailblazer, I was second in line with Daniel, Maddie and Kyle next. Lucy, Cathy and Irmgard followed behind Kyle. Helmuth ended the line, carefully watching for anything out of the ordinary. The whole place was out of the ordinary, so we were cautious and moved slowly. The ground was difficult to navigate. The lighting was poor, unspecified shadows lurked around us. The damp, rocky floor was uneven and pitted. Any misstep could result in a sprained ankle, or worse.

Shaggy was weeping against a wall. She scooted herself inside a small crevice to hide from the Stretchwoman, although she was not yet aware of the monster's identity. Curley and Candy wagged their tails and sniffed each other's butts excitedly. We formed a U-shape around Shaggy. She explained what happened to her. Sam, Helmuth and Irmgard added to her story. They described it from their perspective.

Sam informed Shaggy about the Stretchwoman's identity. He welled up when he talked about his mother. His tears turned to full-blown sobbing as he apologized to Shaggy and confessed that he should have known. He blamed himself for all of the misfortunes. Candy and Curley whimpered as Sam's cries escalated.

Shaggy stood up, put her arms around Sam's waist and pulled him close. She said, "This is NOT your fault. I love you. Now, let's finish this."

With that, the sides of the cave rumbled, debris slid down like a mini avalanche. Trista's anger increased at every display of affection, attachment or bonding.

Cathy detected an eerie ball drop from the crumbling wall. Yukon trotted over, sat beside it and cried. Cathy picked it up and studied it. The object appeared to be constructed out of bones. The surface was cracked and broken, but white and smooth. On a closer examination, she could see stick-like arms and legs jutting out from the top and bottom. Something shiny lie inside the orb. We advised Cathy to leave it alone, but she felt an urgency to continue her quest. She stuck her finger between the gaps in the bones and manipulated the object out. It was Janet's wedding ring.

Cathy dropped the ball and held the ring to her heart. She screamed, "No, no, it can't be. Please tell me it's not. Please, no."

Yukon howled. Lucy hugged Cathy. We all stood silent, afraid of what lie ahead for us.

Another voice whispered, "Is anyone there? I'm over here. Can you hear me?" This timid voice was followed by a deep loud bark. *It must be Nina.*

I yelled, "Nina honey, it's Babs. We're here to help you. Keep talking so we can find you. Try to make Tucker bark again!" Nina's voice took on a more excited, hopeful tone. She yelled, "Yes, it's me. I'm afraid. I'm here, I'm here!"

And, just like a good dog knows, Tucker barked again. And again, and again. We stepped into our places in line. Cathy was reluctant to join, wallowing in her grief. Lucy put her arm around Cathy's shoulders as we ventured forward. Cathy continued to mumble under her breath.

We discovered Nina a few yards down a tunnel. Tucker stuck his head out from their hiding place and barked loud enough to wake the dead. In this case, I hope it wasn't actually loud enough to wake the dead.

Nina was rolled in a fetal position, afraid to move. Paul-Anthony and I stayed back with the children while Helmuth bent down and picked up Nina. Her face was filthy, tears dripped down creating dirty smudged lines from her eyes to her chin and down her neck. She laughed a nervous, relieved cackle. I was concerned for her mental health, but had no time to address it at that moment.

We stopped at the largest area in the cave to discuss our next move. Cathy and Nina couldn't add to the conversation, but their dogs were patiently attending to their needs. Nina sat cross-legged with Tucker on her lap. She was hardly visible. She spoke to him with her head buried in his massive chest. Yukon wouldn't move from Cathy's side, but his ears were perked and he was ready for action.

Daniel took out a package of homemade dog biscuits from his backpack and distributed them to the dogs. Dakota, let hers fall to the floor, seemingly remembering the effect it had on The Plainledge Animal Shelter last time we landed in The Dark Place.

Amazingly, the homemade dog biscuits lit up the cave. This was a huge win for us. Nina lifted her head from Tucker's fur and smiled. Cathy remained sullen, but I noticed a small flicker of hope when she gazed at Yukon.

The biscuits affected the Stretchwoman in a negative manner. She shrieked with rage. The lights blinked, but she had no power over the dog biscuits. We were so excited, we erupted in applause. We took a moment to absorb the small victory. It lasted just a few moments when the figure emerged from the top of the cave.

She pounced. She stretched out her arm and grabbed Cathy by the back of her neck before any of us could respond. Cathy dangled in mid-air. She couldn't speak, but her eyes were full of fear. She grasped for us, the Stretchwoman cackled and pulled Cathy further away. Yukon advanced, barking wildly. Dakota stepped in front of him, blocking his ability to attack. They faced each other, growling for the alpha position. Dakota stopped barking, took a step closer to Yukon and licked his jowls. She placed her paw on his head and bowed before him. Yukon took note of the situation and understood Dakota's message. They both backed up and stood by Lucy.

Daniel took his slingshot from his backpack and loaded it with Karen's homemade dog biscuits. He pulled back the slingshot and the biscuits soared through the cave. Two landed on each of the monster's arms and one anchored in her right eye.

The shrieking filled the cave. We covered our ears as pieces of the walls crumbled around us. The dogs crouched and placed their paws on their ears. It would have been a cute sight if not for the dire situation. The Stretchman dropped Cathy. Yukon gripped Cathy's shirt in his mouth and dragged her to us. The Stretchwoman was enraged. She caught the falling debris and launched it toward us. Rocks, dirt and chunks of wreckage blasted us like huge pieces of hail in a rainsquall. Each little bit of the monster's house sliced fresh wounds in our bodies, shredding us. Blood soaked through the dogs' fur. We were losing hope.

I spotted Daniel. He sat Chestnut down and crammed his slingshot with the homemade dog biscuits. I gave him credit for his attempt, but I knew it would only slow her assault.

Before he discharged his weapon, his eyes rolled back and he turned toward us through the rock-pelting shower and said, "Chestnut said to use the bandanas."

My best friend, Yukon and I were a little bit scared, but we were mostly angry and willing to kill that beast and save our humans. My own heart broke when Cathy faced the monster's cruelty and found Janet, crushed into a hideous ball. I echoed Yukon's howls. His Cathy was in a terrible state of grief. My human, Lucy, tried to comfort Cathy. Humans aren't as good with comforting as we dogs are, but I gave her credit. She was generous with her love and affection.

I was relieved to find Shaggy, Nina and their dogs alive. I played with Candy and Curley a few times at The Plainledge Animal Shelter when Helmuth visited. Tucker and I ran around in the field together. Nina had not yet rescued him, so I spent extra time with him. We are both big dogs, so we could play rough together and never worried about inadvertently hurting each other. I am stronger and better looking, but don't mention that to Tucker. We were good friends and enjoyed our playtime together.

I forced myself to stand against Yukon for a chilling minute. He was ready to defend Cathy and attack the Stretchwoman. I understood his loyalty, but was afraid for his life. I signaled my yearning for him to stand guard without attacking. Fortunately, he realized my intention before reacting hastily.

We refocused when Chestnut gave instructions to Daniel. We used our keen olfactory senses to locate the dog biscuits in the overstuffed backpacks. The way our humans packed, you would think they were going on vacation for a week. We gathered the biscuits as fast as we could. We ate a few along the way, but who could resist? Not only were they delicious, but they energized me and gave me more motivation.

We quickly rummaged for the bandanas in our backpacks. We struggled to feel for the dog biscuits as she continued her assault. Our hands were cut up and bleeding. We flipped the pack upside down and emptied the contents. The dogs were able to sniff out the biscuits. They placed them in their mouths and dropped them at our feet. They repeated this, holding as many biscuits in their mouths as possible, aiding in our defense. They behaved quickly and efficiently. They didn't even eat any of the biscuits. What good dogs.

Daniel yelled, "Now…Chestnut said *now*."

We hastened to heap the bandanas with the dog biscuits. There were no instructions, no one said a word, nor did anyone look to each other for guidance. We simply acted. We piled the biscuits into the bandanas, tied the corners into knots and propelled the packages in the monster's direction.

The explosion was cataclysmic. The bundles hit their mark, bursting open. Dog biscuits took wing and stabbed at the beast at every angle. The crunchy cookies performed like firecrackers on the Fourth of July. They ignited, setting the Stretchwoman in flames. She screeched, horrific, hair-raising screams.

The monster started to spin, creating energy. The rapid rotation caused rumbling and vibrations. Dust swirled around us, like a cyclone. The oxygen gave strength to the flames, burning the Stretchwoman's being. A nauseating stench saturated the cave. Her head slumped from side to side. Her face melted; her arms evaporated from her body. Her footless legs dissolved into the ground. The fire dwindled to a smoldering brush. We used the remaining bandanas to fan away the smoke.

Other voices reverberated around us. People singing in praise. Their bodies were non-descript, but lit up like angels. They ascended, floating through the top of the cave. They were finally free of the Stretchwoman's clutches. Their dogs rose with them, wagging their whole bodies, running in the wind.

I think I caught a glimpse of The Rainbow Bridge.

I will never forget the sound of the Stretchwoman wailing. I still have nightmares, the sound of a person slowly burning to death without aid, alone in her bitterness and pain. Although we couldn't save those that were captured and murdered, we were able to release them and set them free.

Samael was the first to notice her and the mirror. Trista's body lay on the ground twitching. Her antique mirror must have emerged from the walls during the explosion. It was cracked, broken; smothered in grime. Trista's breathing was hushed and shallow. The mirror expanded and contracted in unison with Trista's breath. Sam walked over. We stayed back, allowing him to approach his mother alone. The dogs did not advance. Shaggy took a step forward, and then decided to allow Sam to venture forth alone. Curley and Candy remained with her, one at each side.

Sam looked down at his mother. She appeared helpless, and vulnerable, and she was suffering. She opened her blistered covered lips, stretched her hand out, to normal lengths and whispered his name. He bent on his knees and took hold of her hand.

She said, "The inner evil is reflected on the exterior."

A red glow caught Sam's attention, and he glimpsed over at the decrepit mirror. He saw a strong young man holding hands with an evil, angry monster. He thought that the opposite was also true. The exterior could also reflect the inner goodness.

He watched as the cave engulfed his mother. The mirror glowed with a bright light. The cracks vanished, the wood beamed, the frame radiated. We huddled together, as if we were taking a selfie, and gazed into the mirror.

Our reflection revealed a group of courageous, loving people bonded together with their beautiful, loyal, furry companions. Although we were bruised and filthy from the eruption, the mirror displayed our inner beauty, the loving nature of our souls and the loyalty between the humans and their dogs.

No one noticed the man's reflection in the background. It looked similar to the Stretchwoman, except it was a man, a *Stretchman*.

About the Author

Debra Zaech is a Licensed Social Worker, a University Assistant Dean and a senior lecturer of Psychology.

She wrote and teaches a course on dogs and human bonding. She is married with four children and a Bernese Mountains dog.

The Stretchman

Look for us wherever books are sold.

Made in the USA
Columbia, SC
07 April 2023

14481413R00186